HALLOWEEN MURDER

After snapping a selfie to prove she'd made it to the end, Abby circled the perimeter of the clearing. Still no sign of the farmer anywhere—not that she was surprised by that, as quiet as it was. Finally, she approached the closed door on the front side of the shed and called out, "Mr. Minter, are you in there?"

The only sound was the splash of raindrops hitting the mud puddles. Finally she opened the door and peeked into the dim interior. At first, she didn't see anything except a large basket of mini pumpkins sitting on a rickety-looking table, no doubt the promised prizes. Then she noticed a boot lying on the dirt floor below the table. On second look, the boot was attached to a leg sticking out from beneath a patchwork quilt.

She retreated several steps as her mind flashed back to that day in her backyard when she and Tripp had discovered a dead body wrapped in a quilt. A bad feeling settled in her stomach, and there was no way she wanted to take one more step deeper into that shed.

Hovering near the door, she softly called out, "Mr. Minter, is that you?"

As tempting as it was to believe that the leg and boot were part of the decorations in the maze, meant to scare the visitors, her gut instincts had her convinced otherwise . . .

Books by Alexis Morgan

DEATH BY COMMITTEE

DEATH BY JACK-O'-LANTERN

Published by Kensington Publishing Corporation

DEATH BY JACK-O'-LANTERN

Alexis Morgan

KENSINGTON BOOKS
KENSINGTON PUBLISHING CORP.
www.kensingtonbooks.com

KENSINGTON BOOKS are published by

Kensington Publishing Corp.
119 West 40th Street
New York, NY 10018

All Kensington titles, imprints, and distributed lines are available at special quantity discounts for bulk purchases for sales promotion, premiums, fund-raising, educational, or institutional use.

Special book excerpts or customized printings can also be created to fit specific needs. For details, write or phone the office of the Kensington Sales Manager: Attn.: Sales Department. Kensington Publishing Corp., 119 West 40th Street, New York, NY 10018. Phone: 1-800-221-2647.

Kensington and the K logo Reg. U.S. Pat. & TM Off.

First Printing: September 2019
ISBN-13: 978-1-4967-1954-6
ISBN-10: 1-4967-1954-9

ISBN-13: 978-1-4967-1957-7 (eBook)
ISBN-10: 1-4967-1957-3 (eBook)

10 9 8 7 6 5 4 3 2 1

Printed in the United States of America

Chapter One

"Do you want to run that by me again?"

Abby McCree focused her temper on beating some innocent egg whites into a froth while she waited for her tenant to explain himself. She noticed he'd made sure to put the width of the old oak kitchen table between them. That was smart on his part, because otherwise he might just end up wearing the meringue if she didn't like what he had to say.

Meanwhile, Tripp Blackston leaned back in his chair, his legs stretched out in front of him and crossed at the ankles. His relaxed look didn't fool her for an instant. The former soldier had blazing-fast reflexes. If she went on the attack, he'd be out the door and running before she could stop him.

He reached down to pet her traitor of a dog, who was sprawled on the floor by his feet. Sometimes she suspected that the mastiff mix preferred Tripp's company to hers, but maybe it was because Zeke knew a soft touch when he saw one. She glanced up just in time to catch Tripp slipping the dog another treat—the third since the pair had invaded her kitchen.

"Well?"

After patting Zeke's massive head again, Tripp finally started talking. "As I already told you, my veterans group wants to hold a fundraiser sometime next year. The goal is to substantially increase our budget in order to fund some new projects we want to take on. Important ones."

She didn't doubt that for an instant. The group was known for pitching in to help whenever they could.

Evidently Tripp found explanations to be thirsty work, because he stopped talking long enough to help himself to a can of pop from the refrigerator. Rather than waiting for him to gather his scattered thoughts, she tried to help the conversation along.

"So have a garage sale. That's what all the other groups here in Snowberry Creek do." She pointed at him with her whisk. "I'll even donate all the stuff I've cleaned out of the attic to the cause. I was going to call one of the local charities to come pick it up, but all those boxes can sit out in the garage until you're ready for them."

Tripp settled back in his chair and tossed Zeke another treat. "Sorry, but the board has already rejected that idea for a couple of reasons."

"Which are?"

"Like you said, every group in town holds garage sales. The frequency results in diminishing returns. There's no way we can raise enough money that way."

"And the other reason?"

"Well, we'd like to combine the fundraiser with a special event of some kind. You know, as a way to thank the people in town for their support of our group."

Abby rolled her eyes. "So what you really hope to do is shake everyone's hand and raid their wallets at the same time."

"That's a cold-blooded way to look at things." Then he grinned. "However, I can't argue with your assessment of the situation. The idea is to make the event so inviting, folks won't notice what we're up to."

She added vanilla and sugar to the bowl and resumed beating the egg whites. "So what does this nefarious plan have to do with me?"

Tripp shifted position, leaning forward, elbows resting on the table. "Well, that's where it gets interesting."

She picked up speed with the whisk, almost splashing the egg whites out of the bowl. Since when was "interesting" a synonym for "infuriating"?

"How so?"

"Well, they asked us if we knew anyone who was both really creative and really organized. Of course, I immediately thought of you."

It would be a real shame to waste all her hard work, much less the eggs and sugar. However, the temptation to cut this conversation short by dumping the entire bowl full of fluffy white goo on Tripp's head was almost too strong to resist.

"Why would that be?"

"Several reasons. First, the ladies of the quilting guild are still raving about what an amazing job you did organizing their big garage sale. From what Glenda and Jean said, it was the best one they've ever had. I know the fire department and police department appreciate all the extra quilts the group has made for them to give to kids when they respond to an emergency."

He wasn't wrong. The garage sale had turned out better than anyone had expected, especially her. "Yeah, well, you can write it off to beginner's luck."

He shrugged his shoulders. "I also know that since you took on Mayor McKay's Committee on Senior Affairs, the whole group feels reenergized. I was talking to Connie Pohler at city hall. She said this is the first year that committee has taken on organizing the annual trick-or-treating event on Main Street. They're expecting such a huge turnout that she asked if the veterans group could help with escorting the grade school kids on their rounds and with chaperoning the games at the middle and high schools."

Abby had to laugh. "That sounds like her. I bet Rosalyn McKay is grateful every day that she was smart enough to hire that woman to be her assistant. Connie has a real talent for 'volunteering' people. I swear, you walk into city hall to ask a simple question about property taxes and somehow walk out in charge of a major town event. You're even grateful for the chance to help out."

She should know. That's how she had ended up working on the trick-or-treat event in the first place.

Tripp was still talking. "I think Connie missed her calling. If she'd gone into the military, she'd be running the Pentagon by now."

He might just be right about that. "At least she uses her powers for good and not evil."

"Yeah, she does." Tripp's smile faded a bit. "So back to our fundraiser. We all agreed you'd be perfect to head up the committee."

She sighed and set down her whisk. "I'm sorry,

Tripp, but you of all people know that I'm not in a position to take on any more commitments right now. First of all, I still have the rest of my term on the quilting guild to serve out. Thanks to the sudden influx of money from Dolly Cayhill's estate, the group has become a lot more active than it was. As for the seniors group, the mayor originally asked me to fill in just until Fred Cady, the next chairman, recovers from hip replacement surgery. He was supposed to take over back at the beginning of September, but now it looks as if he won't be up to it until mid-November at the earliest."

A less trusting person might think that was deliberate on Fred's part. The postponement meant he wouldn't be taking over until well after all the hustle and bustle of the town's upcoming Halloween Festival celebration.

She did her best to look sincerely regretful. "Please tell your friends that I'm flattered they thought of me, but I really can't take on anything else right now."

Tripp clearly wasn't buying her excuses. Either that or he didn't care how busy she was. "Sorry, Abby, but it's too late. I already accepted on your behalf."

Okay, maybe it was time to start pelting him with globs of meringue. "What were you thinking? You know you can't make a commitment of that magnitude without asking me first."

He slowly rose to his feet, came around to her side of the kitchen, and planted his size thirteens right in front of her, his massive arms crossed over his chest.

"I was thinking you owe me, Abby. You know, what with the dead body in the backyard, not to mention my rushing to the rescue when you managed to put yourself right in the crosshairs of a killer. The stress alone probably shaved five years off of my life expectancy."

Darn, he had to go and play the hero card. Still, he was exaggerating. After all, he had spent twenty years as a former Special Forces soldier, which probably put him somewhere in his late thirties. Despite his claim to the contrary, she figured he'd lost two years—three at the most.

That didn't mean she would make it easy for him. "Fine, you win, but only if you agree to be my cochair. I'm not doing this by myself."

He looked as if he was about to argue the point. She did her best to look as serious as death and gave him an ultimatum. "You and me as cochairs—that's the deal. Take it or leave it."

While he mulled over her offer, clearly still looking for a way to weasel out of it, she started spreading the meringue on the coconut cream pie she'd made with Tripp in mind. Right now, she still wasn't sure if he was going to end up eating it or wearing it. After sliding the pie into the oven to brown the top, she set the timer.

"Well, what's it going to be?"

"Fine. Cochairs. The first meeting is in a week. They'll expect at least some preliminary suggestions of what we can do."

She started cleaning up the mess she'd made on her baking spree. "Okay then. You make a list of ideas, and I'll do the same. We'll get together before the meeting to narrow it down to the most viable suggestions."

"Sounds good."

He started toward the door but then turned back. "I know this isn't what you wanted, Abby, but there is one bit of good news. At least the members of this group are used to taking orders and working as a team."

"That would be a nice change. I'll deny saying this, but I swear it's like herding kittens with the other two groups."

Meanwhile, Zeke had parked himself right in front of the door, and he whined softly. Tripp gave him a good scratching. "I didn't forget, boy."

The two males looked at her with the exact same hopeful look on their faces. "I promised Zeke I'd take him for a run at the park this afternoon. Is that okay with you?"

Evidently Tripp wasn't the only soft touch in the room. "That's fine. And the pie should be cool enough for you to take home by then." She shot him a nasty look. "Not that you deserve a treat right now, but I'd hate to see all my hard work go to waste."

He clipped on Zeke's leash. "Thanks for taking on this project, Abby. You won't regret it."

So not true, but it was too late to back out.

"I have a couple of errands to run, so make sure you have your key with you so you can let Zeke back in and get the pie. If it's still here when I get back, I might just decide I made it for me."

He winked at her. "Not a chance of that happening. See you later."

She watched from the window as Zeke led the charge up the driveway with Tripp right on his heels. A few seconds later, the timer dinged, and she set the pie out on the counter to cool. It looked delicious. Too bad she'd already promised it to Tripp, but then, she'd made coconut cream knowing it was one of his favorites. Like many of her other friends, he frequently benefited from her love of baking. In this particular instance, however, if he hadn't dropped by with his little bombshell about the committee, she would've used delivering the pie as an excuse to check in on him, not that she would admit that to him.

They hadn't known each other all that long, and Tripp was clearly a man who valued his privacy. Still, discovering a dead body in the backyard had a way of bringing people closer together. She liked to think that they were now friends, maybe even with the occasional hint of the possibility of something more when he'd surprised her with a kiss. Not that she was looking to dive into the deep end of the dating pool so soon, but the couple of times he'd kissed her still replayed in her dreams on a regular basis.

Abby had only moved to Snowberry Creek a few months back after the sudden death of her favorite aunt. She'd also just gone through a tough divorce. As part of the divorce settlement, her now ex-husband had bought out Abby's half of the small import business they'd built together, leaving her in her early thirties, single again as well as unemployed. She was still working on what came next in her life. Aunt Sybil had always rented the small mother-in-law house on the back of the property to a college student, so Abby had inherited both of her aunt's houses along with her dog and her tenant.

But back to Tripp. Lately, he'd been acting withdrawn. She wouldn't exactly say he'd been avoiding her, but she missed the time they'd spent working in the yard together or just enjoying a cold drink out on the back porch at the end of the day. Tripp's college classes kept him busy, but she had good reason to think there was something else going on in his life right now.

Back when she'd been caught up in trying to clear her late aunt's name, Tripp had confessed that he sometimes had trouble sleeping at night. When that happened, he prowled the yard trying to vanquish his inner demons so he could go back to bed. The one time she'd seen him during one of his midnight patrols, he'd been barefoot and wearing a T-shirt and flannel pajama bottoms.

But twice lately, Zeke had woken her up after midnight to draw her attention to Tripp slipping out of his house dressed in his old uniform and combat boots. He'd been carrying a heavily laden backpack as he'd headed up the driveway. She and Zeke had followed his progress from window to window until he disappeared into the shadows. They'd ended up sitting at her window in the dark watching for Tripp's return. He'd stayed gone for almost three hours, finally returning shortly before dawn. The only change she could see was that his pack looked empty.

So both weird and worrisome.

It didn't help that she hadn't been sleeping well since discovering his nighttime escapades. The least little noise, real or imagined, jarred her awake. Then she'd sit on the edge of her bed and watch out the window for any sign that Tripp was out wandering around again. Eventually, she'd give up and lie back down until something else woke her up. It didn't make for restful nights.

Sighing, she checked the depressingly long list on the front of the refrigerator to see what she should be doing next. At least she could cross off a few things. The laundry, vacuuming, and dusting were all done.

The pie hadn't been on the list, so she added it at the bottom and immediately drew a line through it. Maybe that was cheating, but she got a lot of satisfaction from seeing that the completed jobs outnumbered the ones left to do.

With that done, she gathered up everything she needed to take with her as she made her rounds through town. Her first stop would be the fire department to drop off the latest batch of quilts for the first responders to hand out to children at accidents and fires. She had another bunch for the police department, but she'd drop those off when she got to the meeting at city hall regarding the Halloween Festival, which was now just over two weeks away.

She had been counting the days, looking forward to finally having a little downtime after the big celebration was over. Now, thanks to Tripp, she'd be lucky if she even had time to catch her breath before having to launch right into organizing whatever the veterans group settled on as their big fundraiser.

"Take it one day at a time" had become her mantra. If she thought too much about everything she had to get done, she'd end up in a corner sucking her thumb and whimpering.

Rather than dwell on that charming possibility, she picked up the first box of quilts and carried it out to the car. On the second trip, she grabbed her purse, the canvas bag with the library books she needed to return, and the final box of quilts.

Five minutes later, she drove over to Main Street and the first of her stops. The only positive note was that if everything went smoothly, she'd have time to stop at Something's Brewing to pick up an iced coffee before the meeting. No doubt she'd also give in to temptation and try out one of Bridey's latest creations, especially if her friend had made another gooey butter cake. Evidently she'd gotten the recipe from someone who'd grown up in St. Louis, and the response from the folks here in Snowberry Creek, Washington, had been enthusiastic.

Already, imagining biting into the delicious concoction had improved her mood. Who wouldn't love a thick layer of sweetened cream cheese and butter on top of a coffee cake? With that happy thought, she drove to the fire department to drop off the quilts.

Unfortunately, nothing went smoothly at all. Her stop at the fire department took longer than expected, which put her behind schedule. By the time she pulled into the parking lot in back of city hall, she had to hit the ground running to avoid being late for her meeting. Under normal circumstances, that wouldn't have been a big deal, but she didn't trust the rest of the committee members not to volunteer her for something if she wasn't there to defend herself.

She'd seen it happen to someone else, and the last thing she needed was to get saddled with another project for the upcoming festival. While she liked Connie Pohler a lot, the woman's idea of a small favor was the stuff of nightmares as far as Abby was concerned.

Luckily, the meeting hadn't yet been called to order when she walked into the conference room located down the hall from the mayor's office. Bridey's husband, Seth Kyser, smiled as she slipped into the empty seat next to him.

"Did I miss anything?"

He laughed. "We didn't sign you up for another project, if that's what you're asking."

Then he reached down to pick up a cardboard drink tray from the floor on the other side of his chair and handed it to her. "Bridey thought you might need these."

Bless the woman, it was an iced coffee and a huge piece of the cake she'd been craving. "Thank her for me. I might just make it through the day after all."

He winked at her and then turned to answer a question from the man across the table. Abby glanced around the table and was relieved to see she wasn't the only one who was using the last few minutes before the meeting was called to order to finish off a quick snack.

"Boy, that cake looks a lot better than what I'm having. What kind is it?"

Abby smiled at the woman sitting next to her. "It's called gooey butter cake—one of Bridey Kyser's latest experiments. Would you like a bite?"

Not that she really wanted to share.

"That's okay. My husband and I are trying to watch what we eat. I'm Kristy Hake, by the way. I don't believe we've ever been officially introduced. I own the beauty shop down the street, and Dean is a retired carpenter. He keeps himself busy doing a lot of handyman work around town."

"It's nice to finally meet you. I've heard a lot of good things about you from Glenda Unger and Jean Benson."

Kristy brightened up. "That's nice of them. They're two of my favorite customers."

When Connie Pohler entered the room talking on

her cell phone, Kristy leaned in closer. "This is your first year helping with the festival, isn't it?"

She didn't wait for Abby to respond before continuing. "I always head up the pie-eating contest, and Dean is in charge of the games and activities for the kids at the middle school and high school."

"I'm helping organize the trick-or-treating on Main Street, and the quilting guild is putting together all the candy bags for that."

Before they could continue the conversation, the meeting was finally called to order. Abby sipped her coffee and did her best to avoid making eye contact with Connie as the woman asked for status reports and then listed the jobs she still needed someone to take on. The meeting dragged on for almost two hours, but Abby made it through without getting tagged for anything else.

On the way out, Seth held the door open for her. Neither of them said a word until they reached the parking lot. Then he made a pretense of looking all around them. "I like Connie a lot, but it sure doesn't pay to let her corner you when she's on the hunt for volunteers. Think we made a clean getaway?"

She laughed. "So far, so good. I have to stop at the library and the police department, but just in case, I'm tempted to put those things off until tomorrow. Maybe by then she'll have found all the victims . . . I mean volunteers she needs."

"Dream on, lady. Even if she has a full roster for Halloween, there's always Thanksgiving, Christmas, and New Year's to think about."

Even if he meant that assessment to be funny, it didn't make it any less true. "Maybe I'll just mail my books back to the library."

They'd reached her car. "Need a ride back to the coffee shop? I'm going right by there."

"Thanks, but the walk will do me good." He looked a bit sheepish. "I ate two pieces of that gooey butter cake before the meeting, and that was on top of the pumpkin spice cookies Bridey had me sample this morning."

Seth set off across the parking lot toward his wife's shop. Abby watched him for a few seconds, still trying to decide whether she should risk another trip back into the building. If the books weren't overdue and she hadn't promised the quilts would be delivered today, she might have gotten in and driven away.

Knowing her conscience wouldn't rest easy if she gave in to cowardice, she grabbed the box of quilts and her book bag out of the car and headed back inside. She made it in and out of the library in the back of the building in record time, but the front desk in the police department was empty. While she waited for the officer on duty to reappear, Connie walked in and headed straight for her.

"Hey, I'm glad I caught you."

Pasting a smile on her face, Abby turned to greet her. "What can I do for you, Connie?"

One look at the list clutched in Connie's hand told her she might regret asking that question. All she could do was wait to see how much trouble she was in now.

Chapter Two

Connie glanced at the paper in her hand. "I just wanted to make sure that you have everything you need for your committees."

"As far as I know. I have meetings scheduled with each of them later this week. We'll go over the plans in detail to make sure we haven't forgotten anything. We'll also be putting together bags of treats for the businesses to hand out to the kids on Halloween."

"Perfect!" Connie's smile was a bit apologetic. "I know heading up two different activities for the festival is a lot to ask of anyone, but it's such a relief to have someone in charge who stays on top of things. Without naming names, I can tell you that's not always the case."

Then she patted Abby on the shoulder and was off and running again.

"I'd give anything to have that woman's energy, or at least a way to syphon some off now and again to help me get through the day."

Abby turned to smile at Gage Logan, the chief of police, who had just walked into the room. "Me, too. Although right now I'm just glad she wasn't looking for another sucker . . . oops, I meant *volunteer* to take on running the entire festival."

His deep laugh rang out across the room. "So true. I'm on the hook to help out at the high school on Halloween night from eight until eleven. Before that, I'll be helping escort the munchkins on Main Street with the veterans group."

"Tripp mentioned that Connie had 'volunteered' a bunch of you for that duty. Sounds like fun, though. I can't wait to see all the kids decked out in their costumes."

"Yeah, they can be pretty cute."

He gave her a long look. "Have you decided what you're going to wear?"

His question left her speechless. "Seriously? We're expected to dress up, too? No one said anything to me about that."

"It's become a tradition over the years, but they probably forgot that this is your first Halloween Festival here in town."

Great, one more thing to add to her ever-growing to-do list. Sighing, she said, "I guess I'll figure out something. How about you? I'm guessing going dressed as a police officer would be considered cheating."

He grinned. "Yeah, I tried that one year. My daughter gave me grief for weeks. Along about September every year, she starts nagging me to think of something new. Seems she doesn't want me to be an embarrassment in front of all of her friends at the high school. Coming up with this year's costume, though, was a slam dunk."

"How so?"

Gage glanced around the lobby to make sure they were still alone. "Don't tell anyone, but the veterans all decided we'd come dressed as G.I. Joes or Janes. We've already bought the squirt guns we plan to carry."

Okay, that was funny. Had Tripp offered up his own personal collection of action figures as inspiration for the group? She knew he had a bunch of them, because she'd bought the set for him at the quilting guild's garage sale after she'd seen him admiring them.

She offered Gage a hopeful look. "I suppose it's too late for me to enlist. You know, as a mascot or something."

"Yeah, sorry, but I'm sure you'll come up with a great idea."

He glanced at the box of quilts she'd set down on the floor while she was talking to Connie. "Are those for us?"

"Yep, and Glenda said to tell you we'd have more for you in a few weeks."

"Tell the ladies we really do appreciate getting these. It means a lot to the kids who receive them. It's amazing how much better they feel when we give them one of the teddy bears and a quilt to cuddle up with."

"We enjoy working on them."

He picked up the box. "Just a warning, though. Rumor has it that the county sheriff and his deputies are jealous. You may be hearing from them to see if you can make some quilts for them, too."

She knew better than to blindly volunteer the ladies for more work without discussing it with them first. "I'll add it to the agenda for our next meeting. If there's enough interest, I'll get back in touch with you to get the name of someone to contact at the sheriff's department."

"Sounds good. Now, I'd better get back to work."

He glanced back one last time. "Good luck with the costume."

"Thanks a lot."

Although at least now she knew she needed to come up with something to wear. It would've been awful to have shown up for the big event and been the only person not in costume. One more thing to worry about. At least with her errands done, she could head back home. A nap was sounding pretty good about now.

After all, this could be another night where she stood watch and waited for Tripp to return from his mysterious midnight wandering.

"Well, Zeke, there he goes again."

The dog whined softly and wagged his tail. It was hard to tell if he was worried about his buddy or jealous because he wasn't getting to tag along on Tripp's late-night walk. That got her to thinking. Even if Zeke didn't get to go exploring with Tripp, there was no reason she couldn't.

It might not be the smartest thing she'd ever decided to do, but she was worried about him and needed to know what was going on.

After exchanging her pajamas for sweats, she pelted down the stairs to the kitchen, where she grabbed her cell phone and keys off the counter and then dug a flashlight out of the drawer. After putting on shoes and a jacket, she charged out the front door and down the sidewalk to the street. There, she paused to look both ways and finally spotted Tripp about three blocks away as he walked under a streetlight. She hesitated a few more seconds. He was a grown man, a trained soldier, and a very private person—all good reasons to believe he could take care of himself.

Regardless, driven by a compulsion she couldn't seem to override, she set off after him. If she could get some idea of where he was going and what he was up to on his mysterious forays, maybe she could start sleeping through the night again. She hoped so.

It took considerable effort on her part to close some of the distance between them, leaving her breathing hard. If she hadn't hustled, though, she would've missed seeing where he turned off the street to disappear into the trees—part of a national forest that surrounded the town of Snowberry Creek on two sides.

She always enjoyed the dense woods that formed a backdrop for the town, and she often walked Zeke along the trail that led deeper into the trees. In the daylight, the dappled shade was cool, and the air was fragrant with the spicy scent of the enormous cedars and Douglas firs.

But in the dark of night, the place took on a more sinister appearance. To make matters worse, all the scream queen movies she'd watched back in high school started playing out in her head. Hoping she wasn't crossing into too-stupid-to-live territory, she took a deep breath and kept right on walking.

To keep Tripp from realizing he was being followed, she kept the small flashlight aimed on the path just a step or two in front of her feet. Every so often, she paused to listen for any sign that her quarry was nearby. If he was, the man had some serious stealth skills going on. The deep silence gave her the creeps, and the goose bumps on her skin had nothing to do with the temperature of the cool night air. Then the sound of a twig snapping from somewhere off to her left had her spinning around to head right back home where she belonged.

What on earth had she been thinking?

For sure, she hadn't been thinking that someone would reach out of the darkness to clamp his hand across her mouth and drag her deeper into the shadows. She fought with everything she had, but the man who was holding her was far stronger than she was. He smelled bad, too, making it likely that it had been a long time since he'd showered or put on clean clothes.

Not that either of those things mattered right now. Who cared if her attacker practiced good hygiene? It was more important that she break free and get the heck out of Dodge, or at least back to her house, where she could barricade herself inside. Her foot made hard contact with the jerk's shin, but her best kick had no effect on him at all. Neither did biting the hand he had over her mouth, although it must have hurt, from the way he cursed and tightened his grip.

It was impossible to keep track of time or distance as he half carried, half dragged her through the trees. Each terrifying step took them farther and farther away from any chance of crossing paths with anyone else, someone who could call for help. God, she didn't want to die out here in the forest. She had meetings scheduled. Obligations that had to be met. A dog who depended on her. A tenant she wanted to kick for his midnight ramblings.

She gradually became aware of a faint scent of

wood smoke. Were they nearing a campground? Hope was such a fragile thing, but she clung to it as the smell continued to get stronger. As the two of them headed down a steep slope, she thought she saw a flicker of fire at the bottom. A campfire, maybe. Finally, the trees thinned out enough that she could see more of her surroundings, which included a solitary tent. So not a campground, but a single campsite. That wasn't good news at all.

Then a deep voice rang out through the trees, freezing her captor in place. "Sergeant Montgomery, report!"

The big body behind hers immediately jerked to attention. "I've captured an enemy scout, Master Sergeant."

Abby fought without success to break free, her terror growing exponentially with the addition of the second man. Meanwhile, the two men continued their conversation. It was only after she slumped in defeat that she gradually realized one of the voices was familiar. Tripp stepped out of the shadows into her direct line of sight. His hard-eyed gaze raked over her, top to bottom. His facial expression was totally blank. He looked so cold and unforgiving, nothing like the man she'd come to know.

Finally, he looked past her to the man who continued to hold her prisoner. "Sergeant, I promise you that woman is not the enemy or a spy. I have no idea what she is doing wandering around out here in the dead of night, but I will find out and report back to you. For now, please allow me to escort her out of your territory. I promise she won't return."

The other man tightened his grip on her, and it felt like he was shaking his head in denial. "Sorry,

Master Sergeant, but the enemy has shown a lot of increased activity recently. I know one of them is a woman, but I haven't gotten close enough to see her face. How do we know this isn't her?"

Okay, so the man wasn't exactly operating in the same reality as she was. Tripp maintained a calm facade as he talked his friend in off the ledge.

"I know you're worried about your territory being infiltrated, Sergeant, but I promise you Abby here is nosy but not dangerous. You remember Zeke? He lives with her. You know he wouldn't stick with someone who wasn't trustworthy."

It was the first time she'd ever heard anyone use a dog as a character reference, but she was all for it if the mastiff mix's opinion of her carried weight with this guy.

"You're sure?"

Tripp gave a sharp nod. "I am. As I said, I'll take responsibility for escorting her out of the area. If you decide to move your camp, leave word in the usual place. I'll find you."

"Yes, sir."

Abby's rubbery legs failed to support her when the stranger abruptly shoved her toward Tripp. At least he managed to catch her before she hit the ground. His hold on her arms was hard almost to the point of bruising. Either he was really angry that she was there or he was still worried about what his companion would do.

"I unpacked the supplies I brought you, Sergeant. I'll check back with you in a few days to see if there's anything else you need. If something comes up before then, you know how to get ahold of me or one of the others."

As he spoke, he turned Abby so that she finally faced her captor. To her surprise, she recognized him from seeing him wandering around in town. He was always dressed in ragged fatigues and combat boots. Between his bushy beard and messy ponytail, it was difficult to guess his age accurately, but her best estimate would be in his fifties somewhere. The lines around his eyes made her think that a lot of those years had been tough ones. He had to be one of the homeless vets that the local support group was trying to help.

Her heart hurt for the man, although she was still afraid of him, even with Tripp standing right behind her. Then the former soldier met her gaze for the first time. That small connection had him relaxing a little, and he gave her an apologetic look before turning his attention back to Tripp.

"I'll be fine, Master Sergeant. You'd better get the lady back home."

Then he smiled just a little. "Ma'am, I wouldn't want Zeke to get upset with me for mistreating his owner. Tell him Sergeant Kevin Montgomery is sorry for the misunderstanding."

Somehow she knew the apology was really meant for her, so she answered before Tripp had a chance to intercede again. "I'll tell him we're good, Sergeant."

Then the man faded back into the shadows, leaving Abby alone with her pissed-off tenant. As they headed back up the slope and toward home, she was pretty sure an already long night was only going to get longer.

Chapter Three

As it turned out, she was wrong about her night-time adventure dragging on into the wee hours of the morning. Tripp didn't rip into her for her stupidity in following him out into the forest. Instead, he remained coldly silent all the way back to the house, where he deposited her at her back door.

He finally spoke after she'd turned the key in the lock, his comments short and to the point. "How dumb can one woman possibly be? You could've been killed out there, if not by Kevin, then by someone else if he really has seen other people prowling those woods at night. For the last time, stay out of my business. I don't want to find your body out there. I already have too many deaths on my conscience."

Then he walked away before she could apologize for once again stirring up the ghosts from his past. That didn't stop her from texting him as soon as she got inside the house.

I'm sorry, but I was worried about you. So was Zeke. Next time I'll try asking you what's going on, even though I figure you probably won't tell me.

She gave Zeke a thorough scratching and delivered Kevin's message while she waited to see if Tripp would respond. Even though she hoped he would, she still jumped when her cell phone chimed to alert her to a new message.

See, you're getting smarter already. Go to bed, and stay there this time.

For once, she didn't argue. She headed back up to her bedroom, where she changed back into her pajamas without bothering to turn on any lights. Before climbing under the covers, she looked out the window toward the small mother-in-law house where Tripp lived. Just as she suspected, he was standing out in the yard staring toward her bedroom window. Unsure if he could actually see her, she waved anyway.

When he raised a hand in response, the knot of worry in her chest eased just a little. A second later, he disappeared into his own place. Sleep was slow in coming. Finally, she coaxed Zeke up onto the bed. With his warm presence curled up next to her, she finally shook off the last of the night's shadows and drifted off.

Abby fought to hide a yawn and made a promise to herself that the next time she decided to take a midnight ramble, it wouldn't be the night before she had a city council meeting on her schedule. They were never any fun, but this one threatened to drag on for a record amount of time.

She glanced toward the man who was responsible for why everyone else was stuck sitting in the high school gym for half an hour past the usual time. Although she didn't know him personally, everyone who'd ever attended one of the regularly scheduled meetings knew who Ronald Minter was. A local farmer, he was on a permanent crusade to let the mayor and anyone else who would listen know everything that was wrong with the town of Snowberry Creek. He came to every meeting with a long list of complaints. All Abby could figure was that it was the closest thing to a hobby the man had.

This time he was complaining about the new speed limit on the road that went past his small farm. As a result of the higher speed, he claimed fewer people were stopping to buy his pumpkins or to visit his corn maze. It was a direct attack on him and his right to earn a decent living wage.

She spent the time considering various options for fundraisers for her upcoming meeting with the veterans group rather than listening to Mr. Minter's rambling critiques of everything he didn't like in the town—the route the homecoming parade had taken, the zoning commission's recent rulings, the condition of the flowers in the baskets along Main Street in town. After texting a few ideas to herself, she looked around the room to see if the meeting was finally winding down.

But no, Mr. Minter was still talking, his voice ringing with righteous indignation. "I tell you, every other day another one disappears. I reported the thefts to the county sheriff's department and got nowhere with them. I even told them the most likely culprit is that homeless guy who hides out in the woods near my place."

He paused to glance around the room. "I get that pumpkins being stolen seems like no big deal to anyone else, but it's my livelihood on the line. He's stealing from me and trespassing on my property. I know most of the farm is in the county's jurisdiction, but part of my property is within the city limits. I want to know what the city is going to do about this guy."

It didn't take Abby long to connect the dots and realize he was talking about Tripp's friend. Should she tell Tripp what was being said so he could warn Kevin to stay away from the pumpkin farm? Finally, Gage Logan signaled to the mayor that he'd like to address the group.

Mr. Minter reluctantly returned to his seat, his hands clenched in fists as he sat down. Gage took his place at the microphone set up facing the council. "Madam Mayor, members of the council. One of my deputies has already spoken to the individual in question. He has agreed to avoid Mr. Minter's property when he comes into town."

He glanced back toward the farmer before continuing. "For the record, we saw no evidence that the man in question has been pilfering pumpkins. I will, however, continue to monitor the situation."

Mayor McKay spoke next. "Thank you for that information, Chief Logan. Now, if there is no other business we need to address, I move we adjourn the meeting."

From the speed with which the motion was seconded and then voted upon, Abby wasn't the only one who wanted to be headed out the door before Mr. Minter or anyone else could prevent their escape. She made it to the exit before the rest of the stampede, stepping out into the lobby of city hall right behind Gage Logan.

She caught up with him. "Gage, I know Tripp

visits that vet. Would you like me to tell him about Mr. Minter's complaint?"

"Okay, but let him know that if it continues to be a problem, I'll give him a heads-up." He offered her a small smile. "One thing, though. I would've thought you'd have learned your lesson about getting involved in police matters, Abby."

Her cheeks burned hot. After all, this wasn't a murder investigation. Rather than point that out, she changed the subject. "I probably shouldn't say anything, but I've been worried about him. Tripp, that is. Not Kevin. I know he prowls the yard at night when he has trouble sleeping, but slipping out in full uniform seems to be taking it to a whole new level. I just learned that he's been meeting with Sergeant Montgomery at night."

The lobby was starting to fill up. Gage nodded toward the door. "I'll walk you out to your car."

He waited until they were outside and safe from being overheard before he spoke again. "I get that you worry about Tripp, Abby. As far as I can tell, he's doing fine. He checks on Kevin at night because he knows that's a hard time for him, too. Having said that, if you ever have cause to think there is something going on with Tripp, don't hesitate to call me. Not as chief of police, but as his friend."

"I will."

Although she was willing to bet that Tripp wouldn't appreciate them talking about him behind his back.

They'd reached her car. Gage stood by while she unlocked the door and got in. She rolled the window down. "Stop by sometime for coffee. I always have a freezer full of cookies on hand for friends."

"I might just do that. Drive careful."

He patted the top of her car and then stepped back as she drove away. Fifteen minutes later, she let Zeke out one last time before they both turned in for the night. Tomorrow was another busy day, starting with tracking down Tripp to work on their agenda for the upcoming veterans meeting.

And if he didn't cooperate, she would make sure he knew that coconut pie was the last piece of pastry he was going to get from her until he got with the program.

Chapter Four

To make good on her promise to touch base with Tripp, Abby had texted him before the first pot of coffee of the day had finished brewing. She'd also put together a suggested timeline for meetings, as well as a list of ideas she'd come up with for the group to consider. Did he appreciate the sacrifice that had been taken on her part, especially before she'd had her first dose of caffeine for the day? Evidently not, since he hadn't bothered to respond. It wasn't because he wasn't up yet. She'd heard him head out for his daily run just as the sun was starting to make its presence known.

He still hadn't answered by the time she drove into town to pick up a few things at the grocery store. As soon as she got back home, she would hunt him down and demand some answers. She'd also make it clear that if he continued to avoid her, she would be contacting the veterans group herself to tender her resignation from the project.

Satisfied with her plan, she decided to stop in at Something's Brewing to get Bridey's price list for catering desserts for events like the one the veterans might be holding. Of course, that was really just her excuse for buying a tall latte and testing another one of Bridey's creations.

After parking her car, she was heading down the block toward the coffee shop when the sound of angry voices drew her attention. Looking around, she spotted two men on the other side of the street who were yelling at each other. They were drawing a bit of a crowd, although no one seemed inclined to intervene. Not that she blamed them for keeping their distance once she recognized both men: Ronald Minter and Sergeant Kevin Montgomery.

There was no way she would want either one to turn his anger in her direction. When Kevin tried to walk away from Ronald, the other man followed right along behind him, still waving his hands in the air and yelling.

"How many times have I told you to stay the hell away from my farm? I've got pumpkins rotting in the field because people don't want to stop when someone like you is always lurking around."

The former soldier shook his head. "Not me. I'm not there in the daylight. Must be the enemy troops I've seen moving through the area."

Ronald looked triumphant. "See, now you've admitted that you trespass, and I've got witnesses. Wait until I tell the cops about that. They'll have to come out and investigate in person now. I already showed them pictures of where you've been sleeping in my corn maze, but they wouldn't do anything. They said there was no proof that those boot prints were yours."

Kevin backed away and turned as if to leave.

Ronald made a grab for Kevin's sleeve but missed. "I don't know why the police haven't run you off or arrested you for vagrancy. I can tell you this much, though. If they don't get the job done, I will. I don't give a damn if you really were in the army or not, and I have serious doubts about that. Regardless, that ratty uniform doesn't entitle you to special privileges."

Kevin finally spun back to face him, stepping close enough to use his size to intimidate the smaller man. "You might not respect me, you little jerk, but you *will* respect the uniform. Men and women died so you can raise those stupid pumpkins that you're so proud of."

To Abby's surprise, several of the people actually applauded Kevin's comment, which only inflamed Ronald's temper. He shot everyone a dirty look. "Fine, clap your hands like a bunch of idiots. I'm willing to bet that none of you would like it much if this guy decided to camp out in your backyard instead of mine. That uniform didn't earn him the right to trespass."

Kevin was breathing hard, his eyes looking wild, just as they had that night out in the woods. She really wished Tripp was there to intervene on the part of his friend before things really got out of hand.

Still, he kept his hands down at his side as he snarled, "Get out of my face, little man, or you'll be sorry."

Ronald didn't heed his warning, but at least Kevin made no move to touch him. If the two actually did get physical with each other, it wouldn't go well for either of them. She pulled out her cell, intending to text Tripp about the situation, when she realized someone had already called the police. The sound of sirens was getting louder by the second. As soon as the flashing lights came into sight, Kevin took off through the gathering crowd and hustled down the street toward the park. Although it was none of her business, Abby decided to stick around a little longer to see what happened so she could tell Tripp about his friend's problems.

One of Gage's deputies pulled up and walked straight over to Ronald. Whoever had called the police must have told the dispatcher exactly who had been involved in the confrontation. At least now that the actual argument was over, most of the spectators began drifting away to take care of their own business.

With the primary target for his anger long gone, Ronald immediately launched into a loud list of complaints to the deputy. Abby shook her head. Did the man really think that accusing the deputy of taking his own sweet time getting there was going to earn him any points with the man? Then he demanded that the police launch a search for the homeless veteran and arrest him for assaulting Ronald on a public street.

Unfortunately for him, though, witnesses immediately stepped forward to make sure the deputy knew that Ronald had started the argument and that no blows had been exchanged. They pointed down the street toward the park and said Kevin had left the scene rather than continue the discussion.

The deputy took a few names and jotted down notes in the spiral notebook he'd pulled out of his uniform pocket. As he did, Ronald prowled back and forth on the sidewalk, continuing to mutter under his breath. Now that the excitement was over, the small gathering continued to disperse until Ronald and the officer were all that remained. That didn't keep Ronald from glaring at everyone in the general area, his fists tightly clenched at his sides. He glared across at Abby and took a step in her direction. "What are you staring at?"

Luckily, the deputy said something, which drew the

man's attention back to him. Regardless, it was definitely time to make herself scarce. She hustled down the block to the coffee shop and crossed her fingers that the angry man didn't decide to follow her.

Once she was safely inside, she peeked back out the front window and was relieved to see Minter getting into a pickup truck. The deputy stood leaning against the fender of his squad car with his arms crossed over his chest as he watched the other man drive away. When the pickup disappeared around the corner, the deputy took one more look up and down the street before finally resuming his patrol.

Bridey joined Abby at the window. "Is there something exciting going on?"

Abby smiled back at her friend. "Not anymore. Mr. Minter had words with Sergeant Montgomery. The situation threatened to turn ugly, but they're both gone now."

Bridey sighed. "I don't suppose it will ever occur to Ronald Minter that he's his own worst enemy. I personally avoid him, and he doesn't come in here."

That was a relief. "I've only seen him at the city council meetings, but I drive past his farm whenever I need to go into Seattle for something. I love seeing the fields full of ripe pumpkins. It looks so festive."

They walked away from the window and over to the counter, where Abby eyed the pastries in the glass display case. The pumpkin-shaped cookies were really cute, as were the ghosts, not to mention the cupcakes decorated to look like witches. It was hard to choose, but finally she pointed toward a tray of small blackberry tarts. "I'll have my usual and one of those for here and another to go."

Bridey dished up the tarts and then made Abby's

latte. "Speaking of pumpkins, have you heard about the big mystery in town?"

Her friend's grin made it clear that whatever was going on wasn't a bad thing. "No, I haven't."

"Evidently someone has started carving pumpkin portraits of people here in town and leaving them on their doorsteps. So far, Mayor McKay found one of her sitting on the steps outside of city hall. The next person to find one was Frannie over at the diner. You wouldn't think it would be possible for a jack-o'-lantern to look so . . . well, *lifelike* isn't exactly right, but you know what I mean. Both portraits were unmistakable." Bridey pulled out her cell phone and brought up a pair of pictures for Abby to see.

"Wow, you're right. I would've recognized them immediately. Whoever carved those is really talented. Any idea who is doing them?"

"Not so far. A few people have asked my husband if he carved them, but it wasn't Seth. His only medium is wood. He swears he's never had any urge to express himself through vegetables."

Okay, that was funny. "I can understand why. It's a lot of work to put into something that isn't going to last much past Halloween."

The bell over the door chimed as a handful of teenagers came streaming into the shop. Abby paid for her order. "I'd better grab a table before the place fills up."

"Good idea. I love the kids, but they do tend to take over the place. I almost forgot that it's a half day at the high school. I'd better go get my assistant. Take care, Abby."

"I will."

As she settled at a small table near the back, her phone buzzed. "Finally, Tripp."

But as she quickly scanned his response to her text, she wanted to throttle him. Obviously the man was either jerking her chain or, worse yet, not taking his responsibilities to the committee very seriously. His best ideas for fundraisers included a lemonade stand and a topless car wash. Next, he'd probably suggest they could go door to door selling cookies and candy. At least he'd gone on to explain that the "topless" part of the car wash equation meant they wouldn't wash the roofs of the cars. Funny, but not helpful.

Rather than respond, she ate her blackberry tart and decided his would make a nice dessert for her evening meal. Of course, he wouldn't know he was missing out on such yumminess unless she told him. After snapping a quick picture of the tart, she sent it to him and pointed out the error of his ways.

Sorry, but no blackberry tarts for those who don't pull their weight, mister.

His response wasn't long in coming.

That's okay. I still have one piece of the coconut cream pie left.

Enjoy it while you can. It will be the last one you get for the foreseeable future. Too bad, so sad.

Her phone remained silent long enough that she thought he wasn't going to answer. She disposed of her trash and got ready to leave. Just before she reached the door, her phone buzzed again.

Seriously, I'm at school studying for a test. Want to meet up tomorrow morning around ten to discuss plans? I promise to behave and work hard.

Cursing herself for being such a soft touch, she texted back.

It's a deal, but I'm holding your tart prisoner until you make good on that promise.

Even knowing it was impossible, considering Tripp was across town at the college, she could've sworn she heard him laughing.

The next morning, ten o'clock came and went with no sign of Tripp anywhere. They hadn't actually said if they were meeting at her place or his, but she'd assumed they'd work at her kitchen table. For one thing, he'd never once invited her into the small mother-in-law house he rented from her.

When the clock ticked past ten thirty, she and Zeke headed across the backyard to knock on Tripp's door. No response—and there were no lights on inside, either. His usual parking spot was empty, another obvious indication he wasn't home.

"Zeke, I don't know what's going on with your buddy, but I have to admit I'm getting worried about him."

The big dog whined and sniffed at Tripp's door. She patted him on the head. "I know, it's not like him to stand us up like this. If he needed to reschedule, he could have just called."

Well, there was no reason to keep lurking outside his door. "Let's go back to the house, Zeke. We can keep an eye out for Tripp while I organize the candy for the goody bags the quilting guild will be putting together this afternoon."

She wasn't always sure how much Zeke actually understood when she talked to him, but it was a sure bet he recognized any and all food-related words. At the mention of candy, he woofed and charged across the yard toward the house. She caught up with him on the back porch.

"Sorry, buddy, but no sweets for you. Do you remember what happened the last time you helped yourself to the candy dish?"

Evidently he did, because his enthusiasm immediately dimmed. Taking pity on her loyal companion, she fed him one of the organic treats that she made for him on a regular basis. She fixed herself a cup of coffee and headed into the dining room to start opening the bags of candy and pouring them into the large bowls she'd set out earlier. Half a dozen of the ladies from the guild were due to arrive at one to spend the next two hours putting together a bunch of goody bags for the merchants on Main Street to hand out on Halloween. The candy had been donated for that purpose, and the committee had volunteered to get it all organized.

Considering the number of kids she'd been told were expected to participate in the town's festival, she was glad the group was getting an early start on the project. She just wished Tripp would take his group's fundraiser as seriously.

Just as she opened the last bag of today's allotment of candy, she heard the familiar rumble of Tripp's truck coming down the driveway. Rather than charging outside to confront him, she kept working. Even if he wanted to offer an excuse for not showing up, she was no longer in the mood to listen.

When Tripp knocked on the back door, Zeke gave a cheerful bark and charged down the hall to the kitchen, leaving her no choice but to follow. She didn't immediately open the door, preferring to glare at her tenant through the window. At least the man had the good sense to look apologetic.

"Come on, Abby, let me in."

She knew a stubborn man when she saw one, so she gave in and opened the door. That didn't mean she was going to go easy on him. "You're late."

"I know, and I'm sorry." He shuffled from one foot to the other. "Worse yet, I can't stay very long. I have a class in a couple of hours."

"Fine."

She started to shut the door, but he reached out to stop her. "At least give me a chance to explain."

Her temper got the best of her. "Why should I? You were supposed to be here over an hour ago. If you changed your mind about wanting to meet, all you had to do was make a simple phone call or even send me a text."

"I was at the hospital."

The blunt statement defused her anger and converted it right into a huge dose of guilt. "What happened? Are you okay?"

He ran his fingers through his dark hair. "It wasn't me. Rudy, one of the guys from the veterans group, called me at six to say he wasn't feeling all that good this morning and asked if I could come give him a ride to the clinic. When I got there, he looked like hell, and I ended up calling nine-one-one. They transported him to the county hospital, and I followed to keep an eye on the situation."

Abby stepped out of the way and opened the door wider. "Is he okay?"

"He should be. They kept him for observation, though. Seems he had a bad reaction to some new medicine his doctor put him on for his heart. We'll know more by tomorrow. Pastor Haliday came to sit with him, and a couple of the other guys will take turns to cover the rest of the day."

"That's good news."

But it was clear the whole event had taken its toll on Tripp. He looked pretty haggard, with those dark circles under his eyes and a day's worth of whiskers shading his jaw. If she had to guess, she suspected he also had on yesterday's clothes.

"Have you even had breakfast?"

When he shook his head, she pointed him toward the table. "Sit down before you fall down. I'll fix you something."

That he didn't argue was just that much more proof of how tired he was. She poured him a cup of coffee and gave him the tart she'd held back for him. "Eat that to get you started."

Deciding it was closer to lunch than breakfast, she made him a huge ham sandwich and heated up a bowl of soup in the microwave. To keep the other male in the room happy, she set some more of Zeke's treats within easy reach for Tripp to dole out as he saw fit.

Seeing how quickly he was inhaling the meal, she made him a second sandwich and then one for herself before joining him at the table. By the time they were both done eating, he looked a great deal better.

"Thanks, Abby. That really hit the spot."

Tripp picked up her plate and his own dishes and headed for the sink. She started to protest, but past experience had taught her that resistance was futile. The man liked to earn his keep.

"I'm glad your friend will be all right."

"Me, too."

After he loaded everything in the dishwasher, he topped off both of their coffee cups before sitting back down. "He's a Vietnam-era vet with no family in the area. One of the things our group is trying to do is to create a buddy system so no one has to feel like they're totally on their own. I'm on Rudy's list of people he can call twenty-four/seven."

Which reminded her—she still hadn't told him about Kevin's argument with Ronald Minter. Maybe now wasn't the best time, when Tripp was already worried about Rudy, but she might not have another chance anytime soon.

"Look, I don't want to worry you, but I thought you might want to know that Sergeant Montgomery was involved in a confrontation in the middle of town yesterday."

Just that quickly, Tripp's shoulders sagged and he sighed. "What did Kevin do this time?"

"I'm not sure he did anything at all. In fact, he wasn't the one who started the argument." She paused to sip her coffee as she thought about what she actually knew for sure. "At least I don't think so. I was on the other side of the street heading for Bridey's shop when I heard shouting. Do you know Ronald Minter, that guy who owns the pumpkin farm and corn maze just outside of town?"

Tripp frowned and then shook his head. "I may have heard the name, but I wouldn't recognize the guy if I saw him."

She snorted. "You're not missing anything. He has a well-deserved reputation as the town grump and for complaining about everything and everyone, especially at the city council meetings. His problems are always someone else's fault. This time he accused Kevin of trespassing and possibly stealing pumpkins out of his field."

Pinching the bridge of his nose as if fighting a headache, Tripp asked, "Dare I ask how Kevin reacted to that?"

"He yelled right back at him but then started to walk away. Unfortunately, that's when Minter told him that he wondered if Kevin had earned the right to wear that uniform, and said that even if he had, it didn't make it okay for him to trespass."

Even from her vantage point across the street, it had been easy to see how that had infuriated the former soldier. "I was really worried that Kevin would lose it. However, to his credit, he didn't. Kevin informed the jerk that he might not have to respect him, but he did need to respect the uniform. Some of the people watching the whole thing unfold actually applauded at that."

"So how did it end?"

"Someone called the police. At the sound of the sirens, Kevin took off running and was long gone before the deputy actually got there. Enough people stuck around to make sure the deputy knew that it was Mr. Minter who started the argument and that no blows were exchanged. The deputy took down some names and information, but that's all. I think Mr. Minter really expected him to track down Kevin and arrest him or something. When he didn't, Minter walked off in a huff. The last I saw of him he was driving away in his pickup."

Tripp finished his coffee. "Thanks for telling me. After I get out of class, I'll track down Kevin and make sure he's all right."

"Did he move his camp after I stumbled into it?"

"I don't know. I haven't been back to check on him since. Even if he did, he usually stays within that same general area. I know he scared you the other night, and I'm sorry about that. So was he. Kevin's really a good guy at heart, but he's been going through a rough patch lately."

Tripp closed his eyes and drew in a slow breath. "Sometimes what we saw and what we did over there comes back to haunt us. He saw action years before I did, but some things never change. I've been trying to get him some help, but as you saw for yourself, he's pretty skittish."

That was putting it mildly. Even though Kevin had scared her, she still felt bad about upsetting him so badly. Maybe she could do something about that. Tripp was already up and heading for the door.

"Wait a second, Tripp."

She took two containers out of the freezer and carried them over to where Tripp stood waiting and looking impatient. "I baked snickerdoodles for my quilting guild meeting this afternoon and made extra. Maybe Kevin would like some."

He gave the second container a pointed look, his mouth tilted up in a small smile.

She rolled her eyes. "And, yes, the other one is for you. Let him know I don't need the container back."

"I will."

Tripp started out the door with the cookies tucked under his arm. But before he'd gone two steps he turned back and surprised her with a kiss on her cheek. "Thanks for the cookies and for your under-standing. Let me get through the rest of today, and

I'll get back in touch to reschedule our discussion about the committee."

"I'll hold you to that. For now, go to class and then check on your friend."

When she stepped out onto the porch, Zeke quickly joined her. Then he woofed softly and followed Tripp across the yard, providing escort until his friend safely reached his front door. Before heading inside, Tripp stopped to pat the slobbery dog on the head and said something that sent Zeke trotting back to Abby.

The dog sat down and leaned against her leg. He whined, clearly concerned about his buddy. She gave Zeke a hug. "I hear you, boy. Sometimes I worry about him, too."

Chapter Five

The last thing Abby wanted to be doing was slogging through a muddy pumpkin patch looking for Ronald Minter. She'd planned to spend the morning working on organizing the candy for the next round of goody bags, which the guild would be putting together later that afternoon. But her elderly friend Glenda had called just after breakfast to ask for her help in picking up an order of pumpkins from Ronald Minter's farm that were intended for an activity at the senior citizens center in town. Someone else was supposed to go with her, but evidently the woman had called to say she was sick.

Abby tried not to think the worst of people, but she had a sneaking suspicion that Beatrice had taken one look at the threatening skies overhead and decided it was a good day to stay home. All things considered, she couldn't blame the woman even if that's what had happened. The rain had been coming down steadily since right after dawn. No surprise there, of course. After all, this was fall in the Pacific Northwest. Gray skies and wet weather were pretty much the name of the game.

Deciding there was no use in both of them getting wet, she'd asked Glenda to wait in the car while she went looking for Mr. Minter. His instructions had been to park by the house, where he'd have the pumpkins all boxed up and ready to go. It was disappointing to find no sign of either him or the pumpkins.

The lights weren't on in the house when Abby knocked on the front door. When there was no answer, she went around back to look for him. He wasn't in the small barn, either. It was tempting to give up and leave, but that would likely result in her having to make yet another trip back to the farm in the near future. She'd hate to get back home only to learn he'd been working out back in his sprawling pumpkin patch.

Standing on a small rise overlooking the fields out back, she scanned the area. No sign of Mr. Minter anywhere. That left the corn maze. Maybe he was in there doing some mysterious kind of corn maintenance. She'd never visited one before, but she figured the twists and turns would eventually lead her to the center of the maze. A sign near the entrance promised that those who were brave enough to make it all the way to the middle of the maze would be rewarded with their choice of a teeny-tiny pumpkin to take home and a map that would lead them to the closest exit. While it wasn't exactly her kind of thing, she bet the kids really enjoyed it. Or at least they would if the rain hadn't just kicked it up another notch.

She glared up at the sky. "Perfect. Glenda, you owe me big-time for this."

Resigning herself to getting even more thoroughly drenched, she set off along the path that led toward the entrance of the maze. At least there was a covered archway where she could get out of the downpour for a few seconds.

Before continuing forward, she called out, "Mr. Minter, are you in there?"

No answer.

She tried yelling his name again, louder this time. "Mr. Minter, I'm here to pick up pumpkins for Glenda Unger."

It was really tempting to head back to the car and tell her friend that either they'd gotten the time wrong or maybe Mr. Minter had been called away on an emergency. But knowing Glenda, the woman would insist on checking out the maze herself before admitting defeat.

Abby started forward, pausing every so often to listen for any signs of life within the high walls of corn. The towering stalks blocked her view in all directions. Mr. Minter could be just on the other side of the row next to her, and she'd never see him. As she walked along, every so often she passed by a scarecrow or a life-sized skeleton tucked into a corner. There were also some rather sad-looking stuffed crows stuck in among the cornstalks. Maybe it was the weather that made them look so pathetic, but she suspected the fake birds had already been past their prime before the rain started.

Getting lost didn't improve her mood in the least. It took her half a dozen attempts to finally make any real progress toward the center of the maze. She hadn't realized how huge the thing actually was. Did Mr. Minter do the same design every year? He didn't strike her as someone who would want to put in the time and effort it would take to come up with a new plan every fall. If he didn't bother to change up the design periodically, that might account for the reduced number of visitors he'd been complaining about.

Not her problem, though. She turned what appeared to be the final corner. The narrow aisle opened up into a large square. A small wooden shed stood right in the middle with a sign over the door that read "Congratulations! Pick your pumpkin prize." There was also a small bench where visitors could snap their picture sitting next to a smiling scarecrow wearing a flannel shirt and bibbed overalls.

After snapping a selfie to prove she'd made it to the end, she circled the perimeter of the clearing. Still no sign of the farmer anywhere—not that she was surprised by that, as quiet as it was. Finally, she approached the closed door on the front side of the shed and called out, "Mr. Minter, are you in there?"

The only sound was the splash of raindrops hitting the mud puddles. Finally she opened the door and peeked into the dim interior. At first, she didn't see anything except a large basket of mini pumpkins sitting on a rickety-looking table, no doubt the promised prizes. Then she noticed a boot lying on the dirt floor below the table. On second look, the boot was attached to a leg sticking out from beneath a patchwork quilt.

She retreated several steps as her mind flashed to that day in her backyard when she and Tripp had discovered a dead body wrapped in a quilt. A bad feeling settled in her stomach, and there was no way she wanted to take one more step deeper into that shed.

Hovering near the door, she softly called out, "Mr. Minter, is that you?"

As tempting as it was to believe that the leg and boot were part of the decorations in the maze, meant to scare the visitors, her gut instincts had her convinced otherwise. But it also wouldn't do to call the authorities and drag them out there in the rain and the mud to uncover a stuffed scarecrow.

Knowing she was going to regret her decision, she lit the flashlight app on her phone and crept closer to the table. Kneeling down, she reached out to touch the denim-covered leg. It felt too solid to be straw stuffed around a wooden dowel. She tugged the pants leg up far enough to touch the skin. So, so cold. The dark stain in the hard-packed dirt that spread out from beneath the leg was also a bad sign.

Bracing herself for the worst, she lifted a corner of the blanket and shined the light farther underneath. All it took was one good look at the knife sticking out of the man's back to have her scrambling away in full retreat. It was tempting to go charging all the way back to the car, but she retreated only as far as the bench outside. There, she called the police station and asked for Gage Logan.

He came on the line in a matter of seconds. "Hey, Abby, what's up?"

"Gage, I'm afraid I need your professional services. I'm out at Ronald Minter's farm, where Glenda and I were supposed to pick up a bunch of pumpkins. When he wasn't at the house or in the barn, I went looking for him in the corn maze."

She drew a ragged breath and tried to control the shaking in her hands. "I found him. At least I think it's him. I didn't want to move the body to check for sure. It's covered with a quilt, but I peeked underneath and touched his leg. It's ice-cold to the touch, and there's a knife sticking out of his back."

After a brief pause, Gage asked, "Abby, where are you now?"

The calm tone of his voice as he spoke helped her regain control. "I'm sitting on the bench outside of the shed in the middle of the maze. The body is inside."

"Okay, I'm on the way, but I'll need to call this into the county sheriff's department. Most of Minter's farm is in their jurisdiction. I'm going to hang up to do that, but I'll call you right back. Will you be okay that long?"

She nodded and then remembered he couldn't see her. "I'll have to be, won't I? I need to call Glenda and tell her what's taking me so long. She's sitting in my car in Mr. Minter's driveway."

"Okay, you do that. One way or another, someone will be there in a few minutes."

When the line went dead, she called her friend. "Glenda, I'm sorry, but it's going to be a while before I get back to you. I'm afraid Mr. Minter has met with an accident."

Okay, that was a lie. A knife in the back was hardly an accident, but she didn't want to upset Glenda any more than she had to right now.

"The police are already on their way and should be here soon. Chief Logan said I should wait where I am. Can you point them in the direction of the corn maze?"

"Of course, but do you want me to come wait with you?"

To ease the worry she could hear in her friend's voice, Abby fought to sound far more calm than she really was. "No, that's all right. I'm pretty sure the police would prefer to have as few people as possible wandering around in here. It may be some time before I can take you back home."

After a long moment of silence, her friend asked, "What are you not telling me, Abby?"

Glenda would find out the truth soon enough. "I'm pretty sure Mr. Minter is dead, but that's all I know for sure. I need to get off the line now. Gage is trying to call me back. But before I go, start the car if you get cold. I left the key in the ignition, and I keep a blanket in the back seat. It might smell like dog, but I don't want you to catch a chill in this awful weather."

"I'll be fine, so don't worry about me, young lady. I'll be here if you need me."

"Thanks, Glenda."

Then she clicked over to Gage. "Sorry about the wait. I was telling Glenda that it would be a while before I can take her home. I'm worried she'll get cold."

"Don't worry about her, Abby. If the deputy sheriff needs to keep you at the scene for a while, I'll have one of my people run Glenda back home."

"That's good, Gage. I know she'll appreciate it."

"I'm about five blocks out, and I can see the county guys rolling in from the other direction. You won't be alone for much longer."

"Good."

He kept up a steady stream of conversation, which helped keep her centered. It wasn't long before she heard a strange voice shouting, "We're at the entrance of the maze and coming in."

She called back, "I'll wait right where I am. If you have trouble finding your way, I can keep calling out if that would help you track me."

"We'll let you know."

Gage was still talking to her. "I'm with Glenda now. She's doing just fine. One of my deputies just pulled in, so he can take her home. I'll be heading your way as soon as I talk to him."

"I think the other officers are getting close, so I'll hang up now, Gage."

Then she called out, "Sounds like you're almost here, deputies."

Sure enough, a man and woman both stepped into sight a few seconds later. She remained seated on the bench, mainly because she wasn't sure her legs would support her right then. At least this time she didn't pass out like she had when she and Tripp had found Dolly Cayhill's body. Maybe she was getting better at handling this stuff, which was in itself an unsettling thought.

"Ma'am, I'm Deputy Sheriff Solkolski, and this is my partner, Deputy Meg Vinter. I take it that you're Abby McCree."

"Yes, I am."

Solkolski walked closer to her while Deputy Vinter remained near the entrance. "Chief Logan said you'd found a body."

She nodded like a bobblehead doll. "I did. It's . . . he's on the floor inside the shed. I peeked under the blanket to make sure it wasn't just another scarecrow." Her eyes clouded up with tears. "I really wish it had been."

The deputy's expression was sympathetic. "Me, too, Ms. McCree. Deputy Vinter needs to go back to the entrance to the maze to guide the rest of our crew in as they get here. While we're waiting for them, I'm going to step inside and take a quick look around. Will you be all right out here by yourself?"

A familiar figure stepped into sight. "I'll stay with her."

Abby surged up off the bench and ran straight to Gage, who wrapped his arms around her. "I'm glad you came."

He looked over her head to the deputy. "I know this is in your jurisdiction, but Abby is a personal friend. I'll keep out of your way, but I'd like to stay with her."

"Not a problem, Chief."

The deputy ducked into the shed but didn't stay there long. "Gage, can you step inside for a second to see if you can give me a positive identification on this guy?"

Abby stepped back away from Gage. "I'll be fine. Go do whatever you can to help."

"Okay, but then I'll take you back to your car to get warm. I asked my deputy to bring you something hot to drink when he comes back."

Gage followed Deputy Solkolski into the shack. They talked for a minute or two, but Abby didn't even try to make out what they were saying. A few seconds later, Gage walked back out. "Okay, lady, let's get you in out of this rain. Once Deputy Vinter points their people in the right direction, she'll come find us to take your preliminary statement. Once that's done, I'll drive your car home for you. I can hitch a ride back out here to get mine with one of my deputies later."

"Sounds like a plan."

They sloshed their way back out of the maze and across the pumpkin field. Several more deputies, and others who she thought were likely the forensics techs, passed them going the other way. Several said hello to Gage by name. He acknowledged their greetings but made no effort to stop and chat.

She had to wonder if he wouldn't rather be back in the thick of things rather than babysitting her. "Am I taking you away from what you should be doing?"

"Not particularly. This area falls in the jurisdiction of the sheriff's department, but we have a pretty good working relationship with them. If they need anything, they'll let me know."

Her car was empty when they got there. Abby was relieved that Glenda hadn't had to sit out in the cold any longer than necessary, but she was even more glad she didn't have to answer any questions right now. To her surprise and relief, Gage pulled her keys out of his pocket. He clicked the button to unlock the car and then opened the passenger door for her before getting in on the driver's side.

While he started the engine to warm the interior, she reached back over the seat to grab the blanket she kept there for Zeke to sleep on. It was covered in Zeke's hair, but right now she needed the extra layer of warmth it provided.

Gage waited until she got settled before asking, "You doing okay over there?"

She thought about it and then went for the truth. "Not really."

After tugging the blanket up higher around her shoulders, she glanced at Gage. "That really was Mr. Minter there under the table, wasn't it?"

He nodded. "Yeah, it was. I have to tell you the same thing I told Mrs. Unger: You'll need to keep what's happened to yourself for a little while. Just until the sheriff's department has a chance to notify his next of kin."

"I will."

The last thing she wanted to do was talk about what

had happened. It was bad enough that the blood-soaked ground and cold feel of that leg would probably haunt her dreams for a while. Heck, she still had occasional nightmares from the Dolly Cayhill case.

"Do you know if he has any family close by?"

"A cousin or two, I think." Then Gage gave her a hard look. "Your part in this ends when you give the deputy a statement. After that, you stay away from the entire affair."

For the first time, she smiled. "Yes, Gage, I learned my lesson. I have no desire to get involved in another murder investigation."

Pointing at a pale streak in his otherwise dark hair, Gage said, "See those gray hairs? They all appeared when Tripp and I found out you'd decided to follow a stone-cold killer all by yourself."

He pinched the tips of his finger and thumb together, leaving just a thin space between them. "We came that close to getting there too late."

And he was never going to let her forget it. Neither was Tripp, for that matter—not that she blamed them. She'd scared herself that day, too. Looking back, she couldn't figure out what had possessed her. Well, other than the driving need to clear her aunt's name, which was a stupid idea. Sybil would never have wanted Abby to put herself at risk for such a foolish reason. Her lifelong friends would never have believed Sybil was capable of murder, and the opinion of anyone else wouldn't have mattered to her.

Abby leaned her head back and briefly closed her eyes. "I just want to go home and forget all of this."

"Looks like you'll get your chance soon."

Abby sat up straighter and looked around. Sure enough, Deputy Vinter was headed their way. Reliving the whole experience wasn't going to be any fun, but the sooner Abby answered all the woman's questions, the sooner she could go home, take a hot bath, and do her best to pretend the day's events hadn't ever happened.

The deputy slid into the back seat. "Whew, it feels good to get in out of the rain for a few minutes. Ms. McCree, I've got a few basic questions for you. Then I'll want you to tell me step-by-step everything that you can remember about what happened. I'll pass the information on to the detective who takes charge of the investigation. If he or she has any more questions for you, they'll get in touch. Okay?"

As soon as Abby nodded, Deputy Vinter launched right in. "Then let's get started."

Her rapid-fire questions were to the point and her attitude professional. Abby appreciated the woman's calm demeanor, which helped her get through the ordeal as quickly as possible. That didn't change the fact that every second of the discussion was like having a horror movie playing out in her head in Technicolor.

And if the deputy noticed the tears streaming down Abby's face, she tactfully didn't say a thing.

Chapter Six

It was almost an hour later before she and Gage were finally cleared to leave. At least Gage's deputy made good on his promise to return with hot drinks. That he thought to bring extras so Deputy Vinter also got one earned him bonus points with his boss.

The drive back to Abby's house didn't take long. By that point the heat in the car had driven off the worst of her chills, but she couldn't wait to get out of her damp clothes and wet shoes.

"Come on inside, Gage. It's still a little early for lunch, but I could use something to eat. If you're hungry, too, I can set out sandwich makings before I go upstairs to change."

He considered her offer. "If you're sure. I don't want to impose."

She mustered up a small smile. "You were kind enough to stay with me when you didn't have to. The least I can do is feed you."

When he followed Abby into the house, Zeke charged into the kitchen and almost knocked her over in his enthusiasm to greet her. Gage made a quick grab for the dog's collar and tugged him toward the door. "Come on, boy. I bet you need a trip outside."

He and Zeke disappeared back outside while Abby made quick work of setting out everything Gage would need to make himself a sandwich. She'd fix one for herself as soon as she got out of her wet clothes. Before heading upstairs, she also put on a pot of coffee to brew. She didn't know about Gage, but she could use another cup or three to get through the rest of her day.

For one thing, the ladies from the quilting guild were due to arrive in just over an hour. She loved them all dearly, but at the best of times it took every ounce of energy she could muster just to keep them organized and on task. At least Glenda wasn't sched-uled to be there. That would make it easier to keep mum about the morning's events. She knew Glenda was bound to have questions, but she wasn't ready to talk about what had happened and what she'd seen.

Upstairs, she peeled off her clothes down to the skin. As good as a hot bath would have felt, it would've been rude to leave Gage on his own that long. She pulled on some warm sweats and thick socks. Just that change was enough to have her feeling better. After using a towel to dry her hair, she pulled it into a ponytail and headed back down to join her guest.

To her surprise, Gage wasn't alone. Tripp had evi-dently invited himself to join them for lunch, but at least he'd had the decency to make her a sandwich, too. Bless the man, there was also a big mug of coffee sitting by her plate, already heavily dosed with sugar and cream.

Zeke's greeting was a little more subdued this time,

so she made it across to her assigned chair more or less intact. It felt good to sit down.

Gage's plate held nothing but crumbs, making her glad she'd offered to feed him. He looked at her over the rim of his coffee cup. "Just so you know, I already told Tripp the bare-bones facts. All things considered, I thought you might need someone else to talk to if I'm not available."

Tripp reached out to put his big hand over hers. "Are you okay?"

"I will be. It was just such a big shock, you know."

She wrapped her hands around her coffee mug, taking comfort from its warmth. "It isn't like I knew the man or anything."

Honesty had her adding, "Well, I have seen him in town and at the city council meetings, of course. He wasn't the most pleasant person around, but no one deserves to die like that."

Tripp met her gaze from across the table and then looked to Gage. "You didn't say how he was actually killed, just that it wasn't an accident."

Gage leaned back in his chair. "Like I told Abby, until the sheriff's department notifies the next of kin, they won't appreciate anyone talking about their case."

No sooner were the words out of his mouth than Zeke went on full alert. He trotted over to the back door and stared at it in expectation. It was telling that his tail wasn't wagging. Whoever was walking up the steps to the porch definitely wasn't a friend.

Tripp frowned. "Were you expecting someone, Abby?"

"Some of the ladies from the quilting guild are due here at one, but they usually come in through the front door."

"I'll see who it is."

But before Tripp stood up a familiar face appeared in the window that made up the top half of the door. Abby groaned the second she recognized her uninvited guest as Reilly Molitor, the reporter from the *Clarion*, the local weekly newspaper. They'd tangled before. The last time he'd stopped by, Tripp had threatened to toss the guy out in the street to see how high he'd bounce.

"What's he doing here?"

Okay, that wasn't the smartest question she could've asked. No doubt the man had a police scanner or some such thing that kept him plugged in to whatever was going on around town. At least when she and Tripp had found the body in her backyard, it had taken Reilly until the next morning to show up on her doorstep.

"Can we just ignore him?"

Gage laughed. "You really think that's going to work? It's not like he can't see the three of us sitting here."

"Fine, but I'm not giving him a statement. If you want to talk to him, be my guest."

When she opened the door, she made sure to keep Zeke between her and the reporter. Her furry friend had served as a rather handy deterrent the last time Reilly had tried to get in her face over an unfortunate incident—if a murder could be called that.

"Can I help you, Mr. Molitor?"

His smile was too polished to be genuine. "I'm sorry to bother you, Ms. McCree, but I wanted to get a statement from you about the murder of Mr. Minter. I understand you discovered the body."

The smile she offered him in return was about as

real as his. "I'm sorry, but I've been instructed not to discuss the case. Any questions you have should be addressed to the county sheriff's office. I'm sure they'd love to talk to you."

Not.

To give the man credit for sheer determination, he stood his ground. "Who do you think gave me your name? If they didn't want me to talk to you, they wouldn't have pointed me in your direction."

If that was true, she didn't think much of the deputies. On the other hand, Gage seemed to respect them, which meant she shouldn't take everything Reilly said at face value. "Have a nice day, Mr. Molitor. I would appreciate it if you didn't come back. Ever."

When she tried to close the door, he blocked it with his hand. "As I told you last time, the story will get published with or without your cooperation. I promise this won't take long."

Zeke picked up on her increasing tension and shoved his big head into the open door, his growl a deep rumble in his chest. At the same time, Tripp and Gage moved up to flank her, reinforcing her determined effort to prevent the reporter from coming inside.

Instead of being intimidated, though, Reilly cranked both his efforts and his smile up a few more notches. "Chief Logan, this is handy. You were next on my list of people to track down."

"Yeah, well, if you want to talk to me, call the office and make an appointment. I'm sure I can find time on my schedule sometime next week. Keep hassling Ms. McCree like this, and it might be next year before me or my staff will be willing to talk to you."

Reilly finally looked a bit deflated. "Oh, come on,

Gage. You know my deadline for this week's edition is tomorrow. My editor will have my head if I fail to get all the details before then."

Evidently he'd tried the "poor, pitiful me" routine before, because Gage wasn't buying it. "Like the lady said, talk to the sheriff's department. This isn't my case."

"But if you were there, Gage, you're a witness, too. There's no reason you can't talk to me."

"You mean other than I don't want to?"

By that point, Reilly was sputtering in frustration. "But, but, but . . ."

Gage laughed. "I'm just jerking your chain, Reilly. I'll tell you what. If you promise to leave Abby alone and give me a ride back out to Minter's farm to pick up my squad card, I'll tell you what I can on the way. But to be honest, it won't be much."

When the man hesitated, Gage shrugged. "No problem. I'm sure Tripp here will give me a ride."

After pulling Zeke out of the way, he shut the door and turned his back to the window. Holding his hand in front of his chest, where Reilly couldn't see it, he held up his fingers one at a time, counting off the seconds. He'd barely made it to four before Reilly knocked again.

"Fine, I'll drive you, Chief, but you know this isn't fair."

Abby wanted to hug the lawman, but now wasn't the time. "Thanks, Gage. I owe you. The next time I run into you at Something's Brewing, it's on me."

"Sounds like a deal."

He picked up his hat and stepped toward the door. "For what it's worth, Reilly is pretty good about keeping his word. However, if he does show up to bother you again, I want to hear about it."

Gage paused to give Reilly a pointed look, who just rolled his eyes and walked away. When the two men were gone, Abby cleaned up the kitchen while Tripp finished his coffee. "You're welcome to hang around, but I'm thinking you might want to make yourself scarce pretty soon. The quilting guild is having a work party here this afternoon, and Jean will be coming. I'm not saying she'll come armed with one of her tuna casseroles or anything. But if she sees you, she might just get inspired."

Abby knew Jean was fond of her, but the elderly woman really doted on Tripp. Right now he had a particularly pained expression on his face as he gulped down the rest of his coffee. "Seriously, Abby, I really need to figure out how to convince that woman she doesn't need to feed me."

It was hard not to laugh. "What was her latest secret ingredient?"

He winced. "You know how she uses crushed potato chips for a topping?"

Abby snickered as she nodded, already guessing where this line of conversation was headed.

"Well, seems she ran out of the regular flavor. Can you imagine what barbecue chips taste like dipped in tuna?"

Yuck—no wonder Tripp looked a bit sick. "You've got to give the woman credit for being creative."

Tripp snorted. "That's one way to put it."

He drained his cup before heading for the door. "Let me know if you want company or anything after the ladies leave. I'll be around this evening. I can do my homework over here as well as I can at home."

"I should be fine, but I appreciate the offer."

Tripp paused to sneak Zeke an extra treat. "I delivered the cookies to Kevin, by the way. He really appreciated them."

She'd been worried about him. "Was he all right after his argument with Mr. Minter?"

"Yeah, he said he'd make himself scarce for a few days and that he planned to do what he could to avoid the man. I guess he won't have to worry about that anymore."

"No, he won't."

In fact, no one would.

And despite how unpleasant Mr. Minter might have been, that was a real shame. For sure, the city council meetings wouldn't be the same without him there with his monthly list of complaints, some of which were actually legitimate. She also suspected there was probably a long list of people in the area who had exchanged hot words with the man over the years. But that didn't justify such awful violence.

She really hoped the sheriff's deputies found the culprit quickly and brought him or her to justice. Mr. Minter deserved that much.

The rest of the day passed in a blur. She and the ladies made quick work of the goody bags and finalized plans for their part of the festival's celebration. It was hard not to laugh as Jean found several excuses to wander into the kitchen, where she peeked out the back windows toward Tripp's place.

At least she'd arrived without one of her casseroles ready to deliver to him. Poor guy. He was unfailingly polite to Jean and even made a valiant effort to eat whatever she brought him. As far as Abby was concerned, that was definitely above and beyond the call of duty.

After the ladies left, Abby made quick work of washing the dishes and wrapped up the last few lemon bars to give to Tripp. She poured herself another cup of coffee and headed to the living room to watch one of her favorite cooking shows.

But speaking of him, they still needed to get together to talk about their upcoming meeting with the veterans group. Time was running out, and she didn't want to walk in without at least some solid ideas to offer them. It would also be nice to have a chance to pull some definite numbers together before the meeting.

She muted the television and tried calling him. But there was no answer, which was odd. He'd said he'd be home all evening. After hanging up, she sent him a quick text asking him to call her or at least give her a date and time to meet.

An hour later, she was ready to turn in for the night. She perched on the edge of the mattress and looked out the window to see if he was home. His truck was in its usual spot, but his front windows were dark. Maybe he'd gone to bed earlier than normal. She hoped he hadn't had to go hiking out to the woods to check on Kevin again.

Rather than staying up to all hours, she decided to delegate worrying about Tripp to her furry companion, who could sleep all day whenever he wanted to.

"I'm going to bed, Zeke. Only wake me if it's a real emergency."

With his sometimes uncanny way of understanding her, the big dog jumped up on the bed and settled where he could watch over the backyard. Satisfied Tripp was in good hands, she turned out the light and went to sleep.

Errands and meetings kept Abby running for the next two days, too busy to track down her favorite, if only, tenant. Her frustration with the elusive man had reached an all-new high. The only bright spot was the increasing buzz about the mysterious pumpkin carvings that had continued to appear around town. She had to wonder how Gage Logan felt about being immortalized in vegetable art. His was only the most recent portrait to show up. It had mysteriously appeared outside of the back entrance to the police department. To date, there hadn't been even a hint about the artist's identity.

She suspected Gage would've preferred to hide the huge pumpkin, maybe by taking it home for his daughter to enjoy. However, Reilly Molitor had taken it upon himself to prowl the city right after dawn each morning looking for the latest addition to the collection. Once he spotted a new portrait, he snapped a few pictures and rushed back to his office to post them on all of the newspaper's social media.

While Gage might not agree, a lot of people seemed to think being chosen as one of the artist's subjects was quite the honor. Regardless, it was adding a whole new spice to the town's usual Halloween celebration. It had occurred to her to wonder if somehow Connie Pohler was behind the whole thing, using the portraits as a way to increase support for the festival. If so, her efforts were a brilliant success.

Abby made a quick stop at the bookstore to pick up the latest novel by one of her favorite authors. With a murderer on the loose, she wanted to get home before dark where she planned to spend the evening with the doors locked and a glass of wine within easy reach. The only question was whether to head straight home or if she should stop in at Bridey's for a little pick-me-up first. In the end, it was no contest. She also planned to confront Tripp as soon as she could find him. If she finally managed to corner him, she was going to need all the energy she could get.

She had just reached the coffee shop when she spotted Gage headed her way. She still owed him that coffee she'd promised him for deflecting Reilly's attention away from her the day she'd discovered Mr. Minter's body. Instead of going in, she waited outside the shop to invite him to join her.

"Hi, Gage. I was heading inside to take a breather before heading home. I'd love to buy you that coffee I owe you, and I'll even spring for a treat to go along with it although I can't stay for long. I'm really hoping to catch up with Tripp this afternoon. I don't know where that guy's been hiding, but he hasn't been answering my text messages or anything. You haven't seen him, have you?"

Instead of his usual friendly smile, Gage looked wary as he coasted to a stop a few feet away. "I take it you haven't heard."

"Heard what? If you're talking about the sheriff's department, I haven't heard from them since Deputy Vinter took my statement. Have they made an arrest?"

She wasn't sure why his grim expression released a

flock of butterflies in her chest, but it did. His answer didn't help. "Not yet, but they have a suspect in mind. I'm the one who made an arrest in the case. They left me no choice."

She looked back down the street toward city hall, which housed the police department and the jail. "Gage, you're scaring me. Who are you holding?"

Although she knew the answer before he said the name.

"Tripp. And for the record, he left me no choice, either."

Chapter Seven

Abby couldn't remember the last time she'd been this angry. If they weren't standing out on the street, she might have given into the temptation to throw something right at Gage's thick skull. "What do you mean he gave you no choice? You know full well Tripp couldn't kill anyone."

All right, that wasn't exactly true. They both knew he'd been in the army for twenty years, most of it in the Special Forces. He probably knew all kinds of ways to kill someone under the right circumstances. However, stabbing someone he didn't know in the middle of a pumpkin farm didn't even come close to fitting the bill.

Meanwhile, Gage was holding up his hands in front of his chest, palms out, maybe in an effort to calm her down. "Abby, I didn't arrest Tripp for the murder."

Now he was just confusing her. "But you just said—"

"Okay, I'm making a muddle of this. Finding out you didn't know Tripp is in jail threw me for a loop, but there's a lot about this case that's driving me crazy."

He glanced around and realized they were drawing a bit too much attention from passersby. "Why don't we have that cup of coffee you mentioned, and I'll explain everything that I can."

It was tempting to refuse. What she really wanted to do was march down the street to the jail and demand to see her friend. But Gage had always played fair with her, and he'd been Tripp's friend for years longer than Tripp had lived in Snowberry Creek. From what she understood, the two men had served together at some time in the past, creating a bond that had withstood the passage of time. It couldn't have been easy for Gage to toss his friend in a cell and lock the door.

With that in mind, she ratcheted her temper down a few notches. "Coffee sounds good; probably decaf would be a smart choice right now. I also think we both need a few of Bridey's baked goods to go along with it."

For the first time, Gage smiled. "If you promise not to tell my daughter—although she'll probably find out anyway. Ever since we lost her mother a few years back to cancer, Sydney has taken to nagging me about my diet. I swear she has spies planted all over town who let her know whenever I snag a brownie or two to get through the day. You should've heard the lecture she gave me the last time she found out I'd had a double cheeseburger and a shake from Gary's Drive-In. The fact that I skipped the onion rings and French fries didn't carry any weight with her at all. She shows me no mercy. It's amazing how determined a teenage girl can be once she gets her mind set on something."

Despite the sad note about Gage's wife, that story was worth a little smile. "Fine, I promise I won't tell her. And if anyone does ask, I'll swear I forced them on you."

But as they waited to give Bridey's assistant their order, she added, "Of course, I haven't promised not to tell her how often you end up at my kitchen table eating cookies with Tripp."

Gage laughed. "You're a lot meaner than you want people to think you are, Abby McCree."

"Don't you forget it."

They both placed their orders, and then they settled at a table in the back corner, away from the few other people in the shop. Abby used artificial sweetener in her coffee to help compensate for the huge chocolate chip macadamia nut cookies she'd ordered. Yeah, it was a bit silly, but logic didn't play a big part in her need for chocolate in times of stress.

She waited until they'd both finished one of their desserts and had had a few sips of coffee. "Tell me what happened."

Gage glanced around the coffee shop as if making sure no one was listening. "To be perfectly clear, you know I don't make a habit of discussing the details of a case with civilians. I'm making an exception this time for two reasons. First, you're already involved, since you're the one who discovered the body. Second, from what Tripp told me, you've met Kevin Montgomery at some point and also witnessed the argument between the sergeant and Mr. Minter a couple of days before the man died. Am I right about those last two things?"

"Yes."

"Tell me what you can about both incidents. Start with how you met Kevin."

Sighing, she agreed, even knowing how Gage would

likely react to hearing about her middle-of-the-night adventure. Although she did her best to paint the incident in the best possible light, he was staring at her as if she'd sprouted a second head by the time she was finished. Knowing she was only postponing a long lecture on the subject, she launched right into what she'd seen when Kevin and Ronald Minter had argued.

As soon as she was finished, she took a big bite of her other cookie to avoid having to answer any questions he might have. That didn't stop him from asking them anyway.

"So to make sure I have this straight, you took off in the middle of the night to follow Tripp without any idea of where he was going or who he was going to meet. Not only that, you didn't even bother to take Zeke, who could have at least offered you some form of protection out there."

His anger was a cold chill that washed over her from across the table. "Yes, Gage, that's exactly what I did. I've already promised Tripp I won't do it again. In my defense, I've already told you I've been worried about him. There wasn't time to stop and make better plans."

Gage clearly didn't buy that excuse. "It didn't occur to you that Tripp is a highly trained soldier who can take care of himself? Or that if he had been walking into danger, your being there would have only made the situation that much more difficult for him? Because I'm telling this to you straight up—Tripp wouldn't have hesitated a second to sacrifice his own life to keep you safe."

She almost choked. "Why would he do something like that?"

"Because that's how he's wired, Abby. He would do that for anybody, but even more so because you're his friend."

She considered Tripp a friend, too, but she wasn't sure she had it in her to throw herself in front of a bullet for him. That thought didn't set so well with her. It was bad enough she'd put herself at risk; that she could've also put Tripp in jeopardy made it so much worse. Rather than continue this line of conversation, she tried to switch topics. "So how did he end up in jail?"

Gage leaned back in his chair, his eyebrows riding low and his arms crossed over his chest. "I'll let you divert me this time, because I'm more worried about him right now than I am you. But if I ever hear of you doing something that stupid again, we will continue this discussion. And for the record, I have an empty cell right next to his with your name on it."

She knew he was kidding. Most likely, anyway. But to be sure, she asked, "On what charges?"

There wasn't an ounce of humor in his expression when he said, "For being criminally too stupid to live."

Okay, then. "Fine, I'll do better."

He gave her a sharp nod to acknowledge her surrender before continuing his explanation. "The detective handling the murder case caught wind of the argument between Minter and Kevin. He's already interviewed several witnesses, but only the ones my deputy talked to. Since your name wasn't in his report, it's a pretty safe bet that the detective doesn't know you were there, too."

That was a relief. It wasn't as if she'd actually seen

how it all started or anything. "So that made Kevin a person of interest."

Gage smiled just a little at her attempt to use some official cop talk. "Yes, it did, but the argument wasn't the only thing that ties Kevin to this case. The weapon is the same kind of knife he's been known to carry. On top of that, the quilt that covered the body is believed to have belonged to him."

She grimaced. Poor Kevin, which meant poor Tripp as well. "What a nice, tidy package."

"Yeah, it is. That doesn't mean it isn't the truth. In my experience, the most obvious answer is usually the right one."

That was true, if the cop shows on television were to be believed. "So if the detective suspects Kevin, why did you arrest Tripp?"

Gage's big fist slammed down on the table hard enough to rattle the dishes. "Because of that same protective streak I mentioned. The detective wants to talk to Kevin, but no one has seen him since the day of the argument. My people have been keeping an eye out for him, and I let the veterans group know that we need to talk to the guy and why. It will go easier for Kevin if he comes in willingly."

He still hadn't circled around to how Tripp had ended up in jail. Rather than rush him, she let him tell the story in his own good time.

"When I asked Tripp if he knew where Kevin might be hiding out, he said the sergeant had moved his camp without telling him where. At the time, I had no reason to think he was lying to me about that."

"But now?"

"Someone made an anonymous call to the sheriff's

department saying that Tripp had been seen sneaking into the woods out near where you followed him that night. The person alleged he'd overheard Tripp warning Kevin that the cops were hunting for him and to retreat to his secret camp and stay there."

She wanted to deny that he would've done anything so foolish. Unfortunately, it actually sounded like something Tripp might do, especially if he thought his friend was being railroaded for a crime he hadn't committed.

"Any idea who this unknown person might be?"

"No. The detective let me listen to the recording, but I didn't recognize the voice. As a rule, though, I don't rush to trust a supposed witness who points a finger in someone's direction but is too cowardly to identify themselves."

Did the detective in charge of the case feel the same way? There was no good reason to press Gage into gossiping about his professional colleague when it wouldn't change anything. "But it still led them right to Tripp."

"It did. The detective dragged him into my office for a friendly little chat. Tripp admitted he and Kevin are friends and that he occasionally takes supplies out to the sergeant's camp to help him out. He said he can't remember the last time he was out there."

Should she tell Gage what she knew? Maybe. She already knew how he reacted when she held back information that he thought was important to a case. Then there was that empty cell he'd mentioned.

"I gave Tripp some cookies for Kevin. He told me he appreciated them, so I know Tripp went back at least once after the night I was there. I also told him about the argument with Mr. Minter. He was going to check on Kevin after that, but I don't know if that's when he delivered the cookies or not."

"That pretty much jives with what little he would tell me."

"I'm guessing the detective didn't believe him."

"He might have believed that much. I did, for what that's worth. It was when Tripp said Kevin had moved his camp without telling him where he was going that the detective had issues. That fit a little too well with what the anonymous tipster said. Tripp tried to explain that the sergeant had been complaining for some time now that enemy troops had infiltrated the area. It's obvious Kevin has been having some serious issues staying in touch with reality recently."

She nodded. "Tripp said Kevin has been going through a rough patch and that he's been trying to get him some help. The veterans group has been trying to set up a buddy system so none of the vets are ever on their own, and I think Tripp volunteered to be the contact person for Kevin. Maybe not, though. I know Tripp also took a veteran named Rudy to the doctor and then stayed at the hospital with him until someone else could take over."

Gage nodded. "I'm part of the group, too. We've been making a real effort to reach out to every veteran in the area to make sure they all know they're welcome and that we're there for them anytime they need help. There aren't quite enough of us to go around, so it wouldn't surprise me if Tripp took on more than one guy to help."

Then Gage's eyes took on a sly twinkle. "Speaking of helping out the veterans, I hear Tripp volunteered you to head up the big fundraising event for next year."

She groaned. "Yeah, he did, the big jerk. He knew I was trying to wind down my involvement on committees, but he signed me up anyway. Something about me owing him a favor after the whole dead body in my backyard thing."

"And you fell for that?"

She'd already figured out she was being played and had been kicking herself ever since. "You know, I'm beginning to think I have 'sucker' tattooed on my forehead or something. There has to be some reason I ended up running the quilting guild, the Committee on Senior Affairs, and now this project for your group."

Gage leaned back in his chair. "I probably should deny that, but I suspect you are a bit of a soft touch, which isn't a bad thing. It means you care, and a lot of people are benefiting from your efforts and organizational skills. For sure, my deputies and the fire department really appreciate the steady supply of quilts the group has made for us recently. Before you took over, it was more hit-and-miss. And for what it's worth, Connie Pohler mentioned the other day that the seniors group has never been this excited about helping out with the Halloween Festival."

Abby loved flattery as much as the next person, but not all the work she'd had to do to earn it. That was a discussion for another day.

"But again, if Tripp doesn't know where Kevin is, how did that result in him ending up in a cell?"

Gage swept the table clear of crumbs from his cookies and dumped them in his empty coffee cup. "The detective doesn't believe Tripp has no idea where Kevin is or Tripp's claim that Kevin wouldn't hurt anyone. Evidently, the sergeant has a police record that says otherwise."

She thought back to the regret in Kevin's eyes the night he'd taken her prisoner. "I hate to say it, but that doesn't surprise me. I can see why people would be scared of him when he goes off on one of his rants about the enemy being on the prowl. He's also a big man, and surprisingly strong for someone his age."

"Another reason you should give the sergeant a wide berth if you happen to run into him."

"I plan to."

She couldn't resist adding one more detail to her story about the night they'd met. "Do you know what finally convinced him that I was trustworthy? The fact that Zeke belongs to me—or maybe he thinks I belong to Zeke. Evidently the two of them hit it off when they met. He asked me to apologize to Zeke for him bothering me."

Gage laughed. "Well, we've all had good reason to trust Zeke's judgment when it comes to people."

Abby added her own example to the discussion. "He doesn't like Reilly Molitor, and we both know what a pest that reporter can be."

"Yeah, he's a real prize, that's for sure." Gage gathered up their trash. "So, do you want to go see our favorite jailbird? I'm sure he'd appreciate seeing a friendly face about now."

She followed him out the door. "For the record, Gage, I know you're only doing your job, but that doesn't mean I'm happy with you right now. There has to have been some way to keep Tripp from being arrested."

Gage gave her a look of total exasperation. "Yeah, there was. He could've told the truth when the detective asked him where Kevin might be hiding out. Instead, he told the man to do something physically painful with that idea and even took a swing at him. It took two other officers to restrain him, and you've got to know the police don't take such things lightly. The detective gave him every chance to cooperate, but Tripp said he'd rather rot in jail rather than betray a friend. By that point, both the detective and the prosecuting attorney were only too glad to let him do exactly that. I can't go into a lot of detail, but I swear they did everything by the book, and Tripp only made the situation worse for himself. At least they let me toss Tripp in a cell here in town instead of dragging his stubborn self over to the county lockup."

Sighing, she redirected her anger. Tripp had clearly left his friend no choice. "Maybe I can talk some sense into him."

"Yeah, good luck with that."

Chapter Eight

Since moving to Snowberry Creek, Abby had made frequent trips to city hall, and even a few to the police department, but this was the first time she'd entered through the private door that Gage and his staff used. Several people looked up as she passed by, as if assessing her reason for being there. It was tempting to ask for a show of hands to see whether they thought she was a witness, a victim, or a criminal.

She took her cue from Gage and kept her mouth shut as they walked past the rows of desks. Well, right up until she spotted the enormous pumpkin prominently displayed on a low filing cabinet right outside of Gage's office. She ducked around him to head straight for it. When Bridey had taken a picture of his jack-o'-lantern, it hadn't been sporting an official police hat just like the one Gage always wore. Some clever person had also figured out how to arrange the pumpkin in such a way that it appeared to be wearing a Snowberry Creek Police Department uniform shirt, complete with tie and badge.

"Wow, Gage, it looks just like you!"

A rumble of laughter swept across the room behind

them. Unfortunately, there was one person in the room who didn't find it amusing. Gage glared at the pumpkin. "The uniform shirt is a new addition."

He glanced back at the few people in the bull pen area. "If you don't have anything better to do with your time, come see me. I'm sure I can find something to keep you busy."

The laughter died a quick death, and just that quickly the room was filled with the sound of keyboards clicking and phone calls being made. Abby would've felt bad for getting everyone in trouble, but there wasn't a face in the crowd that wasn't sporting at least a small grin.

Gage led her through a door that opened onto a narrow hallway. "He's back this way, Abby."

As they walked, she couldn't resist asking, "You like the pumpkin portrait, don't you?"

He smiled just a little. "Yeah, it's actually pretty cute, but don't tell them that. They're having too much fun jerking my chain about it. Every day I come in, they've added a little something more. My people work hard, and this job doesn't offer a lot to laugh about. If they get a few chuckles at my expense, it's a small enough price for me to pay."

She'd always known that underneath his gruff exterior, Gage was a big softy at heart. It's what made him so good at his job. Her good mood died, though, at the sight of the heavy metal bars at the end of the passageway. Visiting a friend in jail wasn't something she'd ever experienced before, and she wasn't sure of the protocols. The guard sitting on the inside of the locked door stood up and reached for his keys.

"Deputy Chapin, this is Abby McCree. She's here to visit the prisoner. No time limit."

"Yes, sir."

Gage turned his attention back to her. "You can leave your things in the locker next to the desk. The deputy will secure it for you and give you the key. There's a chair around the corner that you can drag over in front of Tripp's cell if you want to sit and talk for a while."

Suddenly this whole thing had become serious as death. "Okay."

She must have sounded a bit shaky, because Gage's big hand came down on her shoulder. "You'll be fine, Abby. When you're ready to leave, Tim here will see you out. Just try to talk some sense into your stubborn friend back there, but don't feel bad if you don't get anywhere with him. He's worried about Sergeant Montgomery, and his sense of honor won't let him betray the guy. If he were just dealing with my department, he might be willing to trust me to make sure that Kevin is treated fairly."

That made sense to her. "Like you said, the evidence is stacking up against the sergeant. If they do arrest him, Tripp probably worries they'll concentrate on proving Kevin guilty instead of looking at other possibilities."

"Exactly. The problem with that thinking is that right now they're focusing most of their efforts just on finding him."

"There is that." She stepped closer to the door. "Well, I guess I'm ready."

Gage patted her shoulder one last time. "I'll be in my office. Stop in before you leave."

"I will."

The deputy unlocked the door to let her in. Once she'd stuck her purse in the locker, he led her around the corner to where the row of cells was located. Tripp was stretched out on the narrow bunk in the one at the far end. From that distance, it was hard to tell if he was sleeping or simply staring up at the ceiling. Her escort carried the chair Gage had mentioned and set it down against the wall facing the cell.

"Blackston, you've got company."

Tripp rolled to his feet in one smooth motion. She hadn't expected him to be happy to see her, but nothing had prepared her for his anger.

"Abby, what are you doing here?"

He stepped back from the door, his fists clenched. "Never mind. I don't want to know. Just go home."

Okay, her emotions had been on a roller-coaster ride since she'd run into Gage outside of Bridey's shop. The tenuous control she had on her temper right then snapped.

Crossing the last small distance to the chair, she sat down and glared right back at him. "I'm not going anywhere until you answer some questions, Tripp Blackston. So you can just quit pounding your chest like some idiot primate who's lost the last little bit of intelligence it had in the first place."

Tripp's attitude didn't improve when Deputy Chapin tried unsuccessfully to smother a laugh. "I'll be around the corner if you need me, Ms. McCree."

"Thanks, Deputy. This will take a while."

He walked away. "No problem. Take all the time you need."

When he was out of sight, Tripp finally turned his attention back in her direction. "You're still here."

"I am."

"Why?"

She studied him for a few seconds before answering.

He looked dreadful. Partly it was that awful jumpsuit they had him wearing. No one would look good in that particular shade of orange. The dark circles under his eyes made her wonder how much sleep he'd been getting. Did being closed in like that set off the nightmares that sometimes had him outside prowling in the middle of the night?

"I'm here because I just now learned you were in jail."

It was surprising how much it hurt that he hadn't bothered to send word. Surely Gage would've called her if he'd realized that Tripp hadn't let her know himself. She could've gotten him a lawyer. Or baked him cookies. Something.

When he didn't say anything, she tipped her head to one side. "Tripp, what's going on? Why didn't you call me?"

He closed his eyes for the longest time before finally opening them again. "Because I didn't want you here."

She winced. Maybe Gage was wrong about her being able to figure out how to help their mutual friend. But then Tripp started talking again.

"Sorry. I didn't mean that the way it came out." He waved his hand around to indicate his surroundings. "This is no place for a woman like you to be hanging out. I get that you wanted to see for yourself that I'm okay. Now that you know I am, you should go."

"You're not getting rid of me that easily, Tripp. Tell me what's going on in that head of yours. Why are you sitting in that cell protecting a man who might very well have killed Mr. Minter?"

Tripp's voice dropped to a low growl. "He didn't."

She crossed her arms over her chest and stared

back at him. "You can't know that for sure. You weren't there the day Sergeant Montgomery and Mr. Minter got into that big argument. I was, and there was a lot of temper on both sides. If their paths crossed again, especially if Mr. Minter caught the sergeant trespassing on his property, things could have gotten ugly really fast."

Tripp latched onto the bars of his cell in a white-knuckled grip. "For the last time, Kevin didn't kill that man."

She understood that he believed that; she just didn't know why. "I know you consider him a friend, but even you admitted the sergeant has been going through a rough patch lately."

The expression on Tripp's face made it clear that her argument had done nothing to convince him he was wrong. "That's true, but I just meant Kevin has a difficult time being around a lot of people. If anything, he's more likely to hide even deeper in the forest whenever the war memories are riding him hard."

The pain in Tripp's expression nearly broke her heart. The hint of fear in his dark eyes was even worse. "You're nothing like him, Tripp."

He was already shaking his head. "You've seen me out prowling the yard at night, Abby. It's just a matter of degree, but I have the same problems sometimes."

Was Tripp saying he needed to believe Sergeant Montgomery wasn't capable of a senseless murder so he could believe the same of himself? As soon as the thought crossed her mind, it was as if a switch had flipped inside her head. If Tripp believed in Kevin, she would do her best to do so as well. Time to change subjects.

"So how long do you plan to stay locked up in there?"

When he didn't answer, she pulled out the big guns. "I was going to ask Gage if I could bake you cookies or maybe cupcakes. Maybe I'll see if Jean can send you one of her tuna casseroles instead."

Tripp looked suitably horrified. "You wouldn't."

"I would. Come to think of it, while you're chilling out in here, I'm going to have to rake my own lawn. As busy as I am with the festival and everything else right now, I don't need to add anything more to my to-do list. I think I'll tell Jean you specifically requested she add anchovies, along with a thick layer of that crushed barbecue potato chip topping you mentioned."

"Not fair, Abby." By that point, he'd backed up to plunk back down on his bunk. "I'm pretty sure that would qualify as cruel and unusual punishment."

She shot him a smug look. "You'd have to ask your lawyer about that. But I'm betting I can have the casserole here, all hot and bubbling, before he can find a way to stop me."

That thought brought a new question to mind.

"What does your lawyer say about you being held here like this when you really haven't done anything wrong?"

His eyes shifted away from her again.

"Tripp, please tell me you asked for a lawyer."

"No, I didn't. I waived my right to one."

"Why?"

One possible reason immediately popped into her head. They had never discussed his finances. All she knew was that he paid his rent on time. There was no way to ask this next question delicately.

She shifted in the hard-backed chair and tried without luck to find a more comfortable position or an easy way to broach the subject of Tripp's ability to pay for an attorney. Finally, she blurted it out and then braced herself for the explosion she was sure would follow.

"Tripp, if you can't afford a good attorney, just say so. I can help with that." She gave him a hopeful look. "You know, a loan or something."

He'd left his bunk behind to pace the width of his cell. Three steps in one direction and then three steps back the other way. But as soon as the words left her mouth, he froze and slowly turned to face her. Instead of blasting her with anger, Tripp stared at her for an uncomfortably long time before finally speaking.

"Thank you for the generous offer, Abby. While I appreciate your concern, I don't need a loan or, for that matter, a lawyer."

Stubborn man.

"Fine."

His mouth quirked up just a little on one side. "So is it going to be cookies or casserole?"

She was about to say that it depended on whether he was ready to hear her ideas for the veterans' fundraiser when he abruptly held up his hand as if to ask for silence. What was going on? Then she heard deep voices arguing and the clang of the jail door opening and slamming shut again.

"Who?" she mouthed at Tripp since he looked as if he was bracing himself for a major confrontation.

He didn't answer, but that didn't matter. The source

of his sudden tension rounded the corner, headed straight for them. He might not be wearing a uniform, but she was willing to bet that she was about to meet the detective in charge of the murder investigation. His suit was perfectly pressed, his shirt snowy white, and his red power tie neatly tied. She had to wonder how many hours a week he spent polishing those gleaming black shoes. Altogether, he presented the perfect image of a successful man.

She wasn't impressed. In fact, she disliked him on sight.

The feeling must have been mutual, considering the dismissing glance he gave her before turning his attention in Tripp's direction.

"Deputy, please escort Ms. McCree out of here."

She hadn't even noticed Deputy Chapin hovering right behind the detective. He didn't look any happier about having the man there than she and Tripp were.

Sometimes the best defense was to go on the attack. She'd learned that from dealing with her ex-husband over the course of their separation and divorce. Abby stood up and moved to plant herself firmly right in front of him. "Excuse me, I don't believe we've met, and I don't—"

Her interruption clearly irritated him. "I'm Detective—"

Abby held up her hand to cut him off mid-sentence. "Please let me finish. What I was going to say was that I really don't care who you are, Detective Whatever-Your-Name-Is, or why you're here. As I'm sure Deputy Chapin told you, I have permission to be here and to stay as long as I like. I'm sure if you want time to talk to Mr. Blackston, Chief Logan will be glad to schedule you an appointment. This particular time slot, however, is already taken."

She wasn't sure what her smile looked like at that moment, but Deputy Chapin backpedaled a few feet. "Now, if you'll excuse us, Mr. Blackston and I were talking. I'm sure you can find something to occupy yourself until we're done. I'm betting if you kick some money into the kitty in the bull pen, they'll even let you have a cup of coffee. If not, there's a nice coffee shop right down the street."

By that point all three men were looking at her as if they hadn't understood a single word she'd said. "I'm sorry, do you need me to repeat that, maybe slower this time?"

She was pretty sure Tripp smothered a laugh, but she didn't dare look back at him to see. Meanwhile, Deputy Chapin did an about-face and headed back toward his desk. Without a doubt, he was going to call in reinforcements. Fine. She could deal with Gage.

"Ms. McCree, this man is my prisoner, and I will determine whether or not he gets to have visitors. Right now, visiting hours are over."

They'd see about that. Rather than let him continue to try to intimidate her, she turned her back on him. "So, Tripp, I'm thinking we should do two events. The first one will be the big fundraiser. The second one will be for everyone in town who would like to attend. It would be a tiered affair, though, with special perks for those who supported the first one the most generously."

Tripp blinked and shook his head. "What?"

Okay, maybe there was something about this place that made it difficult for men to follow a simple conversation. She tried again. "I said we should do two events. They'd be on separate nights but connected by a theme. We can work on what that would be after we run the idea by the group to see what they think."

She could hear the detective breathing hard from right behind her. Just how angry was he? Not that she cared. At least not much, although that row of empty cells next to Tripp's gave her a bit of a chill.

"So what do you think?"

Tripp jerked his head in the direction of the exit, warning her they were about to get more company. Then he said, "I'll go along with whatever you have in mind, Abby. Unfortunately, it doesn't look as if I will be able to attend that planning meeting with you. Please offer the board my apologies."

"I will." Then she gave him a pleading look. "Although I'd really prefer it if you were there, too."

Not to mention back at home where he belonged.

"Detective Earle, I must have been out of my office when you came in. I can't imagine you wouldn't have had the courtesy to tell me you were in the building."

Abby breathed a little easier knowing that friendly reinforcements had arrived. Maybe it was time to make a strategic retreat. But while the detective was distracted by Gage, she reached her hand through the bars of the cell in the hope that Tripp would take it in his. While he might not need it, she did need that brief touch to reassure herself that he was all right. He took the hint and gave her hand a gentle squeeze. A hug would've been better, but she settled for what she could get.

"I know you're worried, but don't be. I'll be fine."

She hoped so. She really did.

The detective reentered the conversation. "Please step back from the cell, Ms. McCree." In another show

of defiance, she held on to Tripp's hand for several
more seconds before finally letting go. She wouldn't do
Tripp any good if she managed to get herself arrested
for whatever trumped-up charge the detective might
come up with for someone who ticked him off.

"Have Gage let me know if there's anything you
need. I'll bring it the next time I come."

He was already shaking his head. "No, you shouldn't
be hanging around a place like this."

"Don't worry, Blackston, she won't be. As long as
you're not cooperating with the investigation, you
don't get perks like visitors."

Once again, Abby simply ignored the odious man.
"Do you want chocolate chip or oatmeal raisin?"

"Either would be fine, as long as it's not tuna
casserole. However, you might ask Gage and his staff,
since I'd like to share with them."

She forced a small smile, when all she wanted to do
was cry. "Bye, Tripp."

Before she'd gone two steps, Detective Earle called
after her, "Ms. McCree, I need to talk to you, too. Now
is as good a time as any. I'm sure Gage won't mind
if you wait in his office until I've finished talking to
Mr. Blackston."

Enough was enough.

"No, actually, this isn't a good time for me, Mr. Earle.
I've already given my statement to Deputy Vinter. I'm
sure she would be only too happy to provide you
with another copy if you've managed to lose yours.
Otherwise, if you find you need to talk to me, please
do me the courtesy to call and make an appointment.
I might find time in my schedule sometime next week,
but maybe not."

He clearly didn't like her refusal to use his title or

when she offered him the same smile that used to put her ex-husband's teeth on edge. "Now, if you'll excuse me. I have other places I need to be."

There was nothing but silence behind her as she made her way back to where Detective Chapin was waiting to let her out. She really hoped that he didn't see how badly her hands were shaking. No such luck. When she muddled her third attempt to stick the key into the lock to retrieve her purse, he gently took it from her and opened the locker door.

"Thank you."

"You're welcome, ma'am. Come on, I'll walk you out."

He silently led the way to the same door where she and Gage had entered the building. He stepped outside with her. "Would you like one of the deputies to drive you home?"

What a sweetheart. "No, I'm parked just down the street. I'll manage just fine."

"If you're sure. I can walk that far with you. You know, to make sure no one hassles you along the way."

Meaning Detective Earle.

"That's okay. I'm sure Gage will keep that conceited jerk occupied long enough for me to make my escape."

"I will admit the detective is a bit full of himself."

She snorted at that assessment.

The deputy laughed. "Okay, more than a bit. However, for what it's worth, he's got a good reputation. He'll do a thorough job and make sure the right person goes down for the murder. Right now, he's just really frustrated with your friend."

"Tripp can have that effect on people. Now, I'd better be going."

As she walked away, Chapin called after her, "If

you're really taking requests, I like chocolate chip cookies the best."

That made her laugh. "I'll see what I can do."

And wouldn't life be grand if all of its problems could be fixed with cookies? In the past, she'd come up with some of her most creative ideas when she was baking. She could only hope this time wouldn't be any different. One way or another, she was going to have to help clear Kevin's name if she was going to get Tripp out of trouble.

She could imagine what he and Gage would have to say on that subject. Still, she had no intention of chasing after Kevin herself. Instead, she'd limit her involvement to asking a few questions around town. Surely they wouldn't object to that.

Yeah, right.

Just in case, she'd give Gage and that jerk of a detective a little more time to do their jobs. If she didn't see them making any real progress, then she'd figure out what she could do to move the process along. She needed Tripp out of that cell and pulling his weight on their committee. And then there were all those leaves waiting to be raked.

Chapter Nine

On the whole, Monday hadn't been the best day in Abby's life. After she studied the calendar on the kitchen wall, it was clear Tuesday was on track to be more of the same. She had a pair of back-to-back meetings scheduled later in the morning, one at city hall and one in the meeting room at the library. At least they were in the same building, so she could walk from one to the other in a matter of a minute or two.

She only hoped she had enough energy left over when she got back to deal with the thick blanket of leaves in the front yard. The backyard was covered, too, but at least it couldn't be seen from the street. While she liked her neighbors, there was an unspoken competition on the block to see who did the best job of keeping their lawns manicured. There was no way she'd ever be able to win that race. At least with Tripp's considerable help, she'd managed to get the overgrown landscaping back under control. Aunt Sybil had always prided herself on her yard, but she'd let things slip a bit as she'd gotten older.

Right now there was someone else in her life who needed her attention. She'd let Zeke outside for his usual morning patrol around the yard, but he hadn't come trotting right back in to inhale his breakfast. What was taking him so long? She'd looked out her back window to see what was fascinating enough to keep him away from his kibble for this length of time.

When she finally spotted him, her heart almost broke. He was sitting on Tripp's front porch and staring at the door as if sheer determination would make his friend appear. How on earth was she supposed to explain to him that his buddy had been locked up in the people pound?

She slipped on her gardening shoes and headed out the back door to coax the dog to come back home with her. Normally he could be bribed with one or two of his favorite treats, and she hoped that would work this time, too. Considering he weighed in at a solid ninety-five pounds, it wasn't as if she could carry him home against his will.

"Hey, Zeke, come on back. Your breakfast is ready."

He gave her a dismissive glance before immediately turning his attention right back to the door.

Holding out her hand, she offered him a bribe. "I've got treats."

No response. Okay, this was getting serious.

Abby sat down on Tripp's porch steps and patted the spot next to her. Finally, Zeke heaved a big sigh and laid down with his heavy head in her lap. His huge brown eyes were just so darn sad. She held out one of his treats, which at least earned her a single thump of his tail. After giving the dog cookie a quick sniff, he licked it up off her palm. She didn't bother wiping her slimy hand on her jeans, since she planned on giving him a second treat as soon as he gulped down the first one.

"I know you miss Tripp, big guy, but he'll be back soon."

She hoped.

As the second cookie disappeared with a quick crunch, she ran her fingers through Zeke's dark fur and gave him a good scratch. "Tell you what, why don't we go on a quick walk before I have to leave for my meetings?"

The dog considered her offer for a few seconds before finally lumbering to his feet. He gave himself a good shake from nose to tail before trotting off in the direction of her house. She followed behind at a slower pace, laughing when Zeke woofed to tell her to hurry up. As soon as she opened the door, he bolted past her to gulp down his breakfast. His bowl was empty and licked clean before she had time to change shoes and grab her wallet and Zeke's leash.

"Let's go."

Rather than walk in the neighborhood, she decided to drive Zeke to the park, where they could take a long ramble along the river. Zeke flopped down in the back seat while she drove the short distance into town. The parking lot was nearly empty, which meant they should pretty much have the trail to themselves.

Zeke waited patiently until she clipped on his leash. Then they were off as he hurried to check out all of his favorite bushes and trees along the path, no doubt catching up on which of his four-legged acquaintances had been by since his last visit. The frequent stops made for a slow walk, but she was all right with that. After all, the outing was meant to cheer up Zeke, so she let him set the pace.

As they rounded a bend in the river, she spotted a couple of familiar faces. Although she hadn't officially met Kristy and Dean Hake until that last meeting of the festival committee, she'd often seen the two of them walking through the park swinging their matching metal detectors from side to side. They seemed pretty dedicated to the endeavor, which made her wonder just how much success they had in finding things.

When they drew closer, Kristy happened to look up. She immediately shut her machine off and headed straight for her.

"Hi, Abby! Who is this handsome fellow?"

"This is my roommate, Zeke."

Kristy held her hand out for Zeke to sniff while she studied him for a few seconds. "I'm guessing he's a mastiff of some kind."

Abby patted his broad head. "That's the general consensus. My late aunt adopted him from the local shelter. I'm not sure they knew much about his past, but he definitely looks like a mastiff, even though he's not as big as the purebreds get."

Zeke gave her a reproachful look, which had both women laughing. "Sorry, boy, I know you're sensitive on that issue."

She pointed toward Kristy's metal detector. "I've seen you and Dean out here before and wondered how much buried treasure you manage to find."

The other woman glanced back in her husband's direction. "Actually, we mainly do it for the exercise and the fresh air. Dean had a bit of a health scare last year, and the doctor told him he needed to get out and walk. That lasted about a month before he got bored with traipsing around the neighborhood. It really scared me when he got sick, so I didn't want him slacking off. We'll be married forty years next month, and he's still my best friend."

Abby was impressed. "Congratulations. That's a rarity these days."

"Thanks. Anyway, a friend of Dean's suggested he take up metal detecting as a hobby. I bought one for myself, too, so we could spend more time together. We take day drives to do some hunting in different places, which makes it more fun. Between the two of us, we've found enough stuff to keep it interesting."

She held out her arm to show Abby the narrow gold chain on her wrist. "Dean found this bracelet walking along a road out in the middle of nowhere. We were driving back from visiting some friends over in Idaho when our car broke down. Dean decided to break out his detector to kill time while we waited for the tow truck. Normally, we turn anything valuable we find over to the local police in case they can track down the owner. However, this was miles from anywhere, so there was no telling how long this bracelet had been sitting there in the dirt."

"It's really pretty."

Kristy looked pleased by the compliment. "I think so, but you should've seen it when we found it. I had the jeweler here in town polish it and fix the clasp."

Zeke must have gotten bored with the conversation, because he stood up and started tugging on his leash. Abby rolled her eyes and shook her head. "I guess I just got my marching orders. Will I see you at the meeting later?"

"I'll be there, but I'm not sure about Dean. There was a death in his family—a cousin he grew up with— so he's having a hard time right now."

. "Oh, I'm sorry to hear that. Please offer him my condolences."

"Thanks, I will. Now, I'd better get back to work before Dean realizes I've been slacking off."

She patted Zeke one more time before hurrying off across the grass to where Dean was methodically sweeping his detector from side to side. He glanced up and smiled when Kristy fell into step beside him.

Abby was happy for the two people who seemed to genuinely enjoy each other's company even after nearly four decades of marriage. She'd hoped she and Chad would have that kind of success, but it hadn't been meant to be. Maybe if they'd done things differently—but she couldn't quite imagine them wearing matching jackets and hunting for lost coins along a river. Besides, it was too late for regrets. Water under the bridge and all that.

"Come on, Zeke, let's do the loop through the trees and then head back."

He woofed his approval of the plan and tugged her along in his wake.

Both of Abby's meetings went remarkably smoothly. Fred Cady had even shown up at the senior affairs meeting to reassure her that he'd be taking over in November for sure. That was something at least.

She planned to grab a bottle of water and get started on the lawn as soon as she got home. Spending time out in the sun together would at least make Zeke happy. The fall rains could return any day now, which would make the raking even harder. Dry leaves were easy to gather into neat piles with her leaf blower, but wet leaves were heavier and more of a mess to deal with.

As she turned into the driveway, she slowed as she passed by the front yard to gauge how long it would take her to do at least that much. Then she hit the brakes and backed up. She rolled down the window to lean her head out and look around. Where had the leaves gone?

Then she heard the sound of the leaf blower coming from the backyard. When she started to move farther up the driveway, she found the way blocked by one of the town's police cruisers. She parked her car and headed around back to find out what was going on. Zeke came charging down off of Tripp's porch to circle around her, barking happily, before bolting right back to where he'd started out. Meanwhile, she was still trying to make sense of the scene before her.

First, there was Gage Logan sitting on Tripp's porch dressed in a flannel shirt and jeans with a beer in his hand. He immediately scooted over to make room for her beside him on the steps. She made her way across the lawn to join him. While she was glad to see him, it was the other person in the yard who held most of her attention.

Tripp was still dressed in that ugly jumpsuit with *Snowberry Creek Jail* stenciled in black across the back. Right now, he was so busy herding leaves across the grass with the blower that she doubted he even knew she was there. Rather than interrupt him, she sat down by Gage on the steps. He opened the small cooler sitting on the side of the porch.

"I've got bottled water and beer."

She didn't make a habit of drinking this early in

the day, but right now a beer sounded good. After popping the top, she took a big swig.

"Thanks, but what's going on here?"

He grinned and winked at her. "You're looking at the grand opening of the Snowberry Creek Jail Work Release Program."

"Really? I hadn't heard such a program was being considered. I would've thought at the very least it would've been mentioned at the city council meetings."

"Well, I thought since it's a pilot program, we'd hold off on making a public announcement until after we see how well it works out."

"And how does your victim . . . I mean your test subject feel about it?"

Gage shrugged. "Actually, it was mostly his idea. Tripp felt bad about you having to pick up the slack in the yard maintenance around here while he was sitting on his backside doing nothing. Then there's the fact he was going a bit stir-crazy in that cell. You can only burn off so much energy walking laps and doing push-ups in such a confined space."

So the two of them had come up with a scheme to get her leaves raked. "Dare I ask what that jerk detective thinks about it?"

Gage kicked his grin up a notch. "Since I didn't tell him, he has been understandably silent on the subject." He nudged her with his shoulder. "By the way, I'm sorry you and Ben Earle got off on the wrong foot. I didn't know that he'd just come from testifying in a trial where the perp is likely to get off with a slap on the wrist. I won't share the details about what the guy did, but it's the kind of case that drives cops crazy. You know he's committed so many more worse crimes, but you've only got the hard evidence to convict him on a lesser charge. In this case, the guy will be back out on the street and up to his old tricks in a matter of months."

Fine, she'd try to cut the man some slack, depending how he treated Tripp. "Your deputy already told me the detective has a good reputation in law enforcement circles. I'll try to give him the benefit of the doubt, especially considering I wasn't at my best, either."

They lapsed into silence as they watched Tripp chasing down the last bunch of leaves. After a minute or two, she asked, "Any breaking news on the case that you can share?"

"Not much. They still haven't found Kevin. The forensics team is processing what little evidence they found at the scene. Considering how many people have been traipsing through the maze, not to mention how hard it was raining that day, I would be surprised if they learn a lot."

The noise of the blower ended abruptly. Abby watched as Tripp started using the broom rake to pick up the leaves to dump them in the yard waste container. Even from where she was sitting, she could tell it was already pretty much full to the brim.

She stood up. "I need to get him some of the biodegradable leaf bags out of the garage."

Gage nodded. "Look, I think I'll stretch my legs a bit. Maybe walk around out front for a few minutes."

In other words, he was going to give her a few minutes alone with Tripp. "Thanks, Gage."

"No problem." Gage set his empty beer can aside. "I can't go far, though, in case someone comes by to check on my pilot program."

She headed into the garage to fetch the bags. By

the time she came out, Gage was out of sight. Tripp was still hard at work. He hadn't acknowledged her presence, making her unsure of her welcome. Well, too bad. He could pretend she was invisible if he wanted to. It was her yard, and she had every right to be there.

After unfolding the big leaf bag, she held it open for him. Tripp didn't comment as he dumped his next load inside. They worked in total silence for a minute or two before she finally broke and dropped the bag on the ground. "I'm sorry. I can't do this. I can't pretend everything is okay."

Zeke had been stretched out in a sunny spot a short distance away, but he lurched back up to his feet and made a beeline for her. She immediately knelt to wrap her arms around him, taking comfort in his warmth. Bless his furry heart, he stood rock still as she fought against the urge to cry.

A second later, Tripp put his hands on her shoulders and gently lifted her up to her feet. She turned into his arms and wrapped hers around his waist. When she sniffed, he muttered something unintelligible under his breath.

"Come on, Abby, don't cry."

"I'm not," she lied. "I think all these leaves blowing around might have stirred up my allergies."

"Funny, you've never mentioned having allergies when we've worked in the yard together before."

Maybe she would have if she'd known she'd need a convenient excuse to explain away a few tears. "Well, you don't know everything about me."

He laughed quietly. "I know enough to know you've got a big, soft heart."

"Yeah, well, that's not a bad thing."

His arms tightened just a little. "No, it's not, but I don't like seeing you hurting, Abby. Not because of me or the choices I've made."

She wasn't the only one with a soft heart, but she figured there was some kind of manly code Tripp ascribed to that said he wouldn't be happy if she pointed that out to him.

It was time to step back. "We should get these leaves bagged up. Gage didn't say how long he could let you hang out here without getting into trouble."

Tripp released his hold on her. "Yeah, I was mostly kidding when I suggested we do this, but he took me seriously. It does feel good to get out of the cell for a while."

She couldn't help but point out the obvious. "You could probably get out for good if you just told the detective what he wanted to know about Sergeant Montgomery and where he—"

When Tripp started to protest, she cut him off.

"Let me finish. What I was about to say is that I know that's not going to happen. It's just who you are. I don't like that you're in jail, even if I do understand why you're there. I might even go so far as to use words like 'noble' or 'heroic,' but I hate to see a Special Forces guy blush."

Which Tripp promptly did. It was hard not to laugh, but she knew better than to press her luck. For his sake, she pointed at the ground. "Now, about these leaves."

Between the two of them, it didn't take long to finish up. Gage even pitched in to help with the last bit of cleanup. He looked around the yard and at the surrounding trees, most of which were cedars and firs. "I'm thinking that should hold you for a while. If it gets bad again, though, give me a call. I'd be glad to park myself on the porch again and watch Tripp work."

Even the man in question laughed at that. "You should take me back, Gage. You've already wasted enough of your day off with me."

"Yeah, although my desk sergeant promised to call if Detective Earle comes nosing around again. We don't want to push our luck."

He headed for the porch. "I'll get my cooler and meet you at the car."

Once again, he was tactfully giving them a minute alone. "I'll drop cookies by for you tomorrow. Detective Chapin put in a request for chocolate chip. I hope that's okay with you."

Tripp brightened up at that. "Beggars can't be choosers, and it's nice to have something to look forward to. Besides, the deputy has been real decent to me. He should have some say in the goodies we get."

She looped her arm through his as they walked back toward Gage's cruiser. "If I get ambitious, any other flavor strike your fancy instead?"

He gave it some thought. "Maybe some gingersnaps?"

"I haven't made those before, so I'll have to see if I have all the ingredients. If I don't, it might be a day or two before I can make those for you."

"I'd tell you not to go out of your way to do that, but I figure I might as well save my breath."

Abby grinned. "Maybe you do know me better than I thought."

By that point, Gage had the back door of the car

open. The sight of Tripp being treated like a criminal made her sick, but at least Gage wasn't dangling a set of handcuffs from his fingers in preparation for snapping them on Tripp's wrists. Maybe he was just waiting until she wasn't there to watch, but she hoped not.

"I'll move my car so you can get out of the driveway."

Once again, her vision blurred, but at least neither of them was close enough to notice. Gage backed out of the driveway, and both men waved one last time before driving away. She blinked to clear her eyes and drove back down the driveway. As she turned off the engine, a single leaf floated down to land on the hood of her car.

She whispered, "See, Tripp, the yard is going to be a mess again before you know it."

Tonight, she'd bake those cookies, but tomorrow she'd start thinking what she could do to help the police with their investigation.

Chapter Ten

Jean set down her cup and looked at the other women seated around the dining room table. "I know we shouldn't gossip, which is why I'm reluctant to share this next bit of information."

Abby almost snorted tea out through her nose at that comment. If her elderly friend had any compunction about gossiping, she'd never seen any evidence of it. Granted, most of the information Jean shared with her friends was pretty harmless. She took great delight in being the first to know about new pregnancies, recent engagements, and who was upset about the neighbor's dog leaving presents in their yard.

Whatever tidbit she'd learned this time had her cheeks flushing pink, meaning that, by her standards, it was pretty racy. Had Jean's fortysomething neighbor slipped outside in his boxer shorts again to pick up the newspaper off his front lawn? The first time that had happened, Jean had claimed to be thoroughly scandalized by the shocking sight. Abby might have believed her if the woman hadn't mentioned more than once how often she kept an eye out to see if he ever did that again.

"It's all right, Jean, you can tell us. We won't tell a soul."

Louise said that with a completely straight face. Abby didn't buy that claim, either. If there was one thing she knew about the members of the quilting guild, it was that their gossip traveled at the speed of light. She'd lost track of how many times she'd heard the same bit of information from several sources, each promising that they were sharing it with only her.

Jean drew a deep breath and nodded as if having just reached a difficult decision. "There's been another pumpkin portrait appearance in town."

The other two ladies seated at the table had been leaning in closer, waiting for the salacious news. Their disappointment was clear as they relaxed back in their chairs. Glenda shook her head and said, "Jean, dear, that's not news. Those pumpkins have been showing up regularly for the past couple of weeks. The pictures appear on the *Clarion*'s website bright and early each morning."

"That's true, Glenda, but it's where this one appeared that is shocking. I won't mention names, but—"

Before she could continue, Abby's front doorbell buzzed three times in rapid order. Everyone immediately fell silent. Well, except for Zeke. He didn't always take his duty as guard dog seriously, but he was on point right now and growling softly.

"Abby, were you expecting company?"

"No one other than you ladies."

Although she had some suspicions about who it might be. Detective Earle had made it clear that he wanted to talk to her. Despite her demand that he do so, she hadn't really believed that he'd actually call ahead for an appointment.

While she remained seated, pondering if she really wanted to know who was standing on her front porch, the doorbell buzzed again. That was followed by a heavy-fisted knock, which pretty much eliminated the possibility of it being some kids selling candy for their sports team.

By this point, Glenda looked concerned. "Abby, aren't you going to see who it is?"

Well, yes, she supposed she was going to have to. "Excuse me, ladies."

One peek out the window by the door had her sighing. There were times she really hated being right. Pasting a bright smile on her face, she shoved Zeke back out of the way and opened the door.

"Detective Earle, I thought we agreed you'd call before stopping by. I'm afraid this isn't a good time."

The steady thump of Jean's walker heading straight toward them meant her friends were about to join them. Great, more grist for the guild's gossip mill.

"Is everything all right, Abby?"

She turned her stiff smile in their direction. "Everything is fine, ladies. Detective Earle just stopped by to see when I'd have time to talk to him."

Which wasn't now—or, better yet, ever.

"I'm really sorry to intrude, Ms. McCree, but I'm afraid we do need to talk."

Stubborn man. "But I don't . . . you see I have . . . I'm sorry, but now isn't convenient. As you can see, I'm in the middle of a board meeting for the quilting guild."

She might have gone right on babbling, but Glenda pushed herself to the front of the other ladies. "Abby, don't worry about us. I'm sure we've accomplished everything we needed to today. We'll head out so you and this nice young man can talk in private."

The detective's expression brightened a little. "Mrs. Unger, it's nice to see you again."

By this point, Abby was confused. "Glenda, you never told me that you and Detective Earle had spoken."

Her friend patted her on the arm. "Just briefly. He wanted to make sure that I wasn't too shaken up by the tragic events at the pumpkin farm."

The other two women's heads swiveled back and forth as if they were watching a tennis match as the conversation continued. If Jean was disappointed that she hadn't been able to finish sharing her scandalous gossip, it didn't show. Clearly learning that two of her friends were being interviewed by the police in connection with the recent murder was so much better.

Luckily, Glenda was far more experienced than Abby at herding their friends along at a good clip. "Louise, will you take the plates and cups back to the kitchen while I help Jean out to the car?"

Abby headed Louise off at the pass. "Don't bother with the dishes. I'll take care of them after the detective leaves. He won't be here long."

Crossing her fingers that this was true, she took charge of helping Jean down the front steps while Glenda and Louise fetched their purses and followed them out the door. Once everyone was safely tucked into the huge sedan, Abby stepped back out of the way and waved goodbye as they disappeared down the road. If she wasn't mistaken, both Louise and Jean remained twisted around in their seats looking back at her to make sure they didn't miss a thing until Glenda turned the corner at the end of the block.

Time to deal with her one remaining guest. She

patted her leg to call Zeke back to her side. "Come on, boy. Let's go."

He trotted back up the steps to where Detective Earle stood waiting. At least he was polite enough to remain outside on the porch until she could usher him inside.

"Come on in, Detective."

She hated that the good manners her late aunt had drilled into her at a young age compelled her to offer refreshments. "I think there's still a cup or two of coffee in the pot, if you'd like one."

He looked surprised by the offer. "If you're sure it would be no bother. It's been a long day already."

That's when she noticed the lines of strain bracketing his mouth and that his eyes looked tired. "It's no problem. How do you take it?"

"With cream."

She pointed into the dining room on her way to the kitchen. "Have a seat at the table and help yourself to some of the leftover snacks from our board meeting."

Zeke played escort, settling himself in a small sunbeam where he could keep an eye on their visitor while she fetched the coffee. When she returned, Ben Earle looked more relaxed. Maybe the decision to play the role of polite hostess had been a good idea. As soon as the detective sipped the coffee, he said, "Thank you. That tastes great."

When he bit into one of the brownies she'd baked that morning, he actually smiled, which took years off his apparent age. "Delicious. I really appreciate this. With the combination of sugar and caffeine, I might make it through the rest of the afternoon."

"Glad I could help."

Sort of, anyway.

She'd already had enough of the sweets, but she nibbled on some brie and a cracker while she waited for the detective to come to the point. Finally, when he'd finished off his second brownie, he leaned back in his chair and took out the same kind of spiral notebook that Gage always carried in his pocket. If all cops used them, maybe they got a discount for buying in bulk.

"I wanted to go over the events of the day in question with you. I know you've already spoken with Gage and with Deputy Vinter, but I would really appreciate it if you'd take me through it all one more time."

She was so tired of the entire affair, but she couldn't very well refuse. For one thing, Mr. Minter deserved justice. For another, if she continued to avoid the subject, the good detective might very well decide she had something to hide or someone she was trying to protect.

She launched right into her story. "I wasn't supposed to be at Mr. Minter's farm at all that morning. Another friend of Mrs. Unger's was going to go with her to pick up the load of pumpkins, but Beatrice woke up ill. When Glenda called and asked if I could go instead, I offered to drive because of the awful weather we were having."

From that point, the detective led her through the entire episode right up to and including Gage driving her home. "And did Gage stick around for a while?"

For the first time she hesitated. How much did he already know? The safest bet would be to assume that Gage wouldn't have held anything back. Besides, sharing sandwiches with two friends was hardly a crime.

"I invited him in for lunch, which I thought was

only polite since he'd gone out of his way to help me get through all of this."

If she sounded a little defensive, so be it. Instead of questioning Gage's actions, the detective actually seemed to approve. "He's good that way. It's one reason I usually like working with him."

"Usually?"

He didn't answer her question, instead asking one of his own. "So, did you suggest Tripp Blackston join the two of you for lunch, or was that Gage?"

Where was he going with this? He stared at her with those world-weary eyes that had seen far too much of the ugliness life had to offer. This was only her second murder case, but the effect they'd both had on her life had been profound. How much worse would it be to deal with such things on a daily basis?

"I didn't call Tripp, but I don't know that Gage did, either. He lives in that small house in the backyard, so he may have seen us drive up and come over on his own. Regardless, I had set out the sandwich makings and then headed upstairs to change out of my drenched clothes. When I came back downstairs, Tripp and Gage were sitting at the kitchen table." She reached down to pet Zeke's big head. "Zeke was there, too."

For the briefest moment, her companion's serious-as-death cop expression slipped a bit as he studied Zeke. "He's a handsome dog. I bet he can be intimidating when he wants to be."

She offered Zeke a couple of baby carrots to chomp on. He gave her a reproachful look for not fetching him his usual treats but took them anyway. "Yeah, but for the most part he's a big sweetie."

"Did you and Gage discuss the case with Mr. Blackston at that time?"

Again, she couldn't lie, but at the same time, she didn't want to add to Tripp's problems. "I honestly don't know how much Gage actually told him. I was still upstairs when they talked about it. Gage did say he'd told Tripp the bare bones of the situation. He wanted him to check in on me later to see how I was doing."

He made a couple of quick notes. "Anything else?"

It probably wouldn't do her any good to ask if she could get a peek at what he'd written down, so she plowed on with her story. "Well, Reilly Molitor, the reporter for the *Clarion*, came knocking at the back door. He wanted to take a statement from me about what had happened. To tell the truth, I was surprised by that, considering it had been such a short time since we'd gotten back to the house. He said someone from the sheriff's department at the murder scene had pointed him in my direction."

The flash of anger on Detective Earle's face seemed genuine. "I hadn't heard that, and I apologize if my team let your name slip. He would've found you eventually, of course, but I don't like my people siccing reporters on witnesses like that."

"Don't worry about it. I'm guessing Reilly recognized my name as soon as he heard it because of the . . . murder victim who was discovered in my backyard a while back. At least Gage was here to run interference this time. Tripp left not long after that, because I was expecting guests for the afternoon. He offered to come back that evening if I needed company, but I didn't call him. I was doing better by then, and I knew he had homework to do."

Which is something she should've asked him about when she'd visited him at the jail, or at least when he and Gage were there dealing with her leaves. It would be a shame if he had to drop out of his classes because of this whole mess. Maybe she'd give Gage a call and ask if she could at least bring Tripp his textbooks and laptop when she dropped by with the cookies she'd promised to bring him.

For now, she stood up. "If there's nothing else, Detective, I do have other things I need to be doing."

He took his time closing his notebook and stuffing it back into his jacket pocket. "Have you seen Sergeant Montgomery since the murder?"

At last, an easy question. "No, I haven't."

The detective finally looked ready to leave. "If you do see him, you will call me or Gage immediately."

Not a question, so she didn't bother to respond. While she'd hate to turn Kevin in to the police, she would if it was the only way to get Tripp out of jail.

"One more thing, and then I'll get out of your way."

"What's that?"

Once again he flashed that rare smile that changed his whole demeanor. "Would you mind if I took another brownie for the road?"

"Help yourself. Take two if you'd like."

He did as she suggested, wrapping the goodies in a napkin before sliding them into another pocket. "Thank you for your help, Ms. McCree. I am sorry that you got caught up in all of this. It's never easy for anyone."

"No, it isn't."

As she followed him toward the front door, she gave in to the temptation to ask one more question.

"Do you have other leads you're following in the case? Other suspects?"

Technically, that was two questions, but he probably wasn't going to answer anyway. She was right. He immediately spun back to stare down at her. "I don't share details of ongoing investigations with civilians."

"Fine."

"And for the record, I reviewed the file of the murder victim discovered in your backyard. I don't know why, but Gage Logan was amazingly lenient about your interference in the investigation. I won't be. We're the professionals. Stay out of our way and let us do our jobs."

Enough was enough.

"On second thought, Detective Earle, I want my brownies back."

He stared down at her outstretched hand, maybe trying to decide if she was serious. When he finally decided she was, he yanked the napkin back out of his pocket and slapped it down on her palm.

"I'll be back in touch if I have any more questions."

She waited until he was out on the porch before answering. "Next time, call first."

Then she slammed the door closed and locked it.

Chapter Eleven

Abby carried two plates of cookies into city hall and headed straight for Jackson Jones, the sergeant who manned the front desk at the police department. She set them down and offered him one of her brightest smiles.

"Hi, is Chief Logan available? If not, maybe Deputy Chapin would have a minute to speak with me."

He studied the foil-covered plates for a second or two before making a quick call. Gage joined them a few seconds later. "Abby, what can I do for you?"

"I brought the cookies I promised, but I wondered if I could deliver them to Tripp myself."

Gage ran his fingers through his hair. "I'm sorry, but that's not a good idea right now. The county sheriff's people have been in and out of here today. Detective Earle is here right now, and if he decides he needs to talk to Tripp again, he wouldn't be happy to see I let you down there."

She made a face. "Yeah, he's not too pleased with me right now."

"Maybe we should head back to my office to talk. This area is a little too public."

Before she rounded the counter, she peeled back the foil on one plate and held it out to the desk sergeant. "I baked these chocolate chip cookies for everyone, if you'd like to take a couple before I set them out."

He grinned and didn't hesitate. "Thanks. They'd likely be all gone before I got a chance to get back there."

She followed Gage down the hall to his office and joined him inside. "I'll get us some coffee."

"That would be great. By the way, I also baked some gingersnaps for Tripp, but I'm sure he'll be glad to share some of them with you, too."

Gage returned a few seconds later with two mugs full of what passed for coffee in the station. After settling into his desk chair, he helped himself to a cookie from Tripp's portion before speaking. "So what have you done to aggravate Ben Earle this time?"

"He dropped by without calling first, but I decided to be nice and let that pass. I answered all his questions and even gave him a cup of coffee. I also let him help himself to the snacks left over from my quilting guild meeting."

Gage motioned her to continue as he took a bite of his gingersnap cookie and then immediately helped himself to a second one.

"When we were done, he asked if he could have another brownie for the road, and I told him to take two. But then I didn't like what he had to say after that."

"Which was?"

"All I asked was if he has any new leads or suspects in the case. Instead of answering me, he said you were too lenient with my alleged interference in the investigation into Dolly Cayhill's murder. He made it clear he wouldn't put up with me asking questions, even ones I thought were only reasonable."

"So how did you respond?"

Her cheeks flushed hot. Her behavior toward the detective hadn't been her proudest moment. "I made him give the brownies back."

She suspected it was hard to knock a man like Gage, a former soldier and experienced cop, sideways. However, apparently that's what she'd just done. He slowly lowered the cookie he'd been about to bite and set it down on his desk. For several seconds, he stared at her as if really seeing her for the first time. Or maybe not seeing her at all. Then he closed his eyes and shook his head.

"Gage?"

It was even more worrisome when his broad shoulders started shaking. Had she actually broken him somehow? Then his laughter came pouring out in huge gulps. She wasn't sure that was any better than the strange silence had been. It took him a minute or two to regain control. By the time he finally wiped a couple of stray tears from his eyes and was back to breathing normally, she was feeling mildly insulted. Yes, maybe she'd behaved badly—okay, in fact *had* behaved badly—that didn't mean she appreciated being the source of such amusement.

"Sorry, Abby, but that's the funniest thing I've heard in . . . well, maybe ever. I would love to have seen the look on his face when you made him fork over those brownies."

She found her own mouth quirking up in a small grin. "I know I should apologize to him, but I was mad. I get that he can't exactly share all the details from his investigation with a civilian, but a simple statement that he was checking into any and all possibilities would have sufficed."

"Really? Because I don't remember you listening all that well when I said something similar to you the last time."

It wasn't like she could deny the truth of that, so she didn't bother trying. "You're right, of course, but I've learned my lesson. I just wanted to know if any real progress was being made. I don't sleep well knowing another killer is wandering loose in town."

Just that quickly Gage went from amused to serious as death. "Has something happened to make you suspect you're in danger?"

Clearly she'd overstated her concern. "No, I'm fine. No rocks through my window. No one trying to break in during the night."

"That's good. If that changes, call me."

"I will."

It was time to hit the road. "Thanks for seeing that Tripp gets the cookies."

"No problem. We can set the other plate out for everyone else."

She started toward the door, but then turned back. "I meant to ask if I should bring in Tripp's textbooks and laptop so he can keep up with his classes."

"He picked them up the other day when we were there."

At least that was one problem solved. "Tell him I said hi."

"Will do."

As they stepped out of his office, she spotted Gage's pumpkin portrait and started laughing. The deputies might look busy, but they obviously found time in their days to further embellish the display. The new additions included a few toy police cruisers, a water pistol, and what looked like the kind of red light cops put on the top of unmarked cars, except in miniature.

Gage mumbled under his breath, "Don't say a word. It only encourages the idiots."

She did her best to muffle the urge to giggle as she set the plate of cookies she'd brought for Gage and his deputies down by the pumpkin. She was about to ask if he played with the cars when no one was around when she spotted Detective Earle standing on the other side of the room. "Oops, it's time for me to disappear."

Gage followed her line of sight. "Too late."

Well, darn. Panic danced around the edges of her mind, but she stood her ground. No way she'd let that man figure out that he had her spooked.

He stopped just short of where the two of them stood. "Ms. McCree, you seem to spend a lot of time hanging around the police department."

His tone made ice sound warm and cozy. She considered how to respond and decided to be the adult in the room. "Detective Earle, I'm glad we ran into each other. I owe you an apology for yesterday."

She took the second plate of cookies from Gage and uncovered it. "Not to mention some cookies. You have your choice of chocolate chip or gingersnap."

It was impossible to read what was going on behind that steely-eyed gaze he offered her, but then there was just a hint of humor in his expression. "Can I keep them this time?"

Abby ignored Gage's small snort of laughter. "Yes, I promise."

Rather than drag out the encounter any longer than

necessary, she decided to beat a hasty retreat. "You two probably have important police things to do, so I'll be going."

She made it to the door to the lobby before the detective caught up with her. "Ms. McCree, a minute please?"

Swallowing a sigh, she turned back. "You might as well call me Abby."

"Okay." He studied her for a few seconds and then said her name as if trying it on for size. "Abby, I didn't mean to anger you yesterday. I understand why you would be curious about the case. You're upset about your friend Tripp, and discovering the body was no doubt traumatic. I just don't want you getting caught in the cross fire when we start closing in on whoever is behind the murder. I could have been more tactful."

"Since you accepted my apology, the least I can do is accept yours." She managed a small smile. "We'll all feel better when this is finally over."

"Yes, we will. Enjoy the rest of your day."

As he disappeared back into the bull pen, she felt bad for him. Yes, they'd both be happier when the truth came out about who had murdered Mr. Minter. The difference was that he'd move on to another case just like it, or even worse. That had her thinking maybe she should bake him his own batch of brownies.

But not until he let Tripp out of jail.

"You poor dear, we heard that you were the one who discovered Mr. Minter had been murdered. Are you all right?"

Thanks to her hearing problem, Mrs. McGill clearly thought she was whispering even though her voice had rung out across the room, immediately drawing everyone's attention to where Abby sat at the head of the table. She'd been through this same sort of thing enough with the members of the Committee on Senior Affairs to know that no further work would get done until she acknowledged the elephant in the room.

She smiled at Mrs. McGill. "It was upsetting, but I'm fine now. The police are working hard to solve the case."

That set off a flurry of comments as people tried to talk over each other.

"I hadn't heard . . ."

"It's a shame, but we all know he was a difficult man to deal with."

"I'm not surprised. They said that homeless man . . ."

"I don't know why the police haven't run him off before now."

At that last one, Abby cleared her throat to get everyone's attention. While she didn't know for sure what Kevin had or had not done, she wasn't going to encourage people to cast blame in his direction without proof. When it finally got quiet, she looked at each of the people seated around the table in turn.

"I am not at liberty to discuss the case, and I am not privy to the details of the investigation. Regardless, I don't think gossiping about Sergeant Montgomery is helpful. He served our country with honor, and I think he deserves the benefit of the doubt."

The muttering immediately resumed, and from the sound of it her defense of Kevin had produced mixed results.

Then Fred Cady raised his hand to get her attention. "Yes, Fred?"

His normally jovial expression was nowhere in sight as he drew a deep breath before speaking. "I knew Ronald Minter for most of his life, and I normally hesitate to speak ill of the dead. Having said that, I feel obligated to point out that if we gathered up everyone who had ever had words with him, the line would reach the length of Main Street. That man had a real talent for aggravating everyone he crossed paths with—neighbors, friends, and even family."

He once again looked around the table. "Don't get me wrong. I'm not saying the police shouldn't consider the sergeant a possible suspect, but he's not the only one who has had problems with Ronald lately. I personally saw Ronald get into it with Jasper Collins a couple of days before Ronald was killed. I have no idea what the discussion was about, but their tempers were both running plenty hot."

Shaking his head, Fred leaned forward to rest his elbows on the table. "Heck, if you're going to try and convict someone for the murder just for fighting with Ronald, I should confess that two weeks back he and I traded some pretty ugly words when I dared to disagree with him over the new speed limit on the road that goes by the front of his farm."

Abby sat up straighter. She couldn't imagine Fred Cady indulging in the kind of violence that had ended Ronald Minter's life, but who was this Jasper Collins? And did the police know about that argument? This wasn't the time or place to press Fred for details, but maybe she could ask Glenda or Jean about the other man later. Better yet, she was supposed to meet Bridey Kyser for lunch at the diner after this meeting ended. She'd know.

"Before we adjourn, does anyone have any last questions about what we're doing at the festival?"

When no one raised a hand, she briefly summarized the plan one last time. "The decorations committee will meet at four o'clock to finish any last-minute details. I've already made arrangements to have the boxes of goody bags delivered ahead of time. I've also sent out another reminder to the merchants telling them when to expect us and to make sure they let us know if they need any of our volunteers to help hand out the candy to the kids."

Ten minutes later she headed out the door, relieved to have checked one major item off her agenda. She'd warned Bridey that she might be late if the meeting ran long, but it looked as if she'd be right on time if she hustled. They both had a narrow window in their schedules to fit in a quick meal before Bridey needed to be back at her shop and Abby's appointment with the executive board of the veterans group. She was rather dreading that particular meeting, but she didn't want to postpone it just because Tripp couldn't be there. She suspected the board wouldn't be surprised by his absence and might even agree with his decision to protect Kevin.

At least she'd managed to come up with an idea for their fundraiser that they might really like. She hoped so, anyway. For now, she wasn't going to worry about it.

Stepping inside the diner, she scanned the room and spotted Bridey seated in a booth in the back corner. She wove her way between tables and waitresses carrying heavy trays to reach her friend. It felt good to slide across the red vinyl seat and relax.

"Have you been waiting long?"

Bridey's smile was bright and welcoming. "No, I just got here. I was worried there wouldn't be anywhere to sit, but this booth opened up right when I walked in. It's a lucky thing, because the only other empty spots were at the counter, and there weren't two seats together."

Abby picked up the menu out of habit although she already knew everything that was on it. Her aunt Sybil had taken her to the diner for a lunch or dinner a few times when Abby had come for a visit back when she was a little girl. Unfortunately, those visits had become less frequent after her parents had gotten a divorce. As far as she could tell, the only things that had ever changed on Frannie's menu over the years were the prices.

Frannie herself showed up to take their orders. "Ladies, what can I get you today?"

Bridey smiled. "I'll have a cheeseburger. Instead of the fries, I'll have a side salad with honey mustard dressing. Iced tea to drink."

Abby set her menu down on top of Bridey's. "I'll have the sourdough burger with fries and iced tea."

Frannie swept up the menus. "Good choice, Abby. You shouldn't have to wait long."

Bridey snickered as the older woman walked away. "She doesn't approve of salads instead of fries. I tried telling her that I have to watch what I eat. I pick up enough extra calories sampling my desserts when I'm working on a new recipe."

They both watched the diner's owner as she stopped to chat with various customers. No one knew for sure how old Frannie was, but estimates ran from early fifties up to late seventies. Regardless of what the actual number might be, the woman had more energy than Abby did on her best day.

"Yeah, I have to limit how often I come here. Everything is delicious, but Frannie either has never heard how bad cholesterol is for people or else she doesn't care."

Enough about that. She didn't want to miss out on this chance to ask Bridey what she knew about the man Fred had mentioned at the meeting.

Dropping her voice down a notch, Abby leaned forward and asked, "Bridey, what can you tell me about a guy named Jasper Collins?"

Her friend frowned. "I'm surprised you haven't met him. He's the branch manager of the bank here in town. What do you need to know?"

"His name came up in conversation earlier this morning, but I didn't know who he was."

Trailing her fingertip through the condensation on the side of her water glass, Bridey said, "When I first moved back to town, I met with him briefly when I needed a loan when I was opening up Something's Brewing. Mostly he leaves that kind of work to one of his assistants. However, Jasper recently decided that he wanted to get to know Seth and me better, maybe because of Seth's reputation as an artist. We ended up at a dinner party at his house along with several other couples I didn't know very well."

She shrugged. "It was pleasant enough, but not really our cup of tea. I've heard rumors he's thinking about running for office, maybe at the county or state level. For sure, I don't think he'd stand a chance against Rosalyn McKay for the job of mayor here in town."

Interesting. "So he was courting possible donors?"

"He didn't exactly have his hand out, but it wouldn't

surprise me. His wife does come from old money, so he might be able to finance a campaign on his own."

Frannie reappeared with their lunches. They waited until she was off and running again before continuing the conversation.

"Why did his name come up at your seniors meeting? I'd guess he's only in his early forties."

Deciding there wasn't any reason not to tell her, Abby said, "The subject of Ronald Minter's murder came up. People were worried about me, I guess. That didn't mean everyone liked it when I defended Sergeant Montgomery. I think they'd rather blame a homeless man than think another one of their neighbors was capable of killing someone. Another man in the group pointed out that Kevin wasn't the only man to have had problems with Mr. Minter in recent days. Evidently he'd overheard Jasper Collins and Mr. Minter having words."

Bridey bit her lower lip. "That doesn't sound like Jasper at all. He's nice enough, if a bit stuffy. I can't imagine him getting into an argument like that, especially in public. It wouldn't fit the image that he's been cultivating."

"I wonder what it was about, or if the police have heard about it."

Then Abby realized her friend was looking pretty worried. "What's wrong?"

"You're not trying to investigate on your own again, are you?"

Why did everyone make that assumption?

Bridey reached across the table to take Abby's hand in hers. "I realize I know you're worried about Tripp and everything, but you really shouldn't be asking questions like this. Please leave it up to the police to investigate, Abby. We came too close to losing you the last time. Promise me you won't confront Jasper Collins about his fight with Ronald."

She really didn't mean to worry her friends, but she just couldn't seem to stop herself from wanting to see how all the pieces of the puzzle would finally fit together. That didn't mean Bridey wasn't right.

"Fine, but I wasn't going to march into his office demanding answers."

Bridey wasn't a fool. She knew Abby was hedging her bets. "That's not good enough. Promise you won't go near the man."

"Fine, I promise."

Bridey stole a fry from Abby's plate. "Thank you. Now, we'd better finish eating. I need to get back to the shop, and I'm guessing you have another dreadful meeting scheduled for this afternoon."

She managed a small smile. "That's my life these days. Another day, another meeting or two."

And as she ate the last bite of her sourdough burger, she silently added, *And another chance to ask questions.*

Chapter Twelve

Someone must have been watching for Abby to arrive at the church where the veterans group met, because a tall man with salt-and-pepper hair and a neatly trimmed beard came striding down the sidewalk to greet her. As he got closer, she noticed he was wearing a clerical collar, which meant she was about to meet Pastor Jack Haliday. From what Tripp had told her, he was one of the original founders of the veterans group. Evidently he'd become a minister after leaving the military.

His smile was warm and welcoming. "Hi, you must be Abby, Tripp's friend."

She shook his hand. "I am. He's spoken often of you, Pastor Haliday."

His eyes twinkled just a bit. "I hope at least some of what he said was good."

"Mostly, but there've been a few things . . ." Then she winked at him.

He laughed, radiating warmth and good humor. She could see why Tripp liked him so much. "Let's head on inside. We'll go through the side entrance to where the group meets. We do want to thank you for stepping up to help us with this project."

His expression turned a little more serious. "Although I somehow suspect it's more likely Tripp volunteered you. I hope he at least asked you first."

While it was tempting to rat Tripp out to his friends, that would only make them feel bad about the situation. She settled for fudging a little on the truth. "We definitely talked about it."

From the skeptical look the pastor gave her, she might not have sold that claim as well as she could have. Even if she hadn't been happy that Tripp had signed her up to help with asking first, she was committed now, especially since he was temporarily unavailable to help out.

As they strolled along the winding sidewalk, Jack asked, "Speaking of Tripp, have you talked to him recently?"

She wasn't sure how many people knew where he was hanging out these days, but she suspected the pastor probably did. "I was able to visit him once. When I stopped by yesterday to drop off some cookies for him, Gage Logan couldn't let me deliver them in person. He assured me Tripp was doing all right, the stubborn jerk. Tripp, that is. Not Gage."

Pastor Jack smiled and said, "I thought I'd drop by later this afternoon to check on him. While I understand what he's doing and why, I'm not sure Sergeant Montgomery would want him to sit in jail just to protect him."

It was tempting to ask if the pastor had seen Kevin since the murder, but she resisted the urge. If he had, she'd feel obligated to tell Detective Earle, or at least Gage. Besides, the pastor might feel just as determined to protect Kevin, especially if he considered him to be one of his parishioners and as well as a member of the support group.

None of that mattered. She wouldn't put Pastor Haliday on the spot by asking.

They stepped into the dim interior of the church basement, where they were greeted by a group of six people—four men and two women. She spotted at least one familiar face. Clarence Reed owned the local hardware store where she shopped.

He waved as he poured himself a cup of coffee from the huge urn sitting on the pass-through counter between the multipurpose room and the church kitchen. "Hi, Abby. Can I pour you a cup?"

"That would be great."

One of the women offered her the chair next to hers and introduced herself. "Hi, I'm Zoe Brevik. I work as a nurse practitioner at the medical clinic here in town."

They chatted for a few minutes while the others got drinks and then drifted over to the table to join them. When everyone was finally seated, the pastor performed the necessary introductions. "And, finally, this is Abby McCree, who has agreed to head up this project for us. Tripp will be her cochair, but he's unable to join us today."

Zoe leaned in closer. "May I say, you're awfully brave to take this on."

Abby whispered back, "Brave, or maybe crazy. I'm not sure which."

Meanwhile, Pastor Haliday went over a few other bits of business before turning the meeting over to Abby. She passed out the information she'd put together for everyone.

"From what Tripp told me, you want to host an event that's both a fundraiser and a thank-you to the community for their support. With that in mind, I came up with what is actually a two-part event. We'd start out with a bachelor/bachelorette auction. The people who bid on and win one of our volunteers would also get free tickets to the dance. Considering it's a veterans group sponsoring the events, I thought it would be fun to stick to a military theme, like a World War II USO-style dance. We could do away with the auction if you don't think it's feasible. Regardless, I'm confident the second one would be a lot of fun, especially if we schedule it on or around Valentine's Day. I know that's working in a pretty short time frame, so we can pick another date. Maybe it could be part of the town's Fourth of July celebration."

She gave everyone a minute or two to scan all the information on the page. It was hard to gauge their reactions, but most of the six were smiling by the time they looked up from reading her presentation.

Jack asked, "So to make sure I'm understanding, the bachelor/bachelorette auction would be held first, to be followed by the dinner/dance a short time later?"

Abby nodded. "Yes. The auction would also help raise funds to cover the cost of the dance. If we promote it right, we should bring in far more than we need. On the night of the dance, we could do a full dinner, but I'd rather keep things simpler and serve drinks and hors d'oeuvres. If you look at the third page, I did a comparison of the costs."

The committee members were definitely looking pretty enthusiastic. "I've already talked to several potential vendors and explained that this would be a fundraiser to help veterans. One of the bigger costume rental places in the area immediately offered to give us a deep discount on the rental fees for the uniforms and vintage clothing. Two of the caterers have also offered to provide refreshments, whether it's just hors d'oeuvres or a sit-down dinner, at about twenty percent over cost, for the same reason."

One of the other men asked, "Where are we going to get volunteers to be auctioned off?"

Tripp was going to kill her for what she was about to say, but too bad. "Tripp will be the first to sign up. I'm guessing that since he's willing, we'll be able to find more people. I was hoping some of you might even know some active-duty military who might be convinced to join the fun."

After she answered another flurry of questions, Jack called for a vote. It was gratifying when they reached a unanimous decision to move forward with the plans. They also set a date to meet again in November to get the ball rolling. Amazingly, each of them also agreed to head up one or more of the various subcommittees that would be required.

Once the meeting was adjourned, Zoe walked out to the parking lot with Abby. "I think your idea is brilliant. I'll talk to the physical therapist at the clinic to see if he'd be willing to join Tripp up there on the stage at the auction. He's former navy and a great guy."

"That would be wonderful. I'm also hoping to convince Gage Logan to participate."

Zoe's eyes widened. "Wow, I was right. You are brave. Don't tell my husband, but I won't mind being there to see the three of them strutting their stuff."

They reached Abby's car. "Well, let's just hope enough people volunteer to make it worth doing. Regardless, I think the vintage dance will be great fun."

"Me, too. See you soon. Tell Tripp hi for me when you see him again."

"I will."

After Zoe walked away, Abby got in her car but didn't immediately start the engine. What should she do next? While it was a relief to be done with the day's errands and meetings, she was in no hurry to get back home. Sometimes she and Tripp went a day or two without crossing paths, but just knowing he wasn't around the place left her feeling out of kilter somehow. Even Zeke continued to be more subdued than normal. Clearly he missed his buddy and their walks together.

Maybe she'd go pick up Zeke and head for the park for another long ramble along the river. That held more appeal than rattling around in the house all by herself. With her plans set, she pulled out of the parking lot. But rather than driving straight home, she took the long way around, which took her past Ronald Minter's farm.

Traffic was light, which allowed her to slow down a little as she drove by. The place looked deserted, lifeless somehow. The crime scene tape didn't help. Seeing all the pumpkins still lying out in the field made her sad. Was no one going to harvest them? But then again, who had the right? She'd never heard who stood to inherit the place. Someone had nailed a piece of lumber that said CLOSED over the sign advertising the corn maze. She shuddered at the memory of sitting outside of that shack with nothing but a dead body for company as she waited for the police.

Gunning the engine, she sped up to put some distance between herself and the farm. It was definitely time to head home.

As she approached her driveway, she noticed a strange car parked out front of the house. What now?

It didn't take her long to recognize the man standing in her front yard. What did Reilly Molitor want now? She considered calling Gage rather than getting out of the car to confront the man herself, but that would be cowardly. Besides, by now, the murder was almost old news. As far as she knew, there hadn't been a break in the case, so there was no reason Reilly would be coming to her for new details.

Then she noticed he appeared to be snapping pictures with his phone. What was up with that? Only one way to find out.

She got out and headed straight for him. As soon as he spotted her coming, he shoved his phone into his pocket and backed away from the house. Considering his welcome both times he'd come by before, she couldn't really blame him for being a bit wary.

Rather than crowd him, she stopped a few feet away from where he stood. "Hi, Reilly. Is there something I can do for you?"

He shook his head and then pointed toward the porch. "I've been taking pictures of the pumpkin portraits that have appeared around town, but there haven't been any new ones for the past couple of days. I happened to be driving by and spotted that one."

She turned to see what he was talking about. Sure

enough, there was a huge pumpkin sitting on her top porch step. "Where did that come from?"

Reilly got brave enough to move up beside her. "No idea. They just seem to appear out of nowhere. As far as I've been able to tell, no one has caught the artist delivering them. You didn't know it was here?"

"No, I didn't, but I've been gone most of the day. When I left, I went out through the back door."

She walked closer to get a better look. "Wow, the detail is amazing. I've seen the pictures you've posted online, and I've seen Gage's a couple of times. Whoever the artist is, he or she's got real talent. I'm not sure how much it looks like me, but it's definitely a work of art."

"They are all amazing." Reilly offered her a small smile. "It's becoming a bit of an honor to get one. It means you're a celebrity here in town."

She wasn't so sure about that. The only claim to fame she had was to have had the bad luck to discover two dead bodies since moving to Snowberry Creek. If that's what it took to be a celebrity, she could live without it.

"Are you going to be okay with me posting the picture with the others?"

It was nice of him to ask, although she had to wonder if he would've bothered if she hadn't caught him in the act. She took a second to think about it before answering. Really, what was the harm?

"That's fine, Reilly."

He looked pleased. "Thanks, I appreciate it. Did you know some of the photos have been picked up by the bigger newspapers in the area? Connie Pohler has also been uploading them to the town's social media, so they're getting a lot of attention. I don't know what the artist's intentions were when he or she started making them, but it's turned out to be good publicity for the whole town."

Abby wasn't sure how she'd been singled out for the honor, but she was all right with it. It occurred to her to ask, "Has everyone who has been honored with one been pleased by it?"

Reilly grimaced. "Not so much. My editor asked me to take down one of the first photos I had posted. Evidently the people in question weren't happy about having their portraits up on our website. After that, I started making sure I had permission, just to cover my . . . uh, all my bases."

She found it curious that someone would have taken such offense. "I probably shouldn't ask if it was anyone I know."

He gave her a sly look. "That's probably true. For the record, the subjects of those particular portraits were mainly upset about where the portraits originally turned up. The artist tends to leave the pumpkins someplace associated with the subject of the portrait. You know, like the mayor's was left at city hall, Gage's by the police station, and Frannie's at the diner."

It took Abby a minute to connect the dots. "So in this case, the pumpkin portraits were someplace the subjects weren't supposed to be."

"Apparently." He glanced at his watch. "Well, I'd better hit the road. I'm supposed to cover the basketball game at the high school this afternoon."

"Have fun with that."

Reilly looked excited by the prospect. "I will. The varsity team has a real shot of winning the division this year."

When he was gone, she dug out her own phone and snapped a couple of pictures of the jack-o'-lantern to send to her parents. Both of them would get a kick out of seeing their daughter immortalized in pumpkin art.

After sending them off, she let herself into the house, where Zeke stood waiting for her. "Come on, boy. It's nice outside, and you've been shut in the house all day. Let's head out to the park for a while. Maybe we'll even grab burgers at Gary's Drive-In for dinner tonight."

The big dog took off running for the kitchen, where she kept his leash and portable water bowl. After grabbing a bottle of water and a few treats to stick into her pack, they went out through the front door. Zeke stopped to check out the pumpkin. After giving it a thorough sniff, he barked and wagged his tail. It was as if he recognized the scent of whoever had left it there and considered the person to be a friend. Not exactly helpful in identifying the mysterious artist, since Zeke couldn't talk. Besides, the only two people Zeke had ever reacted to adversely were Reilly and a murderer. That didn't exactly narrow the possibilities by much.

She opened the door to the back seat and let Zeke scramble inside. He settled on his quilt and waited patiently for her to lower his window enough that he could stick his big head outside to catch the scents on the wind as she drove down the street. His face filled her side mirror, his big tongue hanging out and no doubt drooling on the side of the car. He looked so happy.

His good mood continued as they reached the

park. They headed down the path at a slow jog. It felt good to stretch her legs a bit, and Zeke was definitely enjoying himself. When they reached a fork in the trail, he tried to take the one that led into the national forest. Abby hesitated, but then let him tug her along in his wake. She hadn't ventured into the forest since the night she'd run into Kevin Montgomery and had to be rescued by Tripp.

While she wasn't actually hoping to run into the sergeant, she wouldn't go out of her way to avoid him, either. Not with Zeke there to protect her. They eventually slowed to a walk and then to a stop so she could take a closer look at their surroundings. She honestly had no idea if they were anywhere close to where she'd encountered Kevin that night. For one thing, she'd started out from the other end of the trail.

Zeke sat down and looked up at her with a long sigh. To keep him entertained for a couple of minutes, she filled his bowl with water from the bottle she'd brought and set it down on the ground. When he was done lapping it up, he raised his head with a rivulet of water dripping off his muzzle. It took some fancy footwork on her part to avoid having him use her jeans as a towel.

"Here's one of your cookies, Zeke."

He gulped down his treat while she packed up his water bowl and stuck the empty bottle into her pack. It was time to get moving again; the only question was whether they should finish the loop or turn back toward the river. Zeke answered that question for her when he lifted his head to stare into the distance, a low growl rumbling in his chest. There was no way to know if the danger he sensed walked on two legs or four. Regardless, she had no desire to find out.

When she tugged on his leash, he growled one last time before letting her lead him back toward the river. Her legs were feeling the burn, but she kept up the slow jog until she could catch glimpses of the water through the trees. They hadn't crossed paths with anyone since leaving the main trail, and she'd feel a lot better when they got back to the park, where there were more people.

Just before they reached the last bend in the trail, Kevin Montgomery stepped out of the trees right in front of her. Zeke woofed and charged right toward him. Abby barely managed to hold on to the dog's leash until they reached his friend.

The former soldier went down on one knee to give Zeke a quick hug. "Hey there, boy."

As he continued to pet the happy dog, Sergeant Montgomery gave her a worried look, then scanned the surrounding area. "Ms. Abby, you shouldn't be out here alone even with Zeke here providing escort. I've been looking for Tripp to let him know the enemy has been moving through the area again, but I can't find him. Will you tell him for me?"

So he didn't know Tripp was in jail, which made her wonder if he'd even heard about Ronald Minter's death. As twitchy as he was acting, she was hesitant to be the one to deliver the bad news. Also, did she dare warn him that the police were looking for him?

"Sergeant Montgomery, I don't know how to tell you this, but Tripp is in jail."

He lurched back up to his feet, his hands curled in tight fists. "He was taken prisoner?"

"Not exactly. You see, Ronald Minter—that man you argued with in town last week—was found dead in his corn maze. The police wanted to talk to you, but Tripp wouldn't tell them where you might have moved your camp."

Kevin started to let loose with a string of curse words but quickly reined himself in. It was as if between one breath and the next he had switched gears somehow, changing from the wild-eyed scary guy back into the man he used to be all the time. "Sorry, ma'am, I shouldn't talk like that around you."

She managed a smile. "That's all right, Sergeant. That was a lot of upsetting news to get hit with all at once."

He briefly focused on her before once again resuming his watchful scan of their surroundings. "How did the pumpkin farmer die?"

How much should she tell him? She swallowed hard before answering. "Someone stabbed him in the back with a combat knife. You should know that I'm the one who found the body. I went to the farm with a friend to pick up a load of pumpkins."

Maybe he didn't need to know that, but it drew his gaze back to her again. The sympathy in his faded eyes was unmistakable. "That had to be tough for you to see."

"It was."

Kevin seemed to be mulling over everything she'd just told him. "So they want to talk to me because of the argument and because I carry a combat knife."

As he spoke, she could see the tension ramping up again in the set of his shoulders and the way he rocked forward on his toes as if preparing to run—or maybe attack. She automatically tightened her hold on Zeke's leash in case she needed to make a break for it.

Then Kevin patted his side. "You can see I still have my knife."

He moved slowly as he pulled it out of its sheath, maybe trying to not scare her into running. "I know there's no way to prove I only have the one, but that's the truth. It's the same knife I brought home from the war. Never saw the need to pick up another one."

Oddly enough, she believed that, which made her want to be honest with him, too. "Just so you know, Sergeant, I will have to tell Gage Logan and maybe the detective in charge of the murder case that I've spoken to you."

That didn't seem to upset him. "You do what you have to, Ms. Abby. Don't you worry about me. I can take care of myself. While you're at it, tell that stubborn fool Tripp not to mess up his own life because of me."

"I'll tell him, but I won't promise he'll listen."

Kevin's brief bark of laughter sounded rusty but sincere. "That sounds about right."

Then a noise coming from somewhere behind her had both Zeke and Kevin going back on full alert. She froze as she strained to see if she could pick up anything that might be a clear threat to the three of them. Her imagination must have been running hot, because the ensuing silence seemed ominous, as if there was a clear threat out there. Maybe someone creeping up close enough to listen to their conversation.

Kevin clearly thought the same thing. He still gripped his knife in his right hand, but he placed his left on the dog's head. When he spoke, it was to Zeke rather than to her. "Boy, take your lady back to the park and don't stop until you're both with other people. Go home and stay there. Better yet, stop at the police department first. Tell them you saw me."

Zeke gave the sergeant's hand a quick lick to acknowledge the order and started forward. Abby slowed him only long enough to whisper, "Be careful, Sergeant. If things aren't safe out there for you, go see Gage Logan or Pastor Haliday. Either of them will help you any way they can."

He patted her shoulder. "Thanks for worrying about me, Ms. Abby, but you need to go now. The enemy has already killed once. That will only make it easier for them to do so again."

Then he walked off the path into the surrounding trees. Abby let Zeke tow her down the path back toward the river. When she risked one look back in the sergeant's direction, he'd already faded into the shadows, disappearing from sight. Even so, she suspected he'd keep an eye on her until she reached safety.

Just in case she was right about that, she stopped when the trail rejoined the main path in the park and called out softly, "Be careful out there, Sergeant."

Then she followed his excellent advice and made a beeline back to her car.

Chapter Thirteen

"So you went looking for the sergeant even though you knew better."

Abby hated being double-teamed and didn't think it was fair that Gage and Ben Earle were ganging up on her. Evidently Zeke agreed with her assessment of the situation, because he parked himself between her and the two men, who were clearly unhappy with her right now.

She'd already explained the circumstances of her encounter with Kevin once, but she tried again. Speaking slowly so maybe their overprotective male brains would be able to follow along better this time, she repeated her story. "As I've already told you, I took Zeke for a run at the park. We stayed on the path."

She shot the detective a hard look. "We did *not* go haring off into the woods, and it was broad daylight, with any number of other people within shouting distance."

Well, a few, anyway. But that was neither here nor there. Gage and his buddy had clearly missed the point. "Sergeant Montgomery found me. While he petted Zeke, he said he's been looking for Tripp to warn him that enemy activity in the area is on the increase. I explained where Tripp is and why. The sergeant didn't appear to know about Mr. Minter's death. When I told him what happened, he showed me that he still has his knife. It's the same one he had back when he was in the army. He said he's never seen the need to own a second one. For what it's worth, I think he was telling me the truth."

Neither man commented on that. Either they believed Kevin or they didn't. All she really wanted was some credit for having done her duty by reporting what she'd seen and heard.

"I also told him that if he felt unsafe out in the woods or if he wanted to talk, he should get in touch with you, Gage, or perhaps Pastor Haliday."

Detective Earle started to protest, but she cut him off. "Yeah, yeah, I know it's your case, but the sergeant has never met you. He already knows Gage and the pastor. What's more, like him and Tripp, they've both been in the military and are members of the local veterans' support group. I don't know if you also served, so I went with the two people I knew he'd be more likely to trust. No offense intended."

"None taken."

From the way he muttered his response, though, she doubted he actually meant that. Too bad. She really didn't care.

It was time to put an end to this inquisition. "Now, if that's everything, I'd like to see Tripp before I leave."

She hated that Gage looked to his companion for permission before responding. This was Gage's police department, after all. When Detective Earle finally nodded, Gage stood up. "I'll walk you and Zeke down to the cell. When you're ready to leave, I'll have one of my deputies follow you home to make sure you get there okay."

She wasn't sure how she felt about that but decided not to argue. "Fine. I won't stay long, but I appreciate the chance to check on Tripp. Zeke will be happy to see him, too."

When the three of them were well away from Gage's office, he grinned down at her. "I hear you have your own portrait hanging in Reilly Molitor's official pumpkin portrait gallery."

"I do. It was sitting on my front porch when I got home today. I have no idea when it was delivered. Could've been anytime after I locked up last night. When I left this morning, I went out through the back, so I have no idea if it was already out there or not."

Zeke suddenly lurched forward, trying to drag her down the narrow hallway at a full run. Deputy Chapin was just getting up to unlock the door, but one look at Zeke charging toward him clearly gave him pause.

"Zeke, heel!" she ordered as she gave his leash a hard tug to slow him down. "Hi, Deputy Chapin. I promise my dog is friendly, but I'm guessing he just caught Tripp's scent."

Gage positioned himself on Zeke's other side and took firm hold of his collar. "I've got him. You can open the door."

As he did, something niggled at the edges of Abby's mind. Something about Zeke and scents. Then it hit her.

"Gage, speaking of the pumpkin portrait, I did notice one odd thing. From what I've heard, they seem to appear overnight, meaning whoever is delivering them does so sometime after sundown and before sunrise. If that's what happened, I was most likely home when the pumpkin was delivered."

"And?" he prompted.

"So why didn't Zeke pitch a fit? Granted, although he likes most people, you'd think he still would've raised a ruckus if someone was sneaking around the front porch during the night. Heck, he even wakes me up if it's just Tripp wandering around out in the backyard. But when he sniffed the jack-o'-lantern, he got all happy like he'd recognized a friend's scent on it."

Gage gave Zeke a considering look. "I've heard some folks have started a betting pool over who is behind the portraits. You and I could really clean up if only Zeke could talk."

Deputy Chapin swung the door open. At least Zeke had the good manners to stop and sniff his hand. After giving the man a sloppy lick, he gave Abby an expectant look as if to say, "Well, are we going to find Tripp or not?"

Chapin remained standing. "Sir, do you want me to escort her?"

"No, I'll do it. I plan to let Zeke in to see the prisoner. I'm not sure how Detective Earle would feel about that, and I don't want to put you in his crosshairs."

By the time they reached the last turn before the cells, Zeke's tail was a blur. Finally, Abby let go of his leash and let the dog charge off down the hall to find Tripp. By the time she and Gage caught up, Tripp was already reaching through the bars to hug Zeke, who was trying to bathe Tripp's face with doggy spit and love.

"Hey, boy, it's good to see you."

Gage pulled out his keys. "If you'll back up a bit, I'll open the door."

Five seconds later, Zeke and Tripp were wrestling on the floor of the cell. There were a lot of mock growls and muttered threats. Abby wasn't sure which one came out the victor, but neither of the two combatants seemed to care. Both were grinning and breathing hard by the time they stopped.

Tripp remained right where he was. Zeke flopped down by his side and laid his head on his best friend's leg. It probably spoke poorly of her as a person, but Abby was jealous of her own pet. Surely Tripp should be as happy to see her as he was the dog. He must have sensed some of her disappointment, because his smile dimmed a little when he met her gaze. "I should remind you that I told you not to come here, but I won't. It's really good to see you, Abby. Is everything going okay?"

"Pretty much. I met with the veterans group, and they've given me the initial approval for the fundraiser idea I suggested. There's no need for you to worry about any of that for now. I'll fill you in once you're out of here and get caught up on other stuff."

She had no idea if Gage had heard anything about the plan. If so, he didn't say anything, which was a relief. Tripp wasn't going to be happy that she'd exacted a little revenge by volunteering him to be auctioned off.

Before he could ask any questions, she changed the subject. "By the way, I saw Sergeant Montgomery earlier today. He said for you not to cause yourself problems just to protect him. I said I'd relay the message, but we both agreed it probably wouldn't do any good."

Tripp broke off eye contact and turned his attention back to Zeke. "How was he?"

"Kevin said he'd been looking for you. Evidently whoever he considers to be the enemy has been more active in the area, and he wanted to warn you."

"He's been talking about the enemy for a while now, but I've never seen anyone out there at night except for Kevin himself."

"So there's no way to know if someone is out there or if he's only imagining it."

"That about sums it up. It's part of the national forest, so I guess there could be hikers and backpackers moving through. Kevin's first instinct would be to hide if he spotted anyone."

She wasn't sure about that. For sure he hadn't hidden the night she followed Tripp into the area. Maybe he'd thought she was a direct threat to the two of them. This wasn't the time to point that out. Instead, she glanced at Gage before continuing. "He acted as if he hadn't heard about Ronald Minter's death. He also showed me his combat knife to prove he still had it with him."

They both knew that wasn't exactly proof positive that Kevin was innocent, even if the murder weapon was in an evidence lockup somewhere. Tripp gave Zeke another pat before pushing his head off his lap so he could stand up. "I'm guessing Gage has already given you another 'stay away from the sergeant' lecture, so I'll keep this short. Kevin is my friend, and while I want to believe he would never hurt you, I worry about how he'll react if he has somehow locked onto someone specific as his enemy."

"I know. For what it's worth, he did seem a bit jumpy when he first approached me, but petting Zeke seemed to calm him. After a bit, he became more focused, more *there* with me, if that makes sense. Then he and Zeke heard something coming from the woods behind us, and he got worried again. He ordered Zeke to escort me back to the park, where there were more people. We left right after that."

She hated that Tripp was so worried about his friend when there wasn't anything he could do to help him. "Would you like me to bundle up some food and take it out to the woods for Kevin?"

Gage snapped, "No way."

Tripp glared at her. "Absolutely not."

Well, at least the two men were united in their opinion. She didn't bother to argue. It wasn't as if she would know where to take the stuff anyway. Maybe it was time to lighten the conversation. She pulled out her phone and held it up for Tripp to see. "By the way, Gage isn't the only one who has his very own pumpkin portrait."

Tripp took the phone from her and angled it to catch the light a little better. "Looks just like you, especially around the eyes and mouth. I think you went a little heavy on the orange makeup, though."

"Really? I've always thought it was one of my best colors."

Then she gave Gage a considering look before showing Tripp the picture she'd snapped earlier of Gage's portrait when he was busy talking to Detective Earle. "He, on the other hand, can't carry it off at all."

Tripp cracked up as he studied the second picture. "Wow, Gage, you get all the cool toys. I especially like the squirt guns and the cars. Do the lights and sirens on them work?"

Looking much put-upon, Gage glowered at both

of them. "It obviously doesn't pay to be nice to the prisoners."

Abby studied the photo for a few seconds. "You know, the other officers might not even notice the difference if you stationed the official chief of police pumpkin in your office. Then you could take off for the day and have fun. Maybe slip out for one of those cheeseburgers at Mike's Drive-In that you're so fond of. Sydney couldn't fuss, since you'd have witnesses that you were here at the station the whole time."

For a second, he looked as if he was actually considering the possibilities, but then he shook his head. "It wouldn't work. I suspect Syd has a tracking app on my phone or maybe even my cruiser that goes off whenever I get near Mike's. Regardless, one way or another, she'd find out."

Tripp looked incredulous. "You're seriously worried about what your kid would have to say about you eating a burger? Who's the parent in this equation?"

"I am."

Before Tripp could give him any more grief, Gage repeated, "I am. But after my wife died, Sydney became a bit obsessed about the one parent she had left. If my eating more healthy stuff than I used to makes her feel better, I'm not going to argue."

Okay, then. Although he'd told her the same thing the other day, now she and Tripp both felt bad about giving him grief. Gage picked up on it and shook his head. "Don't get me wrong, I still sneak off to Mike's every so often. I just do my best not to drive Syd crazy."

Tripp gave him an appraising look and then smiled. "You're a good dad."

Abby agreed with that assessment. Her own father had tried to stay involved in her life, but he'd remarried shortly after divorcing her mother and moved out of state with his new wife. If that experience had taught her anything, it was that parenting long-distance was hard.

"We'd better get going. I wouldn't want to push my luck by staying too long." She mustered up a smile for her tenant. "I'll try to get by again in a day or so—that is, if I can't convince you to tell Detective Earle the best places to look for Kevin."

The implacable look on Tripp's face was all the answer she needed.

"That's what I thought. At the very least, I'll drop off some baked goods here at the station as my schedule allows."

But it was so darned hard to take that first step back down the hallway. Once again Gage made up an excuse to give her and Tripp a moment alone. "Look, I'm going to go talk to my deputy for a minute. Catch up with me whenever you're ready to leave, Abby."

The two of them—well, three, counting Zeke—stood in silence until Gage turned the corner and disappeared from sight. Then Tripp edged a little closer to her while remaining inside his cell. "I'm sorry this is so hard for you, Abby. I really don't mean to complicate your life. If you want me to look for somewhere else to live after I get out, say the word."

That was the last thing she wanted. "Don't be ridiculous. Zeke would never forgive me if I made his best friend leave. Besides, Jean might start targeting me with her casseroles if you aren't around."

He looked slightly happier. "Nice to know I serve some useful purpose."

"Yeah, well, you also did a bang-up job with cleaning up the leaves."

He glanced up toward the far corner of the ceiling and then back at her. When she followed his line of sight, she realized he was trying to tell her without words that they were under constant supervision, which meant no hugs.

She nodded and held out her hand. "It was good seeing you again, and I know Zeke was happy to learn you haven't disappeared completely."

He gave her hand a gentle squeeze before turning his attention to the dog. He rubbed Zeke's wrinkled forehead and then scratched behind his ears. "Take care of Abby for me, big guy."

The dog whined softly and then jumped up to put his front paws on Tripp's chest. The impact forced Tripp back a step, but then he held his ground. Gripping Zeke's big head in his hands, he rested his forehead against the dog's for several seconds. Both man and dog seemed to take a lot of comfort from the direct contact.

Finally, Tripp gently shoved Zeke back down onto all fours. "You two better get going. Thanks again for coming."

When she picked up Zeke's leash and tried to lead him away, he sat down and refused to budge. Even throwing her full weight into the process didn't help. It would've been funny, but if she didn't get out of there soon, she might give in to the urge to cry. She hated seeing Tripp in that stupid orange suit, and him staying in that cell wasn't helping anyone, not even Kevin.

Finally, Tripp snapped, "Zeke, get a move on. Now."

Still the dog resisted for a few seconds longer before finally standing up. After giving Tripp a look that accused his friend of betrayal, he slunk out of the cell and docilely followed Abby down the hall, pausing at the corner to look back one last time. Tripp waved and then pulled his cell door closed.

The sound that echoed down the hall was one of the saddest things Abby had ever heard.

She followed Gage out and dutifully made sure the deputy he sent to escort her home had no problem sticking close by until they reached her driveway. She hated that he felt obligated to park and follow her inside long enough to make sure all was well.

She and Zeke watched from the front window as he drove away. When he was gone, she glanced down at her companion.

"What do you say we bake some cookies for Tripp? And meanwhile, I'll do some serious thinking about who killed Mr. Minter. Because until someone is in custody, your buddy won't be coming home."

Zeke's tail did a slow sweep across the floor to show he approved of her plan.

Chapter Fourteen

When a person had important questions, it was always best to go straight to the most informed source for answers. In Snowberry Creek, that meant her closest friends from the quilting guild. They didn't have a board meeting scheduled, but the three of them could be bribed into showing up at her house if Abby promised them tea and dessert. As usual, Glenda acted as the self-appointed chauffeur for the group, picking up Jean and Louise on her way to Abby's house.

Abby met them at the front door. "Welcome, ladies. I appreciate your coming on short notice."

Glenda gave her a long look. "Well, you did say it was important."

"Yes, I did, and I promise it is."

The three of them filed past her and headed straight for the dining room table, where she'd already set out beverages and a plate piled high with lemon bars and the cream cheese spritz cookies that Jean was particularly fond of. Abby waited until everyone was settled with a cup of tea and cookies in hand before explaining why she'd called them together. "You're no doubt wondering why you're here."

Louise spoke first. "We're assuming it has something to do with why Tripp is sitting in jail."

Abby hadn't been sure any of them knew where he was. Regardless of what they thought about that, it would make it easier to explain why she was so interested in any information they could share about Ronald Minter or anything else that might prove useful.

But where to start? Maybe at the beginning.

"As you know, Glenda and I made a trip out to Mr. Minter's farm to pick up some pumpkins. When I went looking for him, I found his body in the middle of the corn maze."

They all clucked in sympathy, and Jean reached out to pat her hand. "We know how horrible that must have been for you, Abby, especially coming so soon after finding dear Dolly's body in your backyard."

Yeah, it had been tough, but she had to get past that awful moment if she was going to help Tripp and his friend. "The detective from the county sheriff's office is in charge of the case. Right now, he seems to think his most viable suspect is Sergeant Kevin Montgomery. He's that homeless veteran we see around town sometimes."

It was Louise who spoke next. "I've actually met him. Sort of, anyway. I was loading groceries into my trunk in the pouring rain when I dropped one of my canvas bags. Oranges and apples went rolling everywhere right as Sergeant Montgomery happened to be walking by. He immediately took the bag from me and started gathering up all of my things for me. He said there was no reason for both of us to get wet and that I should wait in the car. After he picked up everything, he put the bag in the trunk with the others, shut the lid, and then walked away. He wouldn't even let me buy him a cup of coffee or anything, even though I offered."

Abby smiled at her friend. "That was really nice of him."

However, Glenda was frowning big-time. "Why are the police thinking he killed Mr. Minter?"

Picking up where she'd left off before Louise had interrupted her, Abby said, "All I know is that the weapon is apparently similar to the knife the sergeant carries all the time. I know he still has a knife with him. He says it's the only one he's ever owned, and I find myself predisposed to believe him."

Honesty had her adding, "But he's a friend of Tripp's, so I can't say that I'm actually neutral on the subject. In fact, their friendship is the reason Tripp's in jail. The detective got an anonymous tip that Tripp knows where the sergeant is living out in the forest somewhere. He arrested him for obstructing justice."

By that point, all three women were looking pretty fierce. Tripp was one of their favorite people. Jean set her cup down hard. "They're punishing Tripp for no good reason. I think we should go down to the police station and give them a piece of our minds."

While Abby appreciated the passion, she already knew that getting in Detective Earle's face about the situation wasn't going to help. "As much as I hate it, the police are only doing their job. At least Gage arranged for Tripp to stay here in town instead of going to the county jail."

Jean didn't look all that convinced, but at least she

picked up her tea and took another sip. "Then what can we do to help?"

"The other reason they're interested in Kevin is that he and Ronald Minter got into a very public argument only days before Mr. Minter was killed. The police were called in to referee, but the sergeant had already left the scene. Since the two men hadn't actually come to blows, the deputy wrote up a report but didn't arrest anyone. I happened to be across the street on my way to Bridey's shop when it happened, so I know Mr. Minter was very unhappy that the deputy refused to hunt the sergeant down and arrest him. He accused Sergeant Montgomery of all kinds of things."

Glenda shook her head. "I knew Ronald, of course, and I've never known another person with a bigger chip on his shoulder. He didn't always have an easy time of it, but a lot of his problems were his own fault. I'm willing to bet that poor sergeant wasn't the only one to tangle with him lately."

Okay, now they were getting somewhere.

Abby gave each of her three friends a solemn look. "I don't normally want to indulge in gossip, but I'd really like to hear more about what you know."

Jean jumped right in, maybe because she'd never had a chance to finish what she'd wanted to tell them when Detective Earle had interrupted their meeting the other day. "Well, a certain bank manager and Ronald definitely engaged in a heated discussion about a week ago. In this particular case, however, it wasn't Ronald who started it. I was at the bank to make a deposit, and the line was quite long. Ronald was just finishing up his own business at the teller's window when Jasper Collins stepped out of his office.

When he spotted Ronald, he all but dragged the poor man into his office and slammed the door. No one could hear what they were saying, but it clearly wasn't a pleasant discussion."

She paused to sip her tea again, although Abby suspected it was more for dramatic effect than because she was thirsty. "Now, it might have been something about Ronald's account at the bank, but I don't think so."

By this point, Abby wasn't the only one getting frustrated with Jean. Louise made an impatient noise. "Jean, please get on with it. What do you know for certain and what do you just suspect?"

Looking much put-upon, Jean dabbed her lips with her napkin. "Fine. As I clearly said, no one could hear exactly what they were arguing about. However, as the discussion became more intense, we could pick out a few words. It clearly had something to do with pumpkins."

Well, that was disappointing. Abby had been hoping for so much more. Before she could say anything, Jean spoke again. "Now, it could've also had something to do with the mortgage the bank holds on the farm, but I got the impression it was about the actual pumpkins. Ronald kept shaking his head, but Jasper clearly didn't believe whatever he was saying."

Now, that was interesting. "How did it end?"

"That nice Miss Sheffield who works as Jasper's executive assistant stepped into the office and hushed them both. I thought that was quite brave of her, considering how angry both men were by that point."

"And did they listen to her?"

"Evidently, because Ronald stormed out of the office a short time later and walked straight out of the bank. By then, I'd been called up to the teller's window, so I didn't see what happened after that. As I left, I did note that Jasper was talking to someone on his phone, and Miss Sheffield had returned to her desk."

Jean frowned. "Looking back, I'd have to say that she looked a bit upset. You know, with flushed cheeks and her eyes a bit red. She's such a pleasant young woman, and I cannot imagine that working for Jasper is easy if he can't control his temper any better than that."

Glenda reached for the teapot and poured herself another cup of Earl Grey. "I've heard talk that he's considering running for office at some point. You'd think he'd know better than to make a public spectacle of himself."

"Really? I hadn't heard that." And Jean didn't look happy about it. Clearly she didn't appreciate not being in the know. "Well, surely he wouldn't try to run against Mayor McKay. Everyone knows what an amazing job she has done bringing new business to Snowberry Creek since she took over the office."

Glenda clearly recognized the note of jealousy in her friend's voice and looked a bit smug about it. "I think it's far more likely that he'll aim his sights higher than that. What I heard was that he was thinking about a position on the county council, or perhaps even running for the state legislature."

That was interesting. Maybe the argument between the two men meant nothing at all. Regardless, it wouldn't hurt to mention it to Gage the next time she saw him. Unless something unexpected happened, she would likely run into him at the Saturday morning work party when everyone was decorating Main Street for the Halloween Festival.

Louise picked up the conversation. "Speaking of pumpkins, did anyone see the newest pictures that Reilly Molitor has posted?"

Glenda gave Abby a knowing look. "You mean besides our very own Abby's? It really is an amazing likeness." The ladies had stopped on the way into the house to admire her portrait.

"I thought so, too. My parents both got a kick out of it."

Although it still felt a bit odd to have been singled out for such an honor. The experience had given her new sympathy for how Gage must feel with all of his staff having such fun at his expense.

Louise pulled her cell phone out of her purse and started typing on it. "I'm not sure who these two pumpkins are supposed to represent, but I think the expressions on their faces are most unpleasant, especially the man's."

Then she passed her cell phone around the table for all of them to see. "The pumpkins were found sitting on a trail out in the national forest, so the location offers no help in identifying who they're supposed to be."

Jean studied the picture for several seconds but then shook her head and passed it on to Glenda. From the way she was frowning, she apparently didn't recognize them, either. When the phone finally reached her, Abby could see why. They looked like the work of the same artist as all the others, but the expressions looked more . . . what? Exaggerated, somehow. Not quite like more traditional jack-o'-lanterns, but not as refined as the other portraits had been.

Still, they looked a little familiar. Something about the smiles, which definitely had a hard edge to them. Maybe it would come to her later. For now, she'd bring the topic of conversation back to Ronald Minter and his problems.

"So, does anyone else who might have had issues with Mr. Minter come to mind?"

When no one had any suggestions, she asked the only other question she had. "Do you know who might have inherited his farm?"

Jean brightened up. "I heard he had a cousin who is likely to inherit, even though Ronald didn't leave a will. It's even more complicated than that, although I don't know why exactly. Who knows, maybe he owed back taxes or something. I could ask around if you need me to."

Probably not a good idea, especially if it somehow got back to Gage or Detective Earle that she had people asking questions.

"That's all right, Jean. I can always ask Gage the next time I see him."

The older woman looked disappointed, but she didn't argue. Rather than continue the discussion, which hadn't netted her any really useful information, she turned the subject to the upcoming festival.

"So, are you ladies wearing costumes on Halloween? Gage said everyone does, but I haven't come up with a single good idea."

They didn't have any good suggestions on that front, either, but that was all right. She still wasn't sure how she felt about dressing up for Halloween. If all else failed, she'd pick up a simple mask at the local party store and call it good.

Half an hour later she ushered her friends toward

the front door. On the way out, Jean paused to ask,
"Do you think they'd let me bring Tripp one of my
casseroles? I'm worried about the quality of the jailhouse food."

Jean's culinary efforts might be questionable, but
there was never any doubt that her heart was in the
right place. For Tripp's sake, though, Abby hastened
to reassure Jean that he wasn't on a bread-and-water
regimen.

"I was allowed to take him some cookies, but Gage
said that was the limit of what I could bring. They
don't routinely allow prisoners outside food." Not that
she knew that for sure. "But I assure you that Tripp
looked to be in good health when I was there. He'll
be pleased to know that you were thinking about
him, though."

Jean didn't look totally convinced as she headed
toward Glenda's car, which probably meant that Tripp
would be facing an onslaught of casseroles the minute
he got out of jail. Laughing about how he would react
to that, she waved at her friends one last time and
went back inside to plan her next move.

Saturday morning dawned predictably gray and
rainy. Abby studied the sky and considered what to
wear, since she would be spending the majority of the
day outside. Fall weather could be rather unpre-
dictable in the Pacific Northwest, which meant wearing multiple layers was definitely the best way to go.
She settled on her favorite jeans, a cotton turtleneck
under a light sweater, comfortable shoes, and a jacket.
To keep things simple, she pulled her hair back into
a ponytail and put on a baseball cap. A rain poncho

and an umbrella went into her pack, along with a couple of bottles of water and a few granola bars.

"Zeke, I'll be back later. Guard the fort."

He lifted his head long enough to acknowledge her orders. He was back to snoring before she made it out the door. At least the sun came out right as she headed for the park, where the work party was supposed to congregate. No doubt Connie was already waiting there to let everyone know what their assigned duties would be for the day. While Abby didn't mind helping out, she hoped she would get to do something more fun than handing out desserts in the lunch line.

She took the fact that she found a parking spot close to the park as a good omen. After grabbing her pack out of the car, Abby hurried across the crowded parking lot to where a line had formed in front of the picnic table where Connie was already hard at work.

As she waited for her turn, she smiled and waved at a surprising number of familiar faces. It hadn't been all that long since she'd moved to Snowberry Creek after inheriting the house from Aunt Sybil, but the town was already starting to feel like home to her. She and her ex-husband had lived in the same condo for years in a suburb of Seattle, but she'd never had more than a nodding acquaintance with any of their neighbors. Maybe it was the difference between living in a busy suburban area and a small town, but she'd changed, too.

"Hey, Abby! Looks like we're on the same team today."

She turned to smile at Zoe, the nurse practitioner she'd met at the veterans meeting the other day. "Hi, Zoe, that's great. Tell me we're doing something fun, or at least nothing that involves ladders."

Because she'd seen more than a few leaning against the buildings down the length of Main Street.

The tall man standing beside Zoe shook his head. "No, you two lucked out and will be working on the planters. I, on the other hand, will be climbing ladders all day."

Zoe performed the introductions. "Abby McCree, this is my husband, Leif Brevik. Evidently he's not fond of hanging holiday lights."

"It's nice to meet you, Leif." She wrinkled her nose. "I'd offer to trade spots with you so the two of you could work together, but I don't do ladders."

He laughed. "That's all right. You two go have fun playing in the dirt. Besides, if I hurry, I might get to be the one to pass the lights up to one of my teammates."

Another man joined the discussion. He pointed down the street to where a third guy was already pulling a string of lights out of a box. "Fat chance, Leif. Sarge has already called dibs."

"Sneaky jerk. I knew I should've gotten here earlier."

He was still complaining as they headed down the street to join their friend.

"I take it they served together."

Zoe stared after her husband and his friend. "Yeah, they did. The three of them had a tough time when they came home, but they're doing great now. Spencer and his wife run a local business that makes custom cabinets and other types of millwork. Nick and Leif are partners in a construction company."

"So he was kidding about the ladder thing?"

"A little. Mainly, none of the three would be happy unless they had something to complain about."

By this point, Abby was at the front of the line. Connie looked up with a smile. "Abby, glad you could make it. You and Zoe here will be planting mums today. The nursery really came through for us this year with lots of new colors. They should look really pretty when it's all done. Your team is gathering down behind city hall."

She turned her attention to the next person in line before Abby could respond, but that was all right. The woman had a busy day ahead of her, too.

When she and Zoe started back across the parking lot, she spotted Kristy and Dean Hake headed in their direction. She was about to wave and call out to them, but she dropped her hand back down to her side when she got a clear look at Dean's face. He was smiling, but it looked a bit forced, like maybe he was upset about something but trying to hide it. That wasn't what left her staring after them as they walked past without saying a word, though.

She was almost certain she'd seen that exact same smile before—on the pumpkin portrait that none of the quilting group ladies had been able to identify. When she looked back one last time, his expression had changed yet again as he laughed while talking to Fred Cady from the Committee on Senior Affairs. Shaking her head, she hurried after Zoe. Clearly she was imagining things.

Chapter Fifteen

Abby and Zoe joined the group gathered behind the city hall building. She wasn't surprised to see a few familiar faces in the crowd, but it was one man in particular who drew her attention, once she realized who he was. She quickly decided Jasper Collins wasn't the type who liked getting his hands dirty. For one thing, his work boots and gloves looked brand-new, as did the neatly pressed navy blue and gray flannel shirt he had on. It definitely lacked the soft look that cotton took on after being laundered several times. Admittedly, the shirt looked good with his coloring, highlighting the touch of gray at his temples and his bright blue eyes.

A more suspicious person might think the outfit was chosen for how well it would photograph. Sure enough, Jasper quickly picked up a flat of the mums just as Reilly Molitor turned the camera in his direction. Maybe Glenda and Bridey were right about the man having political aspirations. He definitely fit the image, especially with that practiced smile meant to inspire trust.

Zoe nudged her. "You're staring. What's Jasper doing that has you so riveted?"

"Nothing at all. I didn't mean to stare. I was just lost in thought."

She deliberately turned her back on the banker and headed over to help load bags of potting soil in one of the wheelbarrows. She really needed to be more careful. What was worse, Zoe wasn't the only one who had noticed. A woman who looked vaguely familiar had been studying Abby with interest. It finally hit her that she must be his executive assistant from the bank, Lily . . . no, Layla Sheffield.

Abby offered her a quick smile before reaching for another bag, but Layla had already turned her attention back to her boss. What had her looking so stone-faced like that? Another peek in his direction answered the question. He'd set the mums back down and had his arm around another woman. Interesting. Judging by their easy familiarity and the fact that she was close to his age, Abby figured she was looking at Mrs. Jasper Collins. The woman looked just as polished as her husband. Her outfit looked casual but expensive, and those golden highlights in her caramel-brown hair were a bit too perfect to be natural. While she wasn't exactly pretty, she made the most of what she had and pulled off "striking" really well.

Abby reached up to straighten her ponytail, almost wishing she'd taken a little more care with her own appearance.

Yes, it was all too easy to imagine the couple waving from behind a podium as he announced his candidacy or made his acceptance speech after winning an election. At least on the surface, they had the kind of charisma that might appeal to voters. Well, maybe not all voters. She glanced back at Layla, who clearly had issues with the couple. She abruptly turned her back on her boss and walked away.

On the way, she grabbed a pair of gardening gloves from the supply table. She disappeared around the corner just as Zoe rejoined Abby. She was dragging a large child's wagon behind her that was loaded down with mums and gardening tools. "We've been assigned this side of the street. We're supposed to start down by the park and work our way back. Someone will replenish our supplies as we go along."

"Sounds good."

She lifted the handles of her wheelbarrow, and they were off and running. To her surprise, Layla was waiting for them at the edge of the park. She must have walked off some of her bad mood, because she greeted them both with an easy smile.

Holding out her hand, she introduced herself. "Hi. I've seen you both around town, but we've never actually met. I'm Layla Sheffield. I work at the bank."

Abby shook her hand. "Abby McCree, and this is Zoe Brevik."

As soon as Abby said her name, Layla gave her an odd look. "Abby McCree, as in the pumpkin portrait on the *Clarion*'s web page?"

She sighed as she settled another mum into the planter, along with a handful of small plastic pumpkins, ghosts, and skeletons on sticks. "Yes, the very same. I still have no idea why our mystery artist singled me out."

Layla's expression was surprisingly sympathetic. "It would be nice if they could figure out who was carving them. Maybe the intent behind the pumpkins is good, but they can definitely cause unexpected problems for people."

As she spoke, her eyes narrowed as she focused on something in the distance. Had she been referring to the pair of pumpkins that looked so different than the others? Before Abby could ask, someone else joined their group. Zoe had been unpotting the next mum for Abby to plant while Layla pulled the last of the dying summer flowers out of the next planter when Jasper Collins walked up carrying a basket of drinks and snacks.

"Hi, Layla. I can see you and these lovely ladies have been hard at work."

He offered each of them a practiced smile in turn as he passed out the goodies he'd brought. "You might not know it, but Layla and I are business associates at the bank. I don't know what I'd do without her extraordinary organizational skills keeping everything running smoothly."

From the way Layla's face flushed, Abby was beginning to suspect that they were far more than mere associates. That would account for why she'd been unhappy about seeing Jasper with his wife earlier.

That didn't keep the woman from speaking up, though. "Mr. Collins's wife donated all of the flowers we'll be planting this afternoon."

Not that Layla seemed all that impressed by the woman's generosity. Zoe, at least, had the presence of mind to show good manners. "That was nice of her. I'll have to thank her personally. I love how so many people here find a way to all pitch in to make the town look so nice."

When she looked past him, as if searching for the woman in question, the banker shook his head. "I'm sorry, but Bethany couldn't stay to help. Her book club meets today, and it was her turn to host the gathering."

After one more bright smile, he lifted his basket. "I'd better get back to work. Let me know if I can do anything to help."

He seemed to aim that last comment to Layla in particular, but maybe Abby was only imagining it. All three of them watched him make his way to their counterparts on the other side of the road.

"Book club, my foot. More likely Bethany wouldn't risk breaking a nail digging in the dirt. She wrote the check for the flowers because it got her name in the paper again. No matter what they cost, it would be chump change to her." Layla's eyes flared wide. "Sorry, I didn't mean to say that out loud."

Abby cupped her ear with her hand. "Said what? I didn't hear anything."

Zoey grinned. "Me, neither."

Rather than discuss the matter anymore, they got busy planting flowers. They were about halfway done with their assigned planters when the signal went up that lunch was being served. Layla said she'd rejoin them afterward and headed off down the street toward the bank. That seemed odd, since it wasn't normally open on weekends. Of course, as the executive assistant to the bank manager, chances were Layla had her own set of keys.

"You're thinking she's meeting up with Jasper."

Darn it, Abby really needed to work on hiding her thoughts better. "She sure seemed pretty upset earlier this morning when Jasper was with his wife, not to mention the resentment in her voice when she mentioned Bethany buying the flowers. There was also nothing subtle about her heading straight for the bank, so it seems likely."

They both stared at the building as they walked by. Zoe sighed and shook her head. "Yeah, it does. If so, that's really too bad. Layla seems really nice, and getting involved with a married man doesn't often end well for anyone."

They were quickly approaching the line of people waiting to be served lunch, so Abby lowered her voice. "I've heard he might be planning to run for county or state office. A messy divorce won't help him achieve that."

Zoe looked at her in surprise. "I hadn't heard that, but it would make sense. His father and grandfather were both involved in state politics back in the day."

Then her voice dropped to a low whisper.

"Now that I think about it, Leif said he and Nick heard that a set of pumpkin portraits were found outside someone's door awhile back. You know, like yours was left on your porch. The trouble was the guy didn't live there, mainly because he was married to someone else. Given what Layla said about the portraits causing some people trouble, I have to wonder if she was speaking from firsthand knowledge."

If so, Abby hated it for her. Granted, thanks to her own ex-husband's extramarital affair and the devastating effect it had had on her life, she didn't always have a lot of sympathy for the "other woman" when a man decided to cheat on his wife. But maybe Layla really did love the man. If so, watching him with his wife had to hurt.

They were both adults, of course, but that didn't mean the power structure in the relationship was equal by any means. If Jasper really did have aspirations of getting involved in state politics, his wife's checkbook would likely trump Layla's organizational skills.

There were too many people around to continue the discussion, so she and Zoe followed along in the food line in silence. As they picked up trays and flatware, Abby's mind kept whirling with the possible implications of what she'd learned. Was the argument Jean had witnessed between the two men at the bank that day about those pumpkin portraits? Maybe Jasper had made the assumption that Mr. Minter was the secret artist carving all those amazing jack-o'-lanterns.

If so, she knew for a fact that he was wrong about that. Hers had appeared days after the murder.

But what if Jasper had accused Ronald and didn't believe it when he had denied it? Had he confronted the pumpkin farmer one more time with the intention of ending the threat permanently? It would've taken some forethought to make the attack look like Sergeant Montgomery was responsible, but a man didn't become a bank manager at such a young age without being intelligent.

Zoe nudged her with her elbow to get her attention. "I see Leif, and it looks like he saved a seat for me. There's room at the table if you'd like to join us."

"I'd love to."

She shook off all gloomy thoughts about dead men and pumpkins as she followed her friend through the crowd. There'd be plenty of time later to ponder everything she'd learned and how much of it, if any, she should pass along to Detective Earle.

The afternoon passed in a busy blur. She and Zoe finished the rest of their planters by themselves, because Layla failed to reappear after lunch. Maybe that was for the best. She suspected that the woman had been a bit embarrassed by what she'd blurted out about her boss's wife, and maybe even more worried that they might spread gossip about her and her possible relationship with Jasper outside of office hours.

Which left Abby in a quandary. If she told Detective Earle or even Gage about her suspicions, they would be bound to confront the pair. If she was wrong, she would cause two innocent people undue embarrassment. Even if she'd come to the right conclusion about their relationship, she had very little in the way of solid proof to substantiate her theories.

Besides, it was doubtful that many people would look at Jasper Collins and think "murderer." He was a pillar of society and an important man in the local business community.

For now, she'd table the problem until she could come up with some hard evidence that either exonerated the banker and his assistant or proved beyond a reasonable doubt that they were involved with the murder.

She pulled into her driveway, glad to be home. As tired as she was, she'd given in to the temptation to pick up dinner at Frannie's so she wouldn't have to cook. Sometimes fixing meals for one was more than she could face. Baking was relaxing; cooking for herself not so much.

She also hated coming home to an empty house. Well, not exactly empty. Zeke was waiting for her in the kitchen. After giving her a proper greeting that involved sloppy dog kisses, he did a quick patrol of the backyard, stopping at Tripp's door long enough to verify that his friend still hadn't come home.

Seeing his disappointment made her angry on his behalf. Yeah, Tripp was protecting his friend Kevin. She got that, but at the same time, his continued absence was hurting Zeke. The big dog had been abused and then abandoned by his unknown previous owner. It had taken a lot of patience by his first foster family and then Aunt Sybil to teach him to trust people again. She could only hope Tripp's prolonged absence didn't cause a setback.

She slipped him an extra snack when he finally came back inside. His tail wag was definitely a half-hearted effort at best. He settled on the floor at her feet while she ate her dinner. As usual, Frannie's pot roast with all the fixings was perfectly cooked, but Abby was barely aware of how it tasted as she ate. Maybe it was because she was tired, but she suspected her lack of interest had more to do with her dark mood. If she had to put a name to it, she was . . . lonely.

"This is ridiculous," she said to the empty room. "I spent the whole day surrounded by people."

The trouble was that most of them hadn't gone home alone. Well, maybe Layla, but she didn't know that for sure.

A knock at the front door interrupted her little pity party. "Now, who could that be?"

Zeke immediately lumbered to his feet to find out the answer to her question. She followed him down the hall slowly and then flipped on the porch light before peeking out the window to see who it was. A tall man stood near the edge of the porch with his back toward her. Why would he do that? She was reticent to open the door to see what a stranger might want.

When her uninvited guest suddenly turned back

around, she was even more reluctant to answer his summons. What possible reason could Jasper Collins have for showing up both uninvited and unwanted? Unfortunately, since she'd already turned on the light, he knew she was home and most likely still standing close to the door.

Just as she had with Reilly Molitor the other day, she made sure that Zeke was right at her side. Granted, her furry companion rarely took an instant dislike to anyone, but Jasper had no way of knowing that.

It was hard not to laugh at how quickly Jasper backed away as soon as Zeke poked his big head out the door. Abby kept her hand on the dog's collar—not that she had the strength to hold him back if he decided to act up.

Dredging up the good manners her aunt had instilled in her from a young age, she aimed for sounding pleasant rather than irritated that the banker had shown up without calling first. "Hello, Mr. Collins. How can I help you?"

That he looked over his shoulder before answering, as if making sure that no one was watching, creeped her out a little. Finally, he offered her one of his practiced smiles. "I apologize for dropping by unexpectedly, Ms. McCree, but I happened to be in the neighborhood."

Yeah, right. He shifted his weight from one foot to the other before continuing. "I was talking to my assistant, Layla Sheffield, earlier today. She was worried that you might have gotten the wrong impression about our relationship."

Translation: *Abby hadn't been wrong at all.*

Pretending ignorance, she said, "I'm not sure what impression that would be."

Translation: *She was going to make him spell it out for her.*

He sighed. "I just want to make sure for Ms. Sheffield's sake that you understand that she and I are professional colleagues. Nothing more. Unwarranted gossip could harm her reputation, not to mention her career."

Translation: *He would throw the woman under the bus to protect his own backside, not to mention his political aspirations.*

Philandering husbands were never going to be at the top of Abby's list of favorite people, but she reined in the urge to tell him that. Instead, she decided to use the opportunity to press for more information about his argument with Ronald Minter.

"Please reassure Layla that I enjoyed meeting her this morning. She spoke highly of you and your wife, and it was clear that she enjoys working with you at the bank. However, there was nothing about what she said that would have given anyone the impression that you two were anything more than coworkers."

His relief was both obvious and irritating. What had he expected her to say? That she'd already broadcasted the gossip throughout the town? She might not approve of their relationship, but they were both adults.

"I see you got one of the pumpkin portraits, too."

He immediately winced as if he hadn't meant to let that last word slip out. Clearly he'd been immortalized by the same artist and wasn't happy about it. She let that pass for the moment. "Yes, it was left on the front porch the other day. My parents both thought it was a hoot. I know the folks at the police department are having fun with the Gage Logan pumpkin. The last time I saw it, it was wearing one of his uniform shirts, a hat, and a badge. They've also surrounded it with squirt guns, toy cop cars, and its own flashing red light."

"I should stop by there to see it. I'm surprised Reilly hasn't updated the picture of Gage's pumpkin on the paper's website."

She stooped to give Zeke's head a good scratching. "I bet Reilly is dying to learn who is carving the pumpkins. It would be quite a scoop for him if he were to figure that out. I think that's why he's spending so much time prowling through town looking for the latest additions to the collection."

A flash of anger cross Jasper's handsome face. "I can see why everyone is finding all of this so amusing, but it can cause problems if the pumpkins are left in the wrong place. It could give people a mistaken impression."

Straightening up, she gave him a sympathetic look. "Did that happen to someone you know?"

"Yes, it did."

Abby feigned a sympathy she didn't really feel. "I'm sorry to hear that. Somehow I don't think the artist, whoever he or she might be, intended to cause problems."

Jasper didn't look convinced. "I'm going to trust you not to repeat this, but it didn't happen to a friend. It actually happened to me. The jerk left a portrait of me and one of Layla on her front porch. All I can think is that he saw me drop some papers off at her house one morning and decided that's where I live. It took some pretty fast talking on my part to get Reilly not to leave the picture up on the website."

Okay, then. She was still a little surprised that he'd

managed to convince the reporter to take them down. No wonder Jasper was so concerned that she might have spread rumors about him and Layla after such a recent narrow escape.

The banker was still talking. "You know, I actually accused Ronald Minter of being the one carving the portraits. I mean, it was only logical, since he was the only one in town who grew pumpkins. He denied it, of course, but he did think the pumpkins came from his farm."

Abby felt obligated to point out, "The grocery store sells them, too."

"True, but Ronald also complained that someone was sneaking onto his property at night to steal his finest pumpkins. There's no way to prove the portraits were made from the ones that went missing, but he sure thought so."

"Have you told Gage or the detective from the county sheriff's office any of this?"

He looked at her like she was crazy. "Why would I do that? I'm having a hard enough time keeping a lid on what happened as it is."

"But—" she started to protest, when he immediately cut her off.

"Get this straight. I'm not going to say a word about the discussion I had with Ronald, and I'll deny it happened if you tell them. Who do you think they're going to believe? Me, a long-time respected resident of Snowberry Creek, or you?"

He gave her a disparaging look but jumped back another step when Zeke took exception to his tone of voice. The dog had been sitting down, but now he rose to his full height and stared up at Jasper as if reassessing his opinion of the man.

She patted his head with one hand as she tightened her grip on his collar with the other. "I would think such a fine, upstanding man would want the police to have any and all facts that might help them solve Mr. Minter's murder."

"They already know who did it. It's not my problem that they can't manage to track down one homeless veteran."

"I don't think Gage is all that convinced that Sergeant Montgomery is behind the attack on Mr. Minter."

"That's not what I hear. Everyone knows the two of them had a big argument in town. Two days later, Minter was dead. Seems pretty clear to me."

"Well, I think you're wrong."

Not that she could prove it. She stared at the banker, waiting to see what he'd do next. Now that she'd spent some time in his company, it was hard to remember why she'd thought he was good-looking. There was something weak about his chin, and his eyes were a little too close together to look completely trustworthy.

When he just stood there, she drew a deep breath and sighed. "Look, Mr. Collins, I really think it's time for you to leave. I'm sure your wife must be wondering where you are."

Maybe she should have refrained from that last comment, but he'd made her mad. Meanwhile, Jasper remained right where he was and seemed to be engaged in an internal debate about what he wanted to say. Finally, he jerked his head in an abrupt nod. "Fine, I'll leave, but I should make a couple of things clear."

He held up a finger. "First, as I already said, Ms. Sheffield and I are coworkers, nothing more."

Then he raised another finger. "Second, I will deny knowing anything about Ronald and his missing pumpkins."

After he started down the steps, he turned back one last time. "Considering Ronald's temperament, I think it very likely that if he had any idea who was messing with his cash crop, he would've gotten up in their face about it."

She couldn't disagree. "So?"

"So that's probably what got him killed. You might want to remember that and act accordingly. I wouldn't want something to happen to you, too."

Then he stalked off, disappearing into the darkness.

Abby remained frozen in position for several seconds before retreating into the safety of the house with Zeke right behind her. When she locked the door, her hands were shaking more than she cared to admit. So many questions whirled through her mind, leaving her confused and more than a little worried.

She sat in her favorite chair and drew comfort from Zeke, who put his big head in her lap. Stroking his ears, she asked him the one question she really, really wished he could answer.

"Big guy, was Jasper Collins just offering me a bit of helpful advice, or was that more of a threat?"

Zeke seemed to consider the matter and then finally gave his head a hard shake.

She actually laughed. "Yeah, I couldn't tell, either."

Chapter Sixteen

Stepping back out of the way, Abby waited quietly while Bridey studied the results of their handiwork so far. This was the one day a week the shop was closed, so she'd stopped in to help her friend finish decorating the place for Halloween. Bridey tipped her head to one side as if to get a slightly better angle on the view. "I think the front window needs another set of streamers."

Abby dutifully dug out the roll of black crepe paper and another of the orange. After unwinding a few feet, she taped the ends together and began winding the two strands together. Then she held them up to Bridey, who was up on the ladder. She fastened the paper in the corner and then climbed down to reposition the ladder in the center of the huge window. After draping the twisted streamers lower than the first two lengths they'd already hung, she put a tack through the paper to fasten it into the frame above the glass. After another trip down the ladder, she moved to the far side of the window and waited as Abby continued to twist the colors together.

"There, does that look even?"

Abby stepped farther back to get some perspective. "It needs to be about an inch lower."

Bridey adjusted it accordingly and then tacked that end. Abby passed her the scissors to cut the paper off the rolls.

"That looks nice."

Then she held up two round paper pumpkins. "Which one do you want to hang in the middle? The smiley one or the scary one?"

After considering the options, Bridey held out her hand. "The happy one. We can put the scary guy on the counter over there, though. I like him."

"Me, too."

Abby carried the frowning jack-o'-lantern over to where Bridey had pointed and set him down. "He looks pretty dashing there."

"He does, doesn't he?"

Her friend carried the ladder into the back room of the shop. When she returned, she was carrying a plate full of brownies slathered with orange icing. "These are for you."

Abby immediately held out her hand. "I shouldn't accept them since Tripp isn't around to share in the calories, but that isn't going to stop me. They look delicious."

Bridey handed them over. "I take it he's still being stubborn."

"Yeah, he is. I haven't been by to see him again, but I'll probably drop by there on my way home on the off chance that Gage can let me in for a visit."

"Would a bribe help?"

Abby laughed. "I'm sure it would. Based on my experience, it seems the stereotype of cops liking sweets of all kinds is based in truth, at least here in Snowberry Creek."

"Come on in back while I box up a few things for you to take with you. I was experimenting this morning with a few new recipes for Thanksgiving and Christmas, so I have plenty to share."

Following her friend as well as the scents of cinnamon and cloves to the kitchen in back of the shop, she asked, "Are you sure?"

"Even if I wasn't, I'd still give you whatever it takes to get you in to see Tripp. I know you're worried about him." She made quick work of packing up another plate of cookies. "I've got to admit my mood feels off somehow this year despite my best efforts to get in the holiday spirit. I guess that shouldn't come as a surprise considering it's the second time we've had a murderer running loose in the area. Without knowing why Mr. Minter was killed, it's hard to feel safe. I try not to let it bother me, but every so often the thought sends a chill up my spine. It has to be so much worse for you, especially coming on the heels of Dolly Cayhill's death."

It was a shame Abby couldn't find fault with Bridey's logic as they left the kitchen and walked back to the front window of the shop. There, they watched their friends and neighbors calmly going about their business, as if nothing was wrong. Maybe if they'd been there to see the poor man sprawled under that table or how his blood had stained the dirt floor of that shack, his death might have had more of an impact on them.

More to change the subject than anything, she found herself asking, "Do you know Layla Sheffield very well?"

Bridey blinked at the left turn in the conversation but finally answered, "Mainly just as a skinny decaf latte. I see her at the bank, of course, but that's about it. She seems to keep pretty much to herself outside of work. Why?"

"She helped Zoe Brevik and me for a while Saturday when we were working on the planters down the street. She seemed really nice, and I was surprised our paths hadn't crossed before."

"As I recall, Layla only moved here about a year ago, when she transferred from another branch of the bank to take the job as Jasper Collins's executive assistant when his previous one retired. I'm pretty sure it was a promotion for her. Maybe volunteering to help with the festival decorations was her way of getting more involved and as a way to meet more people outside of the ones she works with at the bank."

"That makes sense. After all, that's part of why I do it myself."

Bridey snickered. "Well, that and the fact you haven't figured out how to say no whenever Connie Pohler asks you to take on another project."

That was nothing but the sad, sad truth. "At least I'll be done with the seniors group by the middle of November now that Fred Cady has finally recovered from his hip replacement surgery. Seems like it's been a long haul for him."

Bridey looked surprised. "From what I heard, he bounced back surprisingly fast from the procedure. Seth and I see him out hiking the trail near our house a couple of times a week."

Abby blinked. "What? Seriously?"

She was pretty sure her voice had gone up an

octave between the first word and the second when Bridey cringed and said, "Yeah. Is that a problem?"

Darn straight it was. She'd been had. "That old rascal postponed taking over the group by an extra month because he said he needed a little more recovery time. By some fortuitous happenstance, that meant I had to organize and handle the group's duties for the festival."

Bridey's eyes flared wide as she covered her mouth, no doubt trying to hide a grin or maybe stifle some outright laughter. "I'm really sorry, but you've got to give the guy credit for being crafty. I feel sort of bad for letting the cat out of the bag. What are you going to do?"

It was hard to get mad at someone she actually liked a lot. "I'm not sure, but there will be a reckoning. Regardless, two weeks after the festival, I'm done."

Then she sighed.

"At least with that committee. I'm still heading up the quilting guild until late spring. Then there's the fundraiser for the veterans group that Tripp volunteered me to help with."

Although her friend looked sympathetic, there was no mistaking the glimmer of humor twinkling in her eyes. "You could've told him no."

"We both know that wasn't going to happen, but I am determined that this will be the last project I can take on. I invested the money I got when my ex bought out my half of our small import business for my retirement someday, and thanks to my inheritance from Aunt Sybil, I don't need to go back to work right away. Sorting through everything at the house and cleaning out the attic has kept me pretty busy, but that won't take me much longer to finish up. Eventually,

I'm going to want to find something more challenging to do with my time."

"Do you have any idea what you want to be when you grow up?"

She couldn't help but smile at the way Bridey framed the question. Even though it was couched in a humorous way, it was clear she really wanted a serious answer. After a bit, Abby said, "No, not really. I always hoped there would come a day when Chad and I would start a family. With that in mind, I brought someone onboard to take over some of my duties with our company. I thought that would give me time to be home more with our kids, but that's not what happened. As it turned out, the woman I hired also took over my duties as Chad's wife."

As always, it took her some effort to push past the bitterness. "Right now I don't even have a glimmer of what I want my future to look like. I can't decide if I've legitimately been too busy to think about it or if I've just been keeping myself too busy to avoid moving on."

Bridey gave her a quick hug. "Speaking from my own experience, starting over isn't easy. You don't need to know the sordid details about my first husband, but I suspect we have a lot in common on that score."

Then she paused to look around her coffee shop. "After I walked away from my marriage, I sank everything I had into this place, and I'm not just talking about money. I poured every bit of energy and all of my emotions into making it a success. Looking back, I think I really needed to do that in order to heal and move forward. Rebuilding old friendships and establishing new ones has helped me remember that some people can be trusted. By the time I met Seth, I was ready to try again."

She gave Abby a quick hug. "Eventually, you'll figure it all out. Until then, take pride in everything you're accomplishing, whether it's the time you've put in cleaning out the house or the contributions you've made through your charitable work here in Snowberry Creek."

"Sounds like good advice. Meanwhile, I'll head over to the jail and see what's going on with Tripp."

"Tell the jailbird hi for me. Let him know if he gets tired of living behind bars, I can always hide a file in some of my gingerbread."

Abby feigned horror. "Don't even say that. It's bad enough I have one friend in jail. I don't think Seth would forgive either Tripp or me if you got thrown into the cell next to his for trying to break him out of the pokey."

"The offer still stands." Bridey was grinning as she unlocked the front door to let Abby out. "Thanks again for helping me decorate the shop."

"I enjoyed it. Besides, if you're going to pay me with brownies, I'll be back to help you switch over to Thanksgiving and Christmas, too."

"It's a deal."

The desk sergeant, looked up from his computer screen. "I see you're back, Ms. McCree."

As soon as he spotted the plates in her hands, Jackson Jones offered her a big grin. "You know, those baked goods could be interpreted as a bribe."

She batted her eyes and tried to look shocked by

his good-natured accusation. "Why, I would never stoop to bribing one of Snowberry Creek's finest."

As she spoke, she pulled the plastic wrap off one side of the plate containing Bridey's experimental holiday fare. "Actually, you're being offered a chance to sample in advance some of the treats that will be featured at Something's Brewing for Thanksgiving and Christmas. You know, so Bridey can get some feedback."

"Oh, well, that's different."

He greedily studied the various options for a second or two before picking out a mini cupcake and a turkey-shaped cookie.

"Were you wanting to see Gage or to visit our prisoner?"

She wrinkled her nose. "I was hoping to visit Mr. Blackston, but I should probably clear it with Gage first."

"Must be your lucky day. The last I heard he was down visiting the prisoner. I'll buzz Deputy Chapin and tell him you're headed his way."

"Thanks, Sergeant."

She pointed toward the rest of the bribe that Bridey had put together for her. "On my way, I'll put the rest of this out for everyone to enjoy."

He immediately grabbed another cookie. "Thanks again, and tell Bridey it's nice of her to spoil us like this."

"I'll let her know."

What did it say about her life that she now knew her way around the police department so well? Before moving to Snowberry Creek, she'd never even set foot in such a place. It would be easy to blame Tripp for that, but that wouldn't be entirely fair. She'd paid more than one visit to Gage's office during and after the whole Dolly Cayhill murder investigation.

One of the deputies, who was talking on the phone, looked up and waved when Abby walked into the bull pen. The woman's eyes lit up with interest when she spotted the plate of goodies. Rather than setting it down on the counter, Abby stopped by the woman's desk long enough to let her grab a toffee bar. She mouthed "thanks" while continuing the conversation with whoever was on the other end of the line.

Having done her duty, Abby headed for the passageway that led to where the officer on guard had his desk. Evidently the desk sergeant had called ahead, because the young deputy already had unlocked the door to let her in.

"Ms. McCree, nice to see you again."

Not that Deputy Chapin was looking at her. Instead, his eyes were riveted on the plate of brownies in her hand. "It's good to see you, too."

Meanwhile, she helped herself to some tissues from the box on his desk to use in lieu of napkins. After setting two of the brownies on one for the deputy, she said, "Those are fresh from Something's Brewing. I hope you enjoy them."

"I'm sure I will, but if you keep supplying us with stuff like this, I'll have to add another mile to my morning runs."

"That's why I share them. If I ate them all by myself, I'd be living at the gym." Then she gave him a sly look. "That is, if I belonged to a gym."

He laughed as he picked up a brownie. "Would you like me to walk you the rest of the way?"

"That's not necessary. I'll be fine."

She headed on down the hall. As she reached the

last turn, she could hear the deep rumble of Tripp's voice, and then Gage's. They seemed to be arguing about something, but neither man sounded particularly angry. She slowed down and peeked around the corner to see what was going on.

Gage was sitting on a chair in front of a small table that he'd shoved next to the bars on Tripp's cell. There was a chessboard on the table, and the game looked to have been in progress for a while. For his part, Tripp sat perched on the end of his narrow bed, his eyebrows riding low over his eyes as he studied the chess pieces. Finally, his expression lightened as he reached through the bars and picked up his knight and plunked it down on the board with a grin.

"Checkmate."

Gage looked totally dumbfounded as he leaned in closer to make sense of what had just happened. "You cheated."

Tripp snorted. "No, I didn't. You got careless." Then he glanced in Abby's direction. "Are you going to come say hi or stay over there and spy on us?"

At least he hadn't begun the conversation by telling her she shouldn't have come. That was progress. Gage looked surprised by her sudden appearance, but he didn't seem particularly upset that she'd managed to talk her way in for another visit.

She held up the plate as she approached the two men. "I brought brownies."

Gage pointed toward his prisoner. "He doesn't get any."

Tripp protested. "Why not?"

"Like I said, you cheated. As a duly sworn officer

of the law, I cannot in good conscience reward bad behavior."

Tripp gave him a look of total disgust. "Like I said, you got careless. It's not my fault that I've won three out of the last four games."

They continued to argue as Gage fetched another chair for her while Tripp packed up the chess set to make room for the plate of brownies. When Gage reached for one, Abby slapped at his hand. "We can't eat in front of Tripp. I'm pretty sure that would be considered cruel and unusual punishment."

"Fine, he can have one." Then Gage winked at her. "But you and I can each have two. After all, he is a prisoner. Life behind bars isn't supposed to be all sweetness and light."

She pretended to mull that over before finally nodding. "You're right, of course. We don't want things to be too cushy for him in here. He'll never want to come home."

It suddenly occurred to her wonder if Tripp really considered Snowberry Creek to be his permanent home now. Maybe he thought about it in terms of a college town, only a temporary stop on his way to his future. It was surprising how much that idea hurt.

She doled out the brownies, passing one of the bigger ones through the bars to Tripp before setting two on a tissue for Gage. Having finished her duties as hostess, she picked one for herself and took a big bite. It was hard not to moan in pleasure as the combined flavors of the fudgy chocolate and the cream cheese frosting hit her tongue.

Tripp had already finished his brownie and was

eyeing the two left on the plate. "You outdid yourself this time, Abby. These are fabulous."

Ignoring Gage's half-hearted protest, she handed him a second one. "I'm glad you like them, but Bridey baked these. They were my pay for helping her decorate her shop this morning."

Gage reached for his second one. "I'm surprised you made it all the way here without my deputies robbing you blind. They might not like a prisoner getting spoiled like this."

"Actually, when I told Bridey where I was headed, she packed up a huge plate of baked goods for me to share with everyone in the department. She's been trying out some new recipes for the holidays and had more than she could use in the shop."

"That was nice of her to think of us."

Abby laughed. "Your desk sergeant thought my bringing more treats could be interpreted as more of a bribe."

"There is that."

When he finished his second brownie, he wiped his hands on the tissue and then stood up. "I should head back to my office and do some police work. I'll also inspect the rest of the goodies you brought, so I can speak with authority if I have to deny we're taking bribes these days. You know, in case some concerned citizen lodges a complaint."

Tripp looked disgusted. "More likely you're going to destroy the evidence. It's just another police cover-up. You know, corruption running rampant in a small-town police department."

Gage just laughed. "Abby, I hate to set a time limit on your visit, but I wouldn't stick around more than half an hour or so. We never know when Ben Earle will decide to drop by."

She checked the time on the clock down the hall. "I'll keep an eye on the clock."

When he was gone, she put the plate within easy reach for Tripp. "You can have those, too, if you want them. I've had my fill."

That was a lie, but she also had cookies at home. Tripp didn't exactly have much control over what he got to eat these days.

She finally let herself study his face. He hadn't bothered shaving for a couple of days, or else he'd decided to grow a beard. Either way, the scruff looked good on him. "How are you doing?"

"Fine."

So not true. From the dark circles under his eyes, she was willing to bet he wasn't sleeping all that well. She also suspected that being confined to that small cell had to be hard on a man who always seemed to be in constant motion.

"Has Detective Earle told you if he's made any progress on the case? Is he still trying to blame Sergeant Montgomery?"

Tripp shifted to put a little more distance between the two of them. "Please just let it go, Abby. You don't need to worry about either Kevin or me."

She wanted to punch him. "Are you keeping up with your classes?"

The sudden change in topics seemed to take him aback. "As best I can."

"What's that supposed to mean?"

His expression turned grim and his shoulders sagged. "It sounds like I might have to drop out for the rest of the quarter if I don't get back to class soon."

"Which means?"

"I'll have to repeat the term. That wouldn't be that much of a problem, except they don't always offer all the same classes each quarter. There are a couple I'm enrolled in now that are prerequisites for some others I need to take. It could set me back almost a year."

She wanted to punch him even harder. "Do you really think Kevin would want you to screw up your life like this?"

He didn't respond, mainly because they both already knew the answer to that question—no, he wouldn't.

Despite her misgivings, she might just have to tell Gage what she knew about Jasper Collins's fight with Ronald Minter. She'd hate to cause problems for Layla, but her first loyalty was to Tripp. Rather than discuss the situation with him, though, she reached for the chess set.

"I know we don't have long, but let's see if your luck is still holding." Then she wagged her finger at him. "But for the record, if it turns out that Gage was right about your cheating, you might want to remember I'm all that stands between you and one of Jean's tuna casseroles."

He just smiled and started setting up his pieces.

Chapter Seventeen

Abby walked along the sidewalk as she followed the Hakes' SUV down Main Street. Dean was at the wheel with his wife riding shotgun as they made their way from one storefront to the next. They were dropping off the boxes of goody bags that would be handed out when the kids went trick-or-treating through town on Halloween, now only a few days away. Many of the merchants and businesses in town had donated the supplies to fill the bags, which ranged from candy of all kinds to pencils, pens, stickers, and even coupons for free popcorn at a nearby movie theater.

She thought it was a little funny that the local dental clinic had donated toothbrushes and travel-size toothpaste to the cause. The kids might not appreciate the gesture, but she bet their parents would feel differently about it, especially considering the amount of sugar the kids would be bringing home.

Seth Kyser stepped out of Bridey's shop just as she was reaching for another box out of the SUV. He hurried over to stand beside her. "Let me help you with that, Abby."

She stepped back to allow him easy access to the

box marked for Something's Brewing. "Thanks, Seth, that one is for Bridey's shop. I know she plans to hand out Halloween cookies, but we thought she might like a few of the candy bags as backup in case the turnout is larger than expected."

"I'm sure she'll appreciate having the extra supplies. It seems every year the number of trick-or-treaters goes up." He set the box down on the ground by the door to the shop. "I'll give you a hand with the rest of the block before I take ours inside."

If she'd learned one thing from her recent flurry of committee work, it was to never turn down free labor. "Thanks, we appreciate it."

With both of them working, it sped up the progress considerably. A few minutes later, they reached the front door of the bank. Abby had been avoiding the place since her last encounter with Jasper Collins. They hadn't parted on the best of terms, and she had no desire for a repeat performance. With considerable trepidation, she picked up one of the two boxes designated for the bank and followed Seth inside to set them down. She made it almost back to the door before Jasper appeared in front of her. He glared at her, his temper clearly running on the far edge of hot.

"Ms. McCree, may I speak to you for a moment?"

No way she wanted to talk to the man again. Not now, not ever. If his wasn't the only bank in town, she might have even moved her accounts to avoid him. She pointed at the boxes she and Seth had just brought in. "I'm sorry, Mr. Collins, but now isn't a good time. I have people waiting for me outside. We have more deliveries to make."

He gave the boxes a dismissive look. "They can wait."

Seth stepped closer. "Is everything all right, Abby?"

Other customers in the bank were already watching them with interest, and the last thing she wanted to do was cause a very public scene. "It's fine, Seth. Would you tell the others I'll be right back out? Evidently Mr. Collins and I have a small matter to discuss."

Seth didn't immediately leave, meaning he'd picked up on the tension between her and the bank manager. "I'll let them know, but I'll be right back in to wait for you."

Then he gave Jasper a considering look. "In fact, I think I should stay with you."

As much as she appreciated his offer of support, his presence would only throw gas on what already felt like a volatile situation. "I'll be fine, and this shouldn't take long."

Without waiting for his response, she started toward the open door into Jasper's office. As they passed by an empty desk, she noticed that the nameplate on it belonged to Layla. With a sinking feeling in her stomach, she crossed her fingers that the woman had only stepped away for a moment. She'd feel beyond horrible if Layla had had to resign because of her relationship with her boss. That would be unfortunate for so many reasons.

There was only one way to find out. As soon as they walked into Jasper's office, he closed the door. While that might keep anyone in the lobby from hearing what they said, the customers would still be able to watch and put their own interpretation on the nature of the discussion. This was going to be no fun at all.

It didn't take long for Jasper to launch the opening salvo. "I thought I made it perfectly clear to you that you shouldn't go around starting rumors about me around town. Just what did you tell the police about me? Did you mention Layla?"

"I didn't start any rumors, Mr. Collins. I had no reason to mention either your name or Layla's to Gage Logan in any context."

Jasper glared at her with his hands clenched in tight fists. "I find it highly suspicious that the cops showed up on my doorstep not long after you and I talked, so don't bother to lie about it. You must have told them something."

No, she hadn't, but she'd definitely thought about it, and had yet to reject the idea out of hand. "What makes you think that? Your name has not come up in any conversation I've had with Gage, and I haven't spoken to Detective Earle since you showed up uninvited at my house."

The man wasn't buying it. "Well, someone told them about the argument I had with Ronald Minter. Why else would that detective from the county sheriff's office come around poking his nose into my private business? He didn't even bother calling first, and we had friends over at the time. Can you imagine how my wife reacted to the police showing up at our door?"

Probably not well at all. It would be interesting to know what excuse Jasper had come up with for his rather public disagreement with Ronald. Certainly he wouldn't have admitted it was all about his pumpkin portrait appearing on his mistress's front porch. And while he didn't appreciate the cop showing up at his house, did he think it would have been any better for his reputation if Detective Earle had cornered him at the bank?

"I will not have you or anyone else calling my

character into question, Ms. McCree. Cause me any further problems or embarrassment, and there will be consequences."

"For the last time, I never mentioned you or Ms. Sheffield to either Gage or the detective." It was past time to get out of there. Any number of people could have told Ben Earle about the argument, but Jasper clearly wasn't going to be rational about the situation. She started toward the door. "I've said everything I have to say on the subject. Whether or not you choose to believe me is your problem, not mine."

Jasper practically growled as he continued to speak, and his usual smooth polish was nowhere to be seen. "If there's any blowback from your interference, Ms. McCree, I assure you the problem won't be mine alone. It will be yours as well."

This time she was sure he was threatening her, but there wasn't much she could do about it. Despite the distance between them, she could almost see the tension pouring off him in waves. There was clearly no use in arguing with him anymore, and the absolute fury glittering in his eyes scared her a little. At least he didn't try to stop her from leaving when she walked out of his office, closing his door with the utmost care. It would've given her great satisfaction to express her irritation by slamming it, but that would have only drawn more attention in their direction.

As promised, Seth stood waiting a short distance away. "Are you all right? Should I have a talk with him?"

She struggled to put on a brave front. "No, everything is fine."

Then she sighed. "Okay, not really, but the situation is under control."

At least for now. She would still like to know who had been talking to the police behind Jasper's back.

Seth looked doubtful, but he didn't press for more information. "If he gives you any more trouble, any at all, you let me know, or at least talk to Gage. I couldn't hear what he was saying to you, but his body language was all too clear. Jasper might think he's a big fish in this little pond of ours, but he can't go around harassing people."

"I promise that if I have any problems with him, I'll let Gage know."

When they walked back outside, Kristy was waiting for them, but her husband's SUV was nowhere in sight. She pointed down the street. "Dean went back to get the last load. We're making such good progress that we should finish up before lunch. I'm glad, because we're hoping to take our metal detectors out to the woods for a long ramble this afternoon."

After facing off against Jasper, Abby could really use a break about now, but they needed to get everything distributed as soon as possible. The Halloween Festival was approaching fast, and there were still a lot of details that needed to be finished up if everything was going to be ready on time.

Mustering up a smile, she said, "I'm game if you are."

She realized that Seth was still hovering nearby. "Thanks for your help, Seth. We should be able to finish up pretty quickly. I think we only have another three blocks to cover."

"Anytime."

Before walking away, he gave her another long look. "I meant what I said about you-know-who. Don't let him give you any grief."

"I won't."

Kristy watched the exchange with great interest. "Did you have problems in the bank? I thought they were expecting the candy to arrive today. I know that's what I told Layla Sheffield."

"I didn't see her, but I'm sure someone will let her know that it arrived. I was delayed because Jasper Collins had a question for me about an unrelated matter."

Kristy's normally cheerful expression instantly morphed into one of irritation. "I swear that man thinks he rules the world around here. Dean and I have already sent a formal complaint to the regional officials about him and his obnoxious attitude, but we've gotten nowhere with them."

Asking for more details was tempting, but Abby resisted. After all, it wasn't as if she and the Hakes were close friends. She settled for offering some generic sympathy. "I'm sorry. I know dealing with bureaucracy can be so frustrating."

"Yes, it is. It's beginning to look like we'll probably have to turn the matter over to our attorney to handle, which will no doubt cost us a fortune."

Clearly unhappy about that prospect, Kristy stared back toward the bank. "All we want to do is settle Dean's cousin's estate. It's not like there will be a lot of money involved once we clear all of his debts. It doesn't help that some more distant relatives are trying to muddy the waters."

She gave her head an exasperated shake.

"Heck, we had no way of knowing there was a second mortgage on the house and property. Now we can't sell because the bank—meaning Jasper Collins, of course—has slapped a lien on the title. He hasn't even agreed to let us move ahead with clearing out the house. There's so much work to do just to clean everything before we get the place appraised and then listed on the market."

She gave a snort of pure disgust. "You'd think that fool would be happy someone else is willing to do all the work so the bank can get its money back. Don't even get me started on the effect of all the zoning laws that affect how the place can be listed. We're living on a fixed budget. It's not like we have piles of cash lying around that we could use to pay off the bank loan although that would simplify things. Even then, there's no guarantee that we would actually recoup our investment."

"Sounds complicated."

Not for the first time, Abby was grateful that her late aunt had had all of her affairs in such good order. Abby had had to deal with a couple of disgruntled cousins, but even that had been pretty minor. Meanwhile, Kristy kept watching for her husband's car. She hated seeing the woman look so unhappy, but wasn't sure what she could do to help.

"Sorry, I didn't mean to unload on you, Abby. Even though Dean and his cousin weren't particularly close anymore, they did grow up together. Having to deal with all of these complications just keeps him stirred up all the time, and that worries me. After his health scare last year, I'm concerned about the effect all this stress will have on him."

"I can see why you'd be worried."

Kristy went up on her toes, as if that would give her better visibility. Maybe it worked, because her smile immediately brightened. "There he is."

She waved at Dean as he approached. Before he pulled over to the curb, she leaned in closer to Abby.

"Please don't say anything to him about Jasper Collins. It would only upset him."

"Not a problem."

It took them less than another hour to finish their deliveries. When they were done, Abby waved as Kristy and Dean drove off. As she walked back to her own car, she noticed the clouds rolling in from the west. Hopefully, the rain would hold off long enough for the Hakes to enjoy some time outdoors. It sounded as if both of them could use some downtime indulging in their favorite hobby.

With luck, maybe they'd even find something out there in the woods. She'd noticed the pretty necklace that Kristy was wearing and wondered if that had been another find. On second thought, probably not, considering how closely the chain resembled that bracelet they'd discovered out in the boonies somewhere. More likely she'd seen it in a jewelry store and bought it because of the similarity.

For Abby's part, she was going to head home and take a well-deserved nap. On the other hand, maybe she'd take Zeke for his walk first. Those clouds were looking pretty ugly.

On impulse, Abby had called Glenda after she got home to see if she wanted to grab dinner at a steakhouse out near the highway. After a flurry of phone calls, they had ended up with a foursome when Louise and Jean decided to join them. They were all in high spirits, and the conversation flowed freely over the course of the meal. Abby didn't bring up the subject of Ronald Minter's death, but she listened carefully for any gossip that might shed light on the situation.

Either the ladies hadn't heard anything useful or else they were trying to be tactful by not bringing up a topic that they thought was painful for her. Even Jean didn't ask about Tripp or offer to bring a casserole to him at the jail. After everyone was done eating and had their doggy bags all packed up, Abby insisted on making the meal her treat, telling her friends it was because the outing had been her idea. The real reason that she had pounced on the bill as soon as the waiter had presented it was far more selfish.

Considering the day she'd had, she simply couldn't face another long, involved squabble over who owed what and how much of a tip they should leave for the waiter. Heaven forbid they simply add twenty percent to the total and divide by four. But no, it really mattered to the ladies that Louise had upgraded to sweet potato fries, which cost an extra dollar, and that Jean had settled for water to drink since it was free.

Their first stop on the way home was at Louise's house. From there, they drove the short distance to the apartment complex where Jean lived. Glenda waited in the car while Abby accompanied Jean to her front door. That the older woman didn't argue she could get there on her own was a testament to how really tired Jean was. Abby knew how she felt, despite the fifty-plus years' difference in their ages.

Glenda smiled when Abby got back into the car. "Thanks for walking her inside. I'm afraid she doesn't see as well as she used to."

Then she huffed a small laugh. "Actually, neither do I. That's why I rarely go out at night anymore unless I have somewhere I really have to be."

Aunt Sybil had mentioned having the same problem in the last couple of years of her life and how it had affected her social life. "You know that anytime you need a ride, all you have to do is ask."

"I do, and I appreciate that."

Glenda waited until they were moving before speaking again. "Forgive me for being nosy, Abby, but you've been a bit distracted tonight. Is anything wrong?"

It was tempting to deny it, but she was too tired to put up a brave front. Besides, she knew Glenda could be trusted to keep her secrets if she asked her to keep things to herself. "I hate that the police haven't made any progress in solving Mr. Minter's murder. I'm also worried about the effect all of this is having on Tripp. He's determined to rot there in that cell if that's what it takes to protect his friend."

Before Glenda could comment, she plowed on. "I know that his sense of honor is part of what makes Tripp the man he is, but this could cause him real problems long-term."

Glenda gave her a considering look and then slowly nodded. "You care about him."

Abby tightened her grip on the steering wheel. What could she say that wouldn't have Glenda leaping to conclusions? She settled for keeping it simple. "He's my friend."

She kept her eyes firmly on the road ahead to avoid seeing how Glenda reacted to that statement. She really hoped that her friend wasn't assuming there was more to Abby's feelings about her tenant than simple friendship. That's all it was, though. Really.

Meanwhile, they'd reached Glenda's home. "Do you want me to walk you up to the door?"

"No, I'll be fine."

Then Glenda reached over to pat Abby on the hand. "Thanks for dinner tonight. I know that I speak for Louise and Jean, as well, when I say spending time out with friends gave us all a nice lift of the spirits. Sometimes it's hard to rattle around in my house alone. I suspect it's much the same for you."

Abby couldn't deny it. "While I don't miss my ex-husband after everything that happened, I do miss being part of a couple sometimes. Maybe things would be easier if I hadn't had to walk away from my career, too. After all this time, I still have no idea what I want to do with the rest of my life. I was just talking to Bridey about this same thing the other day. Based on her experience under somewhat similar circumstances, she promised eventually I would know when I was ready to really move on with my life."

"Sounds like she gave you good advice. I do think it's smart of you to get involved like you have here in Snowberry Creek, building friendships and making new connections. Once you have a solid base to work from, I'm sure you'll find your way again."

"I hope so."

"I *know* so."

Then Glenda let herself out of the car and headed up the sidewalk to her front door. Abby waited until the lights came on in the house before heading on home.

Ten minutes later she parked in her own driveway. She had a meeting at city hall early in the morning, so she decided not to pull around back to park. Since Tripp wasn't around, she didn't need to worry about her car blocking the driveway. When she started toward the house, she noticed the porch light had burned out—one more thing to add to her already lengthy to-do list for tomorrow. But as she reached the top step, she heard Zeke barking inside the house.

While he always waited just inside the door to greet her, he wasn't in the habit of raising a ruckus like this.

She froze mid-step, unsure if she should continue forward or retreat back to the car. Considering she'd been gone most of the day, perhaps he was unusually excited that she was home. She could also be over-reacting a little, thanks to a momentary flashback to when a murderer had tossed a rock through her front window and then later tried to break in. Regardless which of those two things was true, right now she was seriously creeped out.

Taking another slow step forward, she glanced all around before unlocking the door. The light she'd left on in the entry spilled out onto the porch. Zeke rushed past, nearly knocking her into the wall in his haste to get outside. Instead of bolting out into the yard to take care of his normal business, he remained on the porch, nose to the ground and sniffing like crazy.

Abby remained in the doorway and tried to figure out what was going on with her furry roommate. Maybe it would help if she cast more light on the area, but she'd need to replace the burned-out bulb first. When she went to unscrew it, she realized it was loose in the socket. It came back on as soon as she twisted it back in tight.

What was going on? It seemed unlikely that it would've worked loose on its own. That left the possi-bility that someone had deliberately unscrewed the bulb. But why? Then she realized Zeke had zeroed in on one spot of particular interest—her pumpkin portrait.

When he started growling, she stepped closer. "What's so fascinating, boy?"

The dog looked up at her briefly before turning his attention back to his target, still blocking her view of the pumpkin. She grabbed his collar and gave him a determined tug to move him out of her way. He was reluctant to give ground, but finally the dog retreated two steps as he continued to express his concern with a soft growl.

When she finally got a clear look at it, she gasped and jumped back as if the big pumpkin could bite. "Come on, Zeke, inside. We need to call Gage."

The dog reluctantly followed her into the house and waited patiently while she locked the door. Then he stuck by her side each step of the way to the kitchen, where she poured herself a large glass of wine while she waited for the police dispatcher to answer her call.

When the woman on the other end of the line calmly asked for the nature of her emergency, Abby swallowed hard and hoped that she didn't sound completely crazy when she described what happened.

"Hi, this is Abby McCree. Could you please let either Chief Logan or Detective Ben Earle know that someone has stabbed my pumpkin? Tell them I think whoever did it used the same kind of knife that killed Ronald Minter."

Chapter Eighteen

To give the woman credit, she didn't laugh. After all, how often did someone call 911 to report squash abuse?

However, the dispatcher did ask several pointed questions. Abby went into greater detail about the loosened light bulb, Zeke's behavior, and the way the pumpkin had been slashed several times and still had a combat knife stuck right between its eyes. Since the pumpkin was meant to be her, it seemed likely the attack had been aimed directly at Abby herself. When the woman finally understood that this wasn't just someone's idea of a funny prank but a real threat, she promised a deputy would be there shortly.

The combined effects of the alcohol and adrenaline hit Abby hard, leaving her pulse racing and chills dancing over the surface of her skin. Maybe chugging a glass of wine hadn't been the smartest thing she'd ever done. Rather than stand around and do nothing, she made a fresh pot of coffee. If Gage or Detective Earle happened to be the ones who showed up to investigate, she was pretty sure they wouldn't mind something hot to drink and maybe even a few cookies to go along with it.

At least it gave her something to do while she waited.

She dug the oatmeal raisin cookies and a few toffee bars out of the pantry and arranged them on a plate, along with some mugs, the sugar bowl, and a small pitcher of cream. Playing hostess under these circumstances seemed a little silly, but she desperately needed to focus on something besides that knife blade in her pumpkin.

When the front doorbell rang a few seconds later, she gave her ponytail a tug to make sure it was neat and tidy. It was tempting to touch up her lipstick, but that would be ridiculous. Even if it would make her feel a little more in control, the cops wouldn't appreciate the delay, nor would they care if she looked a bit frazzled. They'd probably find it strange if she didn't.

A big fist pounded on the door just as she got there. It took her a few extra seconds to undo the locks, but at least they had to know she was trying to let them in. It came as no surprise that the man on her porch wasn't one of the deputies who normally patrolled her neighborhood. Neither was the other one who had just pulled into the driveway.

"Detective Earle, come on in."

He walked into the house to stand a short distance away while they waited for Gage to join them. It was the first time she'd ever seen the man in casual clothing. The jeans and classic rock T-shirt combo that made him seem more approachable probably meant he'd been off duty. If so, he must live close by to have gotten there so fast. She hid a smile when she noticed how he kept a wary eye on Zeke, although she couldn't blame him. Given his size, the dog could look pretty intimidating. He was usually friendly, but these weren't normal circumstances by any means.

Gage stepped through the door. "Abby, I hope you don't mind that I invited Detective Earle to join us even though you live in my jurisdiction. I thought it would save time, since from what you told the dispatcher, it's likely this is tied in to the Minter case that he's investigating."

It wasn't as though Gage actually needed her permission. This wasn't a social occasion where the rules of etiquette applied.

"That's fine."

She hated that her voice cracked, causing Gage to step closer and ask, "Are you all right?"

It was time for honesty, not false bravado. "No, not so much. I'm really hoping you'll look at the pumpkin and tell me I have nothing to worry about, but I'm pretty sure you're not going to do that."

Both men went back out onto the porch to take a closer look at what was left of her portrait. They each snapped several pictures with their cell phones before coming back inside. Detective Earle gestured toward the living room. "Why don't we have a seat while you walk us through what happened? I took a quick peek around outside on my way in, but I'll want to study the area further after we talk. I've also called my forensics team to come by to see what they can pick up."

That surprised her, since this wasn't his jurisdiction. Gage didn't seem to have a problem with his decision, though, most likely because of the possible connection to the murder case. When Detective Earle started toward the living room, she stopped him.

"Let's go to the kitchen. I made coffee."

He looked at her as if he'd heard her wrong. Evidently he wasn't used to being offered refreshments at a crime scene. Should she explain that she'd inherited not only Aunt Sybil's house but her inborn compulsion to feed anyone who came through the door? Once again, Gage came to her rescue. "Abby knows me well enough to know I'd probably show up when she called and that I never turn down a cup of coffee. I'm betting she's also set out cookies, too. It's a thing with her."

Her cheeks flushed hot, but there was no use in denying it when the evidence was sitting right there on the kitchen table for everyone to see.

"Help yourselves."

While Gage filled the three mugs, she got a handful of Zeke's treats out of the jar and set them down in front of the county detective. "I thought you might like to get better acquainted with Zeke. I swear he's really a sweetheart. My friends don't have anything to fear from him."

She patted her buddy on the head.

"Not to mention that his loyalty can be bought by almost anyone who has access to his favorite flavor of dog cookies."

The detective picked up one of the treats and gingerly offered it to Zeke. The dog remained on his best behavior and gently took it into his mouth. Since his fingers survived intact with relatively little mastiff drool, Detective Earle smiled and offered Zeke a second one. Scratching the big fellow behind the ears, he gave Abby an inquisitive look.

"So we're friends now? I had the feeling that I wasn't on your list of favorite people."

Couldn't he have simply accepted her peace offering?

"I'm protective of people I care about and won't apologize for that. I do know that it's not your fault Tripp is in jail—not completely, anyway. Regardless, I can't untangle how angry it makes me that he's there. Having said that, Gage vouches for you, and I value his opinion."

She took a cookie and then pushed the plate closer to his side of the table. "And you came when I called. That counts for a lot with me."

Both men sipped their drinks and waited until they'd finished their cookies before speaking again, maybe to give her time to gather her thoughts. Finally, they each pulled out their ever-present notebooks and pens.

"So take us through what happened this evening."

She gave them a summary of the night's events, making quick work of the time spent at the restaurant with her friends and the trip home. When she got to the part about noticing the porch light being out, she slowed down and went into more detail.

"So you actually touched the light bulb?"

"Yes, because I thought it had burned out. I was going to change it, but then I realized it was just loose in the socket." She frowned. "And not just a little loose, either. If it had been unscrewed any farther, it would have likely fallen out."

From there, she told them about Zeke's reaction and her first look at how her portrait had been savaged. She stroked the dog's dark fur, taking comfort from the soft texture and the warmth of his big body. "It's funny, Gage. He had the opposite reaction the other day when the jack-o'-lantern first appeared on the porch. Zeke took one sniff and then acted all happy."

She hesitated, not sure how they would react to what she was about to say. Gage must have noticed, because he said, "Just spit it out, Abby. You never know what might help us with a case."

"Fine. I took his behavior to mean that the artist behind the pumpkin portraits must be someone Zeke knows and likes. But tonight, his reaction was completely different. He was angry and clearly didn't like the scent of the person who'd been out there."

Neither man scoffed at the conclusion she'd drawn. In fact, after making a couple of notes in his small spiral notebook, Detective Earle asked, "Do you know of anyone specific that Zeke doesn't like and why?"

"There have only been a few times that Zeke has taken an immediate dislike to someone. Once when some old ladies ripped into me a few months back when they thought my aunt had been involved in the death of their friend. He didn't make any threatening moves toward those women, though. He just planted himself between me and them."

When she looked to Gage to confirm her story, he nodded and said, "Yeah, I talked to them shortly after that happened, and they admitted he hadn't actually gone near them."

Now here is where it got dicey. "There is another man who stopped by the other day. Zeke must not have liked the tone of his voice or something, because nothing bad actually happened. After the two of us talked, the guy left. There's no reason to think he would've done something like this."

Gage gave her an exasperated look. "Come on, Abby, don't stop there. We need names. Who was it?"

Her stomach wasn't feeling all that settled right now. Maybe the combination of wine followed by coffee and now two . . . no, three cookies. It was that, or maybe the knowledge that she would cause herself more problems with what she was about to say.

"It was Jasper Collins."

Clearly neither man hadn't seen that one coming. Detective Earle took the lead this time. "Was the banker's visit professional or personal?"

It wasn't that clear-cut. "Both, really."

She sighed as she reached for another cookie she didn't really want. "I'll have to backtrack a little to explain. A few days ago, I was part of the group decorating the town for the festival. Three of us were assigned to work together on putting new flowers in the planters up and down Main Street. It was Zoe Brevik, Layla Sheffield, and me. Layla works for Jasper at the bank."

Both men wrote down the woman's name. Gage looked up from his notebook to ask, "So what happened?"

"Jasper thought I may have gotten the impression from some things Layla said that she might be more than just his assistant. He insisted that wasn't the case and wanted to make sure that I wasn't going to spread rumors about them. I've heard he's considering pursuing a career in politics, and I suspect he was worried about what any gossip would do to his reputation in town. Well, and then there's the fact that he's married. For the record, other than Zoe Brevik, who was there at the time, I haven't said anything to anyone about what was said."

Not that Jasper had believed her, the big jerk. She suspected he would be only too happy to throw Layla under the bus if their involvement interfered with the bright and shining future he had planned for himself. It took some effort to rein in her anger, knowing a lot of it stemmed from her own experience with a cheating husband.

She didn't see the need to mention Zoe had also picked up the same vibes from Layla that Abby had, the kind that indicated the woman was harboring some pretty strong feelings for her boss. That didn't mean Jasper felt the same way about her. He could've been trying to deal with an awkward situation as best as he could while trying to avoid any possible fallout.

"Is that the only time the two of you had words?"

"No, he cornered me again this morning. I was working with Kristy and Dean Hake to deliver bags of candy for businesses to hand out on Halloween. Seth Kyser also pitched in to help me carry the boxes into the bank. When Jasper saw us come in, he insisted he had to talk to me right then."

All this talking was making her mouth dry, so she paused to sip her coffee. "He was furious because the police had come to his house to talk to him about the argument he'd had with Ronald Minter at the bank."

She gave Detective Earle a questioning look. "He was sure I had been the one to point you in his direction. I denied it, of course. I told him I had no idea who your source was. I still don't."

He didn't fill in the missing blank for her. "But you knew about the argument?"

Gage set his coffee cup down harder than necessary to glare at her. "And you didn't tell me why?"

"Because I didn't witness the argument myself. I

heard about it from someone who was there, but all she knew is they looked angry. She couldn't hear what they were actually arguing about."

She really hoped neither of the two men would insist that she reveal her source. Although she suspected Jean would be thrilled to be interviewed as a possible witness, she really didn't want to drag her into this mess.

Gage leaned back in his chair. "Ben, do you need to talk to Abby's unnamed source?"

The other man studied her for several seconds. "Probably not. I've already talked to several people who were there that day, as well as Jasper Collins himself. He insisted it was a business discussion about the status on the mortgage the bank held on Minter's farm. After Minter started yelling, Mr. Collins asked him to leave. It's hard to know if that's a true picture of how things went down, since the other party to the conversation is dead. Several people who were out in the lobby said the only words they could make out referred to pumpkins, so I can't really dispute that they were talking about anything else."

Well, darn. She knew more than the detective did, and now wasn't the time to hold anything back. "From what Jasper told me, they weren't talking about the pumpkins on the farm. Well, not in the way you meant, anyway. Detective Earle, I'm sure you've heard about the pumpkin portraits that keep mysteriously popping up around town."

"If you mean like the one that immortalizes Gage here back at the station, then the answer is yes. Although I have to say, Pumpkin Gage is better-looking." He gave Gage an amused glance before turning his attention back to her. "By the way, if you're going to make a habit of serving me coffee and cookies, you should probably call me Ben."

"Well, Ben, the jack-o'-lanterns normally show up in a place associated with the subject of the portrait. Like Gage's showing up at the police department and mine appearing on my front steps."

Both men nodded.

Feeling as if she was about to jump off a cliff right into a river full of trouble, she set her coffee cup down and met each man's gaze in turn. "Well, evidently Jasper's portrait showed up on Layla Sheffield's front porch sitting right next to one of her."

The only sound after that was the ticking of the clock on the wall.

Chapter Nineteen

Abby waited patiently as the two men struggled to absorb the meaning behind what she'd just told them. Of course, she had no way of knowing for sure that Jasper and Layla had ever done anything improper. Her gut instinct was that they had, but that could still be her own past coloring her interpretation of the present.

It was Gage who finally spoke. "Seriously? Those two?"

She shrugged. "Like I said, Jasper swears there's nothing between them beyond the boss-employee relationship. While he did admit that he'd been at her place really early one morning, he insisted it was to drop off some work-related papers. His best guess is that someone saw him leaving her house and assumed the worst."

Ben was writing like crazy, while Gage continued asking questions. "They're lucky Reilly didn't spot the pumpkins. I can only imagine how Mrs. Collins would've reacted to seeing her husband's portrait posted with another woman's on the local social media outlets."

"That's just it. I'm pretty sure Reilly did post them, but only very briefly. Evidently Jasper threw his weight around and demanded they be taken down immediately. The day Reilly took a picture of my portrait, he made sure to ask my permission to post it. Seems his editor asked him to take down one of a couple when the people involved complained. He never mentioned any names."

Gage looked at Ben. "I'll give Reilly a call and ask him to verify their identities to make sure we're all on the same page."

Abby didn't see the need to mention that Leif, Nick, and Zoe also knew about the incident. After all, she didn't know how they found out. No use in unleashing Jasper's temper on them since Gage could confirm the portraits actually existed by talking to Reilly. He might even still be able to get copies of the reporter's pictures.

There wasn't much more to tell. "So anyway, I think Jasper must have leapt to the conclusion that Ronald Minter was carving the portraits. The only thing that I can figure is that he thought it was a publicity stunt to advertise the pumpkin farm and his corn maze. I don't know why he'd think that, though, since there was nothing to link the pumpkins directly to the farm. Certainly there was no proof that Mr. Minter was involved or that the pumpkins were even his to begin with."

On second thought, there was something else she should probably tell them. "You know, when Mr. Collins was here, he was about to leave, but he stopped to study the pumpkin. You know, kind of like he was thinking hard about something. Then looked back at me and said he wondered if Mr. Minter had some idea of who was actually stealing his pumpkins. If so,

DEATH BY JACK-O'-LANTERN   223

considering the kind of man he was, Mr. Minter
would've likely gone out of his way to confront the
culprit. Then Mr. Collins said that if he had, it might
have gotten him killed."

Abby looked from Gage to Ben and then back
again. "He also added that it would be a shame if the
same thing happened to me. I'm not saying he threatened me, you understand."

Although at the time, it had certainly felt that way.

"I think it was his way of warning me to mind my
own business. You know, for safety's sake."

She managed a small smile. "For the record, other
than the one time I ran into Sergeant Montgomery
that day in the woods, I have not gone out of my
way to have any contact with him or anyone else
connected to the investigation."

Not directly, anyway. She might have asked a few
questions, but she had quit doing that, too. "I really
did learn my lesson last time."

She wasn't sure Gage completely believed her, but
at least he said, "Good to know."

Ben rejoined the conversation. "Considering more
portraits have appeared since his murder, that pretty
definitively eliminates Minter as the artist."

The chills were back, making her wish she could
crawl into bed and pull the covers up over her head.
On the other hand, she was in no hurry for Gage and
the detective to leave.

When the doorbell rang, she jumped. Ben immediately stood up. "Sorry, Abby, that's probably my team.
I'll be back after they get started."

He disappeared down the hall, leaving her alone
with Zeke and Gage, who tilted his head to the side as
if listening for something. At the sound of the door

opening and closing, he gave her a quick smile. "Is the brandy still in the cabinet above the fridge?"

When she nodded, he fetched the bottle and poured a sizable dollop into her cup and then topped it off with more coffee. She sipped the powerful brew and savored the slow burn as it slipped down her throat. It tasted delicious, although she had to wonder what effect more alcohol and caffeine would have on her.

"Feeling better? You looked a little shaky there for a minute."

"Thanks, it helped."

She glanced down the hall toward the front door. "So I was right to report what happened out there, wasn't I? It really is a threat aimed right at me."

Even as she asked the question, she really hoped she was wrong. She should have known that Gage wouldn't sugarcoat the situation. "I wish I could tell you differently, but you're right. It was meant to send a clear threat—or maybe a better description is that it's a warning, a message of some kind."

"But other than scaring me half to death, what could it be telling me? I've already told Jasper repeatedly that I haven't been gossiping about him and Layla. I also wasn't the one who told Ben about the argument he had with Mr. Minter. I know he doesn't believe me, but I don't know what else I can do to convince him."

"Don't worry. Ben and I will have a talk with him."

The subtext of that bald statement was clear—it wouldn't go well for the banker if they found out he was behind the attack on her portrait. It wasn't the first time circumstances had given Abby a glimpse of the warrior Gage was under that thin veneer of a friendly local police chief, and she suspected he shared that trait with Ben Earle. While she appreciated that both men were willing to come to her defense, it wasn't as if they could be there twenty-four-seven to make sure the threat wasn't ramped up to something far worse and more direct.

"And if he denies it?"

"Depends on how solid his alibi is. He shouldn't have trouble accounting for his evening, considering we're not dealing with a huge time frame here. You were gone about three hours at the most. It would be different if you'd been gone all day or had gone out the back door and didn't see the pumpkin until you came home or even tomorrow morning."

"What if he does have witnesses who can prove he couldn't have been here?"

Which in some ways was an even scarier prospect, because it meant that there was someone else out there who apparently hated her.

"Then we'll see where the evidence leads us. I really want to know if the knife is the identical make and model as the murder weapon. There may be finger-prints on the knife, or we might get lucky and get something off the porch light."

She wasn't going to hold her breath that they would be that lucky, but she appreciated knowing two different police departments were taking the situation so seriously. Meanwhile, the two of them lapsed into a companionable silence. After a couple of minutes passed, she noticed how he kept staring in the direction of the front door.

"I'll be fine here on my own, Gage, if you want to see how things are going out front. I'm guessing they've got everything they might need to transport any evidence back to their headquarters, but tell them I have boxes upstairs if they need one for the pumpkin."

"I will."

He stopped to give her shoulder a quick squeeze. "You're strong, Abby. You'll get through this."

"I'm glad you think so."

Then, before he walked away, she said, "There's one thing, Gage. Don't tell Tripp about any of this. I might not be happy with him for being so stubborn, but I also don't want to worry him while he's sitting in that cell."

Gage didn't agree. "Maybe if I did tell him, he'd finally get over his martyr complex. I'm getting tired of him beating me at chess."

Yeah, right. She didn't call him on the lie. The truth was he was worried about the effect the long stay in jail would have on their friend. If nothing else, it had to be playing havoc with Tripp's ability to keep up with his classes.

That was a worry for another day. For now, she'd clean up the kitchen and wait to see what else Ben and Gage had to say about the vandalism before they left for the night. Would they leave her place and head straight over to confront Jasper Collins? She could just imagine how that was going to go over with the man. No matter how it turned out, she hoped they made it clear that he was to stay far away from her, and the farther the better.

She made quick work of clearing the table and then reluctantly walked back to the entryway, so she could watch the activity out on the porch from the narrow window by the front door. From what she could tell, the crime scene techs were packing up. After one pointed at the porch light and said something to Ben, the detective nodded and then knocked on the door.

She hurried to open it.

"Abby, would you have another bulb we can put in place of the one that's in there now? The techs want to take it back to the lab to run some tests—fingerprints and such. We figured you might want us to replace it while we're here, so the front of the house isn't completely dark."

"That's very thoughtful of you. I'll grab one and be right back."

After that, it was only a short time until she waved goodbye to him and Gage and trudged upstairs to see if there was any chance she could actually sleep.

Personally, she wasn't betting on it.

To her surprise, Abby somehow managed to get a decent night's rest. If Zeke hadn't gifted her with a slobbery lick and then snorted in her face, she might have managed to sleep for another hour, maybe even two. She didn't complain about the rude awakening, though, because she was due to meet some people at the high school in a couple of hours to work on the decorations for the festival.

While meetings weren't usually what she'd call fun, this particular work party promised to be better than most. A few of her favorite people would be there, and they'd be doing something more active than sitting around a table and discussing items on an agenda.

She and Zeke made quick work of breakfast, and then the two of them set off for a quick walk around the neighborhood. Between her busy schedule and Tripp being in jail, the poor dog was spending too much time locked up in the house alone.

As they rounded the corner toward home, she patted him on the head. "I promise we'll go for a longer walk after I get back. Maybe even go to the park."

His ears perked up as soon as she mentioned one of his favorite places. He loved the path along the river where he often got to romp with other dogs.

"Better yet, maybe we'll grab some burgers at Gary's Drive-In and eat outside at one of his picnic tables. Then we can walk along the river out there."

Considering "burger" was another of Zeke's favorite words, her promise seemed to give him new energy. Her, too. She loved Gary's Number Three Special, which consisted of a double cheeseburger, fries, and a strawberry shake. Considering the total salt and cholesterol content, it was something she saved for special occasions and desperate circumstances. In this instance, it was dealing with the trauma of having a knife shoved through her forehead, at least figuratively.

Which had her wondering what Gage and Ben had learned from their talk with Jasper and his wife. If neither of them had contacted her by later in the afternoon, maybe she'd give one of them a call. This wasn't a case where she believed no news was good news.

"Come on, Zeke, let's run the rest of the way."

He obligingly let her set the pace as she kicked it into a higher gear. She couldn't come close to moving as fast as Tripp did when he took Zeke out for a run, but she did her best. At least one of them was breathing hard as they turned up the sidewalk to the house.

Just as they reached the front porch, a car turned into her driveway.

Suddenly, her speeding pulse had nothing to do with the run. Instead, it was the fear that Jasper or maybe Layla had decided to pay her a personal visit. She breathed a huge sigh of relief when she recognized Ben Earle climbing out of the car.

"My original plan was to call you after I got to the office. But since your place isn't far off my usual route to work, I thought I'd take a chance you were at home and drop by." He pointed off to the north. "I only live about three miles that way."

She unlocked the door. "You hit it lucky. We just got back from our morning walk. Come on inside."

As she waited for him to join her, she unclipped Zeke's leash. He padded on down the hallway to the kitchen, where she could hear him slurping up water at an alarming rate, no doubt getting as much on the floor as he did in his mouth. With luck most of it would've dripped off his jowls before he got close enough to wipe his mouth on her jeans.

Ben took a seat on the couch as she settled in her favorite chair. "So, what's up?"

"Gage and I double-teamed Jasper Collins last night. Our favorite banker didn't much appreciate the visit, but that's not unusual. Most people don't make a habit of serving police officers coffee and dessert."

He offered her a crooked smile. "Not that I'm hinting for any special treats this morning."

She smiled back. "I could pack up a few things to go."

For a second, it looked as if he was actually considering her offer, but then he shook his head. "I'd better not. My doctor wants me watching my diet, and I like your cookies a little too much to share them with my coworkers."

His stance had been relaxed, but now he leaned forward to rest his elbows on his knees, and all traces of humor disappeared. It was obviously time to get back to business. "Like I said, we met with Jasper and his wife last night."

That much came as no surprise. "Did you learn anything helpful?"

He shook his head. "It's hard to question someone's alibi when they were having dinner with the mayor and several members of the city council. They might have been able to squeeze in a quick stop at your house on their way home, but that wouldn't make sense. There was too much of a risk that someone would recognize their car or that you might have come home at the wrong moment. Neither Jasper nor his wife strikes me as impulsive or stupid."

While disappointing, it really didn't surprise her that Gage and Ben hadn't been able to solve the mystery that easily. Considering Jasper had already confronted her directly on two separate occasions, it seemed unlikely that he'd stoop to sneaking around and slashing her pumpkin just to make a point.

"I appreciate the fact that you and Gage took this so seriously. That means a lot."

That much was true. But what was she supposed to do now besides lock herself inside the house and never go out?

Ben must be a mind reader, because his next words addressed that very issue. "My gut feeling is that this was supposed to get someone's attention—and not necessarily yours. We'll keep pursuing what leads we have, so don't think we've given up on finding the culprit. For now, my advice is just go about your normal routine, but use good common sense. Keep your doors locked and the outside lights on. If you're out working in the yard, keep Zeke with you. I know he's mostly friendly, but I'm guessing he can get pretty fierce when someone he cares about is threatened."

The fellow in question came trotting into the room and made a beeline for Ben. She tried to warn the man about the impending slobber, but it was already too late. The dog plopped his big head on Ben's knee and waited to be petted.

It was hard to tell if the detective didn't notice the growing water spot on his slacks or if he simply didn't care. Regardless, he stroked Zeke's fur, which had the dog moaning with bliss.

"Well, I'd better get going. If anything comes up or if you have any questions, don't hesitate to call me directly. Otherwise, when I have some definitive answers, I'll be back in touch. I'm hoping to get the report from the forensics team soon, but a damaged pumpkin probably won't get high priority."

After gently shoving Zeke's head off his knee, Ben studied the wet spot on his pants and then shrugged. "We did take Jasper aside and tell him to leave you alone, and that even if he hadn't meant to threaten you, what he'd said to you could certainly be construed that way. Then I made it clear that even though I wouldn't reveal my sources, you were not one of the people who tipped me off about his argument with Ronald Minter. We made sure not to mention Jasper's pumpkin portrait in front of his wife, but we did tell him we were aware of it and where it had been found. He appreciated our discretion and said under the circumstances he understood why you would have told us about them and the fight."

"So I shouldn't have any more problems with him?"

"It seems unlikely at this point. But like I said, if something comes up, call me."

"I will."

She followed him to the door and locked it behind him. "Come on, Zeke. I need to get ready to leave."

Rather than follow her upstairs, Zeke sought out his favorite sunbeam on the living room floor and made himself comfortable. Lucky dog. Although it was only midmorning, a nap in the sun sounded good about now. Instead, she'd put on a little makeup so she wouldn't look quite so haggard. Although she'd slept all right, the effects of last night's adventure had left her with dark circles under her eyes and looking a bit pale. At least she'd be spending most of the day working on final preparations for the Halloween Festival. Hopefully, she would be able to relax and not have to worry about who in Snowberry Creek had felt compelled to stab her pumpkin.

And what's worse, whether they had any other knives with her name on them.

With that chilling thought, she picked up her keys and headed for the high school, where she'd spend her afternoon surrounded by people, one of whom might just know the answer to that question.

Despite the bright sunshine, she shivered.

Chapter Twenty

Abby signed in at the main office at the high school and then found her way to the pair of empty portable classrooms that were being used as a staging area for the Halloween night event. She walked in to the familiar sight of the mayor's assistant flipping through a stack of papers on her clipboard. Connie happened to look up at that instant and smiled as soon as she spotted her. "Hey, Abby! Glad you could make it."

"I'm happy to be here."

Surprisingly, that was true on so many levels. Back when she had been married to both her husband and the business they'd built together, she'd been too caught up in the endless pursuit of a healthy bottom line to get involved in anything else. Although proud of their success, she now regretted how much it had cost her—not just in the breakup of her marriage, but in other personal relationships, too.

She'd come to view the various work parties she'd gotten drawn into here in Snowberry Creek as an investment in herself. The people involved came together to accomplish a specific goal, whether it was sprucing up the park or decorating for a holiday celebration. At the same time, friendships were formed, and that made all the difference.

"Abby?"

Connie's soft question jarred her out of her reverie. She gave her head a quick shake. "Sorry, Connie, I didn't mean to drift off like that. Were you saying something?"

"Just that you can have your pick of projects today." She pointed across the room. "That group is painting the boards for the beanbag toss. That bunch is working on the ring toss. Kristy Hake is next door cleaning up the tables we rented for her pie-eating contest. Once that's done, she plans to finish up the posters for the event. I'm sure she'd appreciate some help."

"I'll head over to give her a hand."

Connie checked something off on her list. "When you're done helping Kristy, they'll be bringing in the portable booths that we'll be using for various games and for the face painting. They'll need a good scrubbing as well, if you have time to help with that."

"No problem. I plan to be here all afternoon."

Just then a bell rang out, signaling it was time for the students' mad rush from one class to the next. The sound briefly flashed Abby back to her own days in high school, where life seemed to have been lived at a dead run. As she walked out of the portable room, she paused to watch a group of kids stream out of the building, heading for another cluster of portable classrooms. The buildings were a symbol of the recent growth spurt in the population of Snowberry Creek.

While that made for a healthier tax base for the whole area, she really hoped it didn't change the small-town flavor that she was coming to love so much.

For now, she'd work on shoring up the connections and friendships she already had.

Kristy looked pleased to see her. "Hey, Abby! Glad to see a friendly face."

"Connie said you could use some help."

"That I could. I just got started, and we have about twenty of these tables to scrub. Not all of them are for the pie-eating contest, but I thought we might as well clean all of them while we're at it."

Abby looked around. "Where would you like me to start?"

Kristy pointed to a couple of canvas bags in the corner. "There's another sponge in that first bag, as well as some rubber gloves, if you want to protect your hands. I'll help you set up a couple of tables to start on. I told Dean we should be done around twelve thirty. He's going to bring me lunch and then borrow some kids from the PE class to carry the finished tables over to the storeroom off the gym. I can give him a call and ask him to bring lunch for you, too, if you'd like. He promised me one of Frannie's club sandwiches and a side salad." She frowned and patted her hips. "I'd rather have the fries, but I'm trying to resist them these days."

Abby understood that all too well. "I'll have the same."

After calling Dean to place Abby's order, Kristy stripped off her own gloves and helped her set up several of the tables. As they worked, Abby noticed the other woman's jewelry was a perfect match for the black-and-white top and slacks she was wearing. The earrings were small white flowers with black centers, the bracelet was all flowers, and the necklace was a trio of the same flowers hanging from a simple chain.

"I really love your taste in jewelry, Kristy. Those earrings, necklace, and bracelet are adorable."

The compliment clearly pleased the other woman. "They're just costume jewelry and not worth much, but I love them. I wear a lot of black and white, so they go with several of my outfits."

Abby stepped closer to get a better look. "They give off a vintage vibe. I seem to remember seeing pictures of my mom wearing something similar back when she was in college."

Kristy studied the bracelet. "I don't know how old they are. Dean got them for me as a surprise a while back. He was poking around in some secondhand store he frequents and saw them."

"Well, he has excellent taste, and not just in wives."

That comment had the other woman laughing. "I'll tell him that, although there are days he might argue that point."

Despite Kristy's comment, once again Abby couldn't help but envy the couple. They were so clearly happily married. She could remember when Chad used to buy her small gifts, too. In the early days, when they had little money, it might have been something as simple as one of her favorite candy bars or some grocery store flowers to brighten her day. Like the saying goes, it was the thought that counted.

The truly sad thing was that she couldn't remember when he had quit giving her the small reminders that he loved her. Why hadn't she noticed? If she had, would things have turned out differently for them?

No, she wasn't going to go down that road again. That was the past, and she had a future to figure out. For sure, this was a day for hanging out with people she liked and forgetting all about the events of the previous evening. Determined to shrug off all dark thoughts, she started scrubbing the nearest table.

They worked in silence for a few minutes while a small radio sitting on the windowsill played some classic rock. When they'd finished the first batch of tables, they collapsed them and set up the next four. Before starting in again, Kristy got each of them a diet cola out of a small cooler in the corner.

She held one out to Abby. "Not to bring up a sore subject, but did you get things straightened out with Jasper Collins? I've been thinking about you since you two tangled at the bank."

How much should she share? She decided the less said, the better. "I think we're good. I haven't seen him since, which is fine with me. How about you and Dean? Are things going any better?"

"A little. Our attorney started the paperwork asking the court to let us start clearing out the house sometime next week. At the very least, someone should empty out the refrigerator, and the freezer if there was one. We don't even know whether or not the power is still on. That said, we're not about to pay the utility bills out of our own pocket until we know we can recoup the loss." She rolled her shoulders. "It's all such a hassle that I'm not sure it's even worth pursuing our claim for the estate. I've never been inside the house, and Dean hasn't been there for years. We have no idea if there's even anything worth saving or if it's all junk. Considering Ronnie's cheapskate nature, I'm betting on the latter."

Abby froze for a second. Did she just say Ronnie? And if so, was Kristy talking about who she thought she was?

Only one way to find out. "Dean and Ronald Minter were cousins?"

The other woman wrinkled her nose and nodded. "Yes, they were, on their moms' side. Although not many folks remember they were related. That's mainly because there was a huge falling-out between their parents when the boys were still teenagers. And of course, Dean is such a people person, and Ronnie was the biggest jerk in town."

She sighed. "Considering the circumstances of his death, I was reluctant to mention his name. I know how awful finding his body must have been for you, and I figured you're probably trying hard not to think about it."

Like she could think about anything else right now.

"I appreciate your consideration, but there's no need to walk on eggshells around me. It was awful, but I hardly knew the man."

"Still—"

Abby had no idea what Kristy had been planning to say when she suddenly stopped talking and frowned. She walked over to the window to stare outside. "We'd better get back to work. Dean has gotten here early and is headed this way. We should be able to wash the last few tables and have them ready to go by the time he gets the kids organized to start carrying them out of here."

Without another word, she went back to scrubbing the tables as if the world might end if they didn't finish in the next few minutes. Clearly the subject of Ronald Minter had upset Kristy more than it had Abby, but then, the man had been family. Even if he and Dean had been on the outs for years, his death still had to have hurt.

Between the two of them, they finished the tables quickly and got them stacked near the door for Dean and his crew. With that much done, they pulled three of the classroom desks out from the wall where Kristy had shoved them to make room and gave them a quick scrub, too. When Dean finally joined them with their lunches, they were ready to sit down for a while and enjoy the sandwiches and salads.

Abby let Dean and his wife lead the conversation. He told her several really funny stories about things that had happened at some of the previous festival nights at the high school. One year the former principal had made the mistake of renting a dunk tank and volunteering to be the first member of the faculty to be the target.

Dean's laugh was a deep rumble. "The poor man was half-drowned by the time the varsity baseball and softball pitchers got done with him. Gotta give him credit for sticking with it, though. None of the other volunteers lasted anywhere near that long. That was the one and only time we've had a dunk tank. I always offer to rent one again, but for some reason no one here wants me to do it."

Abby gave him a wry look. "I can't imagine why. Well, other than that it had to be pretty chilly getting dumped in a vat of unheated water in the fall, not to mention after dark and outside."

Dean grinned at her. "Yeah, other than those things."

From there, they moved on to talking about the pie-eating contest. Kristy was the expert on the event. "We have to order more and more pies every year to make sure we don't run out. Seriously, it has become a matter of school pride for the winner to be a member of the varsity football team. But the contestants aren't just kids. We get a bunch of the local men, and even a few of the women. It's really something to see. Sort of gross, but entertaining for sure."

Abby finished the last of her salad. "Despite all the work it takes to put on a festival like this, I'm really looking forward to it. I can't wait to see all the little trick-or-treaters hitting the stores on Main Street. I think it's really sweet of the veterans group to volunteer to provide escort for the munchkins." She meant that. "I'm also hoping to get done with my duties there early enough to spend some time here at the festival."

"It should be fun."

Dean started cleaning up their trash. "My only concern is that the homeless vet the police have been hunting for will show up in town. I've heard the members of the veterans group are all dressing up in camo and everything. It would be easy for that guy to slip into town unnoticed until it was too late."

Now Abby was confused. "Too late for what?"

Kristy reached for her husband's hand with a worried look. "Well, it seems obvious he killed poor Ronald. Who knows why he did such a terrible thing? And what if all the noise and crowds set him off again? There's no telling how many people could get hurt before the police could capture him."

Dean was looking pretty grim. "I have a concealed carry permit, but I don't normally feel the necessity to go around armed here in Snowberry Creek. Still, ever since Ronnie was butchered, I keep a gun with me all the time." He paused to look out the window. "Well, not here at the school, of course, but pretty much everywhere else I go. The man is a trained killer, and he's out there wandering around free."

Abby's first instinct was to leap to Kevin's defense, but she held back. It wasn't as if she could prove he was innocent, and the Hakes were basing their fears on the fact that he was the only suspect the police seemed to be seriously pursuing. All in all, it was hard to understand how he'd managed to elude capture for so long already. Rather than offend her new friends by saying the wrong thing, she concentrated on finishing the last few bites of her sandwich.

When she was done, Dean carried the bag that held their trash over to the door. "I'll take that out to the dumpster after I get the kids organized to haul the tables over to the storeroom. Do either of you need anything else while I'm out and about?"

Abby and Kristy both looked around the room. Finally, his wife said, "Not that I can think of right now. We still have a few cold drinks left. They should hold us until we're done with the posters I need to make."

"Okay, I'll be back in a few with my helpers."

After that, the afternoon went quickly. Abby couldn't remember the last time she had made signs with poster board and tempera paints, but it was fun. After spreading their creations out to dry, they went next door to help with the last few items on Connie's long list of chores.

When they were done, she made sure to walk out to the parking lot with several of the others. Whether it was because of Dean's worry about Kevin still being on the loose or the attack on her pumpkin, she felt far safer being part of a crowd. She hated that recent events made her feel that way, but there wasn't much she could do about it.

All in all, she was rethinking her promise to take Zeke out to Gary's Drive-In for dinner, which was located off by itself outside of the city limits. As she followed the others out of the parking lot and drove through town to her own house, everything looked peaceful and quiet. It was a nice reminder that this was a good town filled with people who came together to make Snowberry Creek be the best it could be.

Darned if she let a few bad apples spoil her new home for her or force her to huddle behind locked doors alone and afraid.

On the other hand, she wasn't all that anxious to sit alone by the river with only Zeke for protection. There were at least one or two other people she knew who loved Gary's burgers as much as she did.

She hit Gage's number on speed dial and waited for him to answer. When he did, she asked, "So tell me, would a meal of a cheeseburger, fries, and a shake constitute a bribe? Because I'm thinking about ordering one for dinner and thought the local police chief, the deputy on guard duty, and a certain prisoner might like me to order a few extra."

To give the man credit, he did hesitate, no doubt thinking about his daughter's reaction if she found out. "Any chance you could make them double cheeseburgers?"

That cracked her up. Evidently when the man decided to cross over to the dark side, he didn't hold back. "As long as I can bring my dog with me, I'm sure that could be arranged."

"See you when you get here."

* * *

Deputy Chapin had already relieved her of a chocolate shake and the bag containing his burger and fries. She carried the remaining three sacks around the corner to where her other two dinner guests stood waiting for her. Seeing Gage had already opened the door to Tripp's cell, she immediately released her hold on Zeke's leash, letting go just in time to keep him from hauling her down the hall at a dead run.

She followed at a slightly more leisurely pace. Once again, Tripp let Zeke take him down, which resulted in a fast and furious wrestling match on the floor. His quarters were a bit crowded for an all-out tussle, but the two males seemed to be enjoying themselves. Gage watched them for a few seconds before turning his attention in her direction with a smile.

"You caught me on the perfect night. Sydney is at a sleepover at a friend's house, so I was on my own for dinner."

When he reached for his wallet, she waved him off. "It's my treat. You're saving me from eating alone, and I was definitely in the mood for some company."

Tripp rolled back up to his feet. "Seriously? You would rather hang out in jail than call one of your friends to go out to a nice restaurant for dinner?"

She gave him a withering glance. "I did call one of my friends, and he happens to work at the jail. Sorry if you don't approve of my taste in dinner companions."

She understood why the idiot didn't like her hanging out there, but she'd made it equally clear she would as long as he was going to insist on living in that vile cell. "Gage, here's your double cheeseburger, as ordered."

After sitting down at the same small table they'd used to play chess, she set out her own food and then gave Zeke one of the plain burgers she'd ordered for him. Tripp would get his dinner when he apologized. Maybe.

He finally sat down on the end of his bunk. "I know I'm just wasting my breath, but this is no place for you to be."

Did that qualify as an apology? No, not really. To show her displeasure, she moved his dinner farther from the bars that separated him from both her and his food. Then she petted Zeke. "Looks like you're going to eat like a king tonight, boy. I'll even let you have a few fries, but the onion rings and the shake would likely make you sick."

Gage was clearly fighting the urge to laugh. For that matter, so was she. It would be interesting to see if she could out-stubborn her jailbird of a tenant. Right now he was staring at the grease-stained paper bag with greedy eyes.

He held his hands up in surrender. "Fine, you win. I admit it. I'm glad to see you and Zeke."

She met his dark-eyed gaze head-on and waited. After a few seconds, he nodded, acknowledging the truth she really needed to hear from him right then. "Really. It means a lot that you bother."

That concession earned him his dinner. Knowing his appetite, she'd brought him two of the huge burgers and then thrown in an order of onion rings for good measure. As he dug right in, she told the men about her day, not that it was all that thrilling.

As soon as she mentioned that she'd spent time

with the Hakes, Gage set his shake down on the table. "How is Dean doing? I've been meaning to stop by and check on both of them."

Was she the only one who hadn't known about their relationship to Ronald Minter? "Kristy worries about the effect all of this is having on Dean. Something about him having had a health problem last year. She's afraid the stress might cause him to have a relapse. She never said what it was, but she's clearly worried about him."

Gage picked up one of his fries and dipped it in ketchup. "As I recall, it was a minor heart attack. He retired from working construction and started doing handyman work around town. He doesn't take on all that many jobs, but I think that's by choice, not because of any health reasons. Mostly he does odd jobs for widows and senior citizens who need small repairs done."

"That sounds like something he'd do. That probably leaves him more time for his metal detecting."

Tripp had finished his first burger and was unwrapping his second. "That always seemed like it would be a huge waste of time. Seriously, does he ever find anything worthwhile?"

"Kristy says they've found a few things. I know one of the bracelets she wears was one of their better finds. She said they started doing it as a form of exercise when Dean got tired of just walking in the neighborhood."

Zeke nudged her arm to remind her that he was still hungry. She gave him another burger and then filled his collapsible bowl with bottled water. Tripp laughed as the big dog splashed as much water on the floor as he managed to drink. It eased Abby's heart to see him enjoying himself.

He leaned out of his cell long enough to pick up the empty bowl. "Let me refill that for you, Zeke. It won't be your fancy bottled water, but it tastes all right."

While he was busy with the dog, Gage leaned in closer to murmur "Any more problems that I should know about?"

She shook her head. "No, everything's been quiet."

Tripp must have had ears like a bat, because he immediately marched out of his cell to loom over her. "What kind of problems have you been having? And don't bother to lie. I'll know."

When she gave Gage a questioning look, he just shrugged, leaving it up to her how much she wanted to tell Tripp. Fine. Maybe knowing someone had vandalized her pumpkin might finally convince him to get his backside out of that jail cell sooner rather than later.

"Someone took a combat knife to my pumpkin portrait last night."

He dropped to one knee to bring himself down to her eye level. "Were you home when it happened?"

"No, I was out to dinner with Glenda, Louise, and Jean. I came home to hear Zeke pitching a fit and noticed the porch light was out. I realized someone had unscrewed the bulb when I went to replace it. That's when I saw the pumpkin had been slashed several times." She shuddered at the memory.

"The worst part was that whoever did it left the knife sticking right between my eyes . . . its eyes . . . oh heck, you know what I mean."

Gage took over. "Ben Earle and I responded to her

call. His forensics team is doing a full workup, but it's too soon for him to have gotten any results."

Tripp glared at his friend. "Tell him to hurry it up. She doesn't need a threat like this hanging over her head. Do something."

Gage didn't appreciate the implied criticism. "Did you not hear me say that Ben and I personally responded to her call? We also went right out to talk to the only suspect we had. Considering his alibi was rock solid, that didn't get us very far. We're also checking with shops in the area to see if any of them have sold that kind of combat knife. Admittedly, that's a long shot. They're too readily available, not to mention they can be ordered online. If Ben's forensics team manages to come up with any solid leads, we'll go after whoever was responsible."

He glared at Tripp, putting a little temper in his next words. "Regardless, don't go pointing fingers at me for not doing enough. Remember, you're the one spending all his time flaked out on that cot and staring at the ceiling."

Tripp rose back up to his full height. "What's that supposed to mean?"

Gage tossed his pack of fries back down on the table and stood up. "It means you're not helping the situation by sitting inside those bars. Maybe you'd serve your friend better if you found him and convinced him to talk to us."

"Why? So that detective can throw him in jail for a crime he didn't commit and close the books on the case?"

Okay, this was getting ugly. Even Zeke had crowded closer to Tripp, offering his friend backup while he growled at Gage. She shoved her chair back and grabbed Zeke's leash. "Stop it, all three of you. This bickering isn't accomplishing anything."

Then she gave Zeke's leash a hard yank and firmly ordered him to sit. Oddly enough, both Gage and Tripp also responded to her sharp order and dropped back down on their seats, too. It would've been funny if they weren't still glaring at each other.

"Please, guys, let's not do this." She gave each of them a sharp look. "I just wanted to relax and enjoy one of Gary's finest with friends. Right now, the burger I just ate feels like a rock in my stomach."

Although the two men didn't apologize to each other, they each mumbled "sorry" to her. At least that was something. She sipped her shake, enjoying the rich flavor of fresh strawberries and real ice cream. As they finished up, she handed Tripp the last two hamburger patties so he could hand-feed them to Zeke.

While the two concentrated on that, she turned her attention back to Gage. She shouldn't prod him about the ongoing murder investigation, but it wouldn't hurt to skate around the edges with a few indirect questions. "Is there anything else I should know? You know, about anything at all?"

Smart man that he was, he knew what she was up to. "If Ben's learned anything new about the murder case, he hasn't told me. One odd thing, though. He decided to talk to Layla Sheffield about her portrait. But when he called her work number, he was told she'd taken a short leave of absence from the bank. He verified that with their personnel department, by the way. If she gave a reason for it, they wouldn't tell him without a court order. Since she's not a suspect in anything, it's unlikely he'd be able to get one."

Interesting. She mulled that over while bagging up the detritus from their dinner.

"And she wasn't at home?"

The lines bracketing Gage's mouth deepened. "No, and no one has talked to her or seen her since the day she helped you plant flowers."

"Not even Jasper?"

"Not even. Evidently she bypassed him and contacted human resources at the regional office to request her leave. The people at the bank here in town learned about it from them."

They both knew the man was determined to protect his precious pristine reputation in town. "Do you believe him?"

"The jury is out on that."

His succinct answer sent a chill straight up her spine. Maybe it was time to go home and hunker down behind locked doors. Tripp must have had similar thoughts.

"Gage, make sure she gets home safely."

She doubted the lawman appreciated his prisoner issuing orders like that, but he didn't argue. Regardless, it was time for her to leave.

Gage stood up at the same time she did. "Look, I'm going to go check in with my deputy and then get a couple of things from my office before heading home for the night. I'll meet you by the back door in a few minutes."

Without waiting for her to respond, he picked up their trash and walked away. Once again, she and Tripp watched him disappear around the corner. As soon as he was out of sight, Tripp stepped out of his cell and held out his arms as if to hug her.

As much as she wanted that small bit of comfort, she protested. "Tripp, the camera."

He immediately wrapped his arms around her, pulling her in close enough to hear his heartbeat. "To heck with the camera. Let them watch."

When she relaxed against him, he eased up enough that she could breathe. "I'm sorry I wasn't there for you last night."

"That's all right."

Even though it wasn't. Not by a long shot.

With that unhappy thought, she broke free of his embrace and reached for Zeke's leash. At least the dog didn't fight her this time and followed her down the hall toward the exit. When Tripp called her name, she waved her hand over her shoulder without looking back. "Sorry, but I really need to get out of here, and so do you."

The last thing she heard was the sound of his cell door slamming shut.

Chapter Twenty-One

Zeke did a slow stretch and then picked a different sunny spot to sleep in next. Abby envied the dog. While she enjoyed spending time puttering around in the yard on a warm fall day, she was anything but relaxed. At least she could work off her excess energy by getting some of the yard work done.

But rather than taking pride in her accomplishments, all she could think about was Tripp. There hadn't been a repeat performance of the Snowberry Creek Work Release Program. Had Gage gotten complaints about him letting Tripp out of jail long enough to clean up the leaves in her yard? She hoped not.

Layla Sheffield was the other person who had been on her mind all morning. She really hoped the woman was all right. Maybe she'd had a family emergency or something, but the timing seemed a little strange.

Reminding herself that it was none of her business, she turned her attention back to deadheading the last of the roses. She was just finishing up when her phone rang. The number on the screen wasn't familiar, but she answered anyway. With the festival so close, she'd been getting calls from people from both the quilting guild and the seniors committee to verify that all the last-minute details were being taken care of.

"Hello?"

A deep voice responded. "It's me, Abby."

"Tripp?"

"Yeah, I borrowed Deputy Chapin's phone. I wanted to say again that I'm sorry about last night."

She wandered over to the steps and sat down in the sun. "For what specifically? There are so many possibilities, and I want to make sure which ones you're talking about."

"Brat."

She smiled. "Yeah, well, I always say go with your strengths."

He chuckled, just as she hoped he would. "How about I tell you what I wanted to apologize for, and you can let me know if I miss anything important?"

"It's a good thing I don't have to be anywhere until later this afternoon. This could take a while, so I'm making myself comfortable here on the front steps and soaking up some rays."

"Like I said, brat."

When he didn't immediately launch into his "forgive me" spiel, she gave him a bit of a nudge. "Time's a wasting, Tripp. I have weeds to pull, a dog to pet, and all kinds of important things to get done."

"Fine." After a much-put-upon sigh, he said, "Mostly I'm really sorry I wasn't there when your pumpkin got destroyed and that you had to deal with that all on your own. I also know you don't understand why I haven't offered to hunt down Kevin for the cops just so I can get out of here."

She immediately cut him off. "You're wrong about

that, Tripp. I understand the reasons why you're doing what you're doing. I just don't agree that it's the best way to help Sergeant Montgomery."

How much should she tell him?

Abby settled for saying, "I know you believe he's innocent. So do I. Having said that, not everyone feels that way, and knowing he's still out there wandering around might be making some people nervous. I won't mention any names, but I know at least one person who has taken to carrying a gun in case he needs to defend himself from Kevin."

Tripp sounded frustrated. "We both know Kevin does his best to stay away from people. He doesn't like the way they stare at him, and he does stick out even in a crowd."

"But that's the problem. Halloween is almost here, and your friends from the veterans group are all going to be dressed in their uniforms that night. Kevin could wander through town and not necessarily be noticed at all. But if someone does spot him out on the street, there's no telling how people will react. I'm worried about him."

Tripp's vocal reaction to that idea ended up being something else he felt obligated to apologize for. "Sorry, Abby. I shouldn't have said that. I hadn't considered that possibility."

"Don't worry about it, Tripp. I've heard worse." Even said worse, when the occasion called for it.

"I'll let Gage know to keep an eye out for Kevin on the off chance he does come into town."

They lapsed into silence, but then Tripp came up with a new topic for discussion. "So, we both know what I'll be wearing on Halloween."

"Are you talking about your lovely orange jumpsuit,

or your camouflage-colored BDUs? Because if I have
a vote, it will be your G.I. Joe disguise."

He let that pass without comment. "I've been curious about what kind of costume you've come up with
to wear."

"It's a secret. You'll have to opt for your soldier suit
and be out patrolling Main Street to find out."

He called her bluff. "In other words, you haven't
figured anything out yet."

No one ever said he was slow on the uptake.
"Maybe that's true, but I can always wear your camo
gear since it sounds like you'll be opting for your jailhouse attire."

That had him laughing. "That's quite an image,
considering two of you wouldn't fill out my uniform."

That was an exaggeration, but he wasn't far wrong.
He was half a foot taller than she was and packed a
lot more muscle on his frame than she'd ever dream
of having. She'd look like a kid playing dress-up in her
dad's uniform.

"I'll come up with something eventually."

"The clock is ticking."

"I know. I can always drive into Seattle and check
out a couple of the party shops. Maybe something will
catch my eye."

"Sounds like a good idea. Maybe they have a
princess dress in your size. I can just see you with a
tiara and scepter. Or, better yet, a pumpkin costume,
or maybe a scarecrow. Worse comes to worst, you can
cut a couple of holes in a sheet and go as a ghost."

"Thanks for all the helpful suggestions."

"Just a second, Abby."

She could hear a murmur of voices in the back-
ground. When Tripp came back on the line, he said,

"Sorry, my time is up. Seems the ever-charming Detective Earle is on his way down to see me. Somehow I doubt he'll be bringing me cookies or one of Gary's burgers."

"Probably not."

She could sense his reluctance to end the call. She felt the same way. Finally he said, "Are we okay?"

"Yeah, we are. Thank the deputy for me for letting you use his phone."

"I will."

As much as she hated that the call was about to end, she felt better for having talked to Tripp again. Her good mood lasted right up until a movement along the front edge of the yard caught her attention. Layla Sheffield had just stepped into sight, staring at Abby and clutching a combat knife in her hand.

Abby swallowed hard and held her phone in a death grip. Struggling to stay calm, she whispered, "Uh, Tripp, do me a favor. Please tell Detective Earle I've just found Layla Sheffield—or, actually, she found me. He knows who she is. He'll want to know that the knife she's carrying looks just like the one that was stuck in my pumpkin."

Tripp yelled, "Detective, get here quick. Emergency."

Then his voice dropped back down to normal volume. "Abby, stay on the line. Get Zeke and lock yourself in the house."

Did he think she hadn't thought of that herself? The trouble was she wasn't sure she'd make it that far before Layla caught up with her. She also wouldn't abandon Zeke. If she called him to her side, who knew how the other woman would react? Knowing the police would already be on their way gave her the courage to stay right where she was.

Rather than ignore the woman, perhaps it would be better to engage her in conversation. "Hi, Layla. It's a nice day, isn't it? Zeke is sure enjoying basking in the sun."

Hearing his name mentioned, Zeke lifted his head to see if the conversation involved food. He lumbered to his feet as soon as Abby pulled one of his treats from her pocket. After giving himself a good shake, he trotted over to join her on the porch. She gave him his cookie and then latched onto his collar—not that there was much she could do about it if he really wanted to resume his nap in the grass. She laid the phone in her lap and started stroking Zeke's head.

Layla had moved a little closer but kept a wary eye on Zeke. "What kind of dog is he?"

"My late aunt adopted him through a shelter, so we don't really know much about his past for sure. However, the general consensus is that he's mostly mastiff of some kind. He's quite handsome, isn't he?"

"If you say so." There was a hint of a smile in Layla's voice, although her facial expression was anything but amused.

Abby continued to talk about the dog, hoping it would keep her uninvited guest focused on something other than the knife in her hand. "I like his jowls. They give him such a distinguished look."

Not to mention they hid his huge teeth. While Zeke might be pretty mellow most of the time, mastiffs were bred to protect. That didn't mean she wanted to risk him getting hurt if the woman suddenly decided to go on the attack, which could happen any second if she were to notice the three police cruisers Abby could see headed their way. Their lights were flashing, but at least they had the good sense not to use the sirens.

To keep Layla's attention focused on Abby herself, she asked, "Was there something you needed?"

She shrugged. "I was thinking about slashing your tires like I just did Jasper's."

Her smile was more than a little creepy. "I slashed his wife's tires first. Made her late for some charity function. You should've heard her squeal like a pig when she realized she wasn't going anywhere soon. Bethany is not the kind to take care of such problems on her own, so I figured she would call Jasper first thing. And don't you know he came running like he does every time she snaps her fingers? Can you imagine the look on his face the second he discovered his car had four flats, too?"

Looking pretty pleased with herself, she laughed. "He's so proud of that car, you know. It suits his self-image of being a mover and a shaker. I wanted to fix that for him, too, by carving 'adulterer' or something in the paint. There wasn't time, though. He prides himself on being the first one in the door every morning, so I had a pretty narrow time frame before the other employees started showing up. Since they'd been told I was called out of town, I couldn't risk being seen."

"That makes sense." At least in a "crazy ex-girlfriend" sort of way.

The police were out of their cars and closing in, but they were still farther away from Layla than she was from Abby. That made the next couple of minutes the most dangerous. "So, why my tires?"

"Jasper broke up with me after he talked to you.

He said you swore that you didn't spread any gossip about us, but we already had another close call with those stupid pumpkins. He said he can't risk Bethany finding out. He makes a good living at the bank, but it doesn't come close to the kind of money he has access to through her family trust. He likes living well, and he's hoping she'll agree to fund his political campaign."

The cops were close enough now that she could recognize Deputy Vinter from the county sheriff's office, as well as two members of the Snowberry Creek Police Department. Good—the more the merrier, as far as she was concerned.

Layla sniffed a little as if fighting back tears. "I finally figured out that he loves her bank account more than he ever loved me. It's so hard to be the other woman in these situations. If news of our affair did come out, we both know I'd be vilified and she'd get all the sympathy. You have no idea what that would be like."

Actually, Abby had firsthand knowledge of that exact situation. The difference was that, in her case, she'd lost everything even though she'd been the wife in the equation. Again, it wouldn't be smart to point that out.

By this point, Layla had eased up her grip on the knife, letting her hand drop down to her side. Maybe she'd simply run out of energy, or else she'd decided that Abby wasn't the right target for her anger.

There was one more question Abby would like to have answered. "So, Layla, I get why you're upset with Jasper and his wife, but why would you destroy my pumpkin portrait?"

"Huh, I didn't know you got one, too."

Her surprise seemed to be too genuine to be faked.

The deputies were almost within pouncing distance, so Abby kept talking. "Yes, I discovered it sitting on my front porch. No idea who left it there. However, night before last, someone totally trashed it. They used a knife that looked a lot like the one in your hand."

Layla lifted her hand again and stared at the knife as if she couldn't quite figure out where it had come from. "How do you know it was like this one?"

"Whoever did it left the knife stuck in the pumpkin."

The other woman studied the knife for a second. "I found this one on the front seat of my car. No idea where it came from, but I figured I might as well put it to good use."

She grinned suddenly and slipped the knife into the sheath hanging from her belt. "It sure did a heck of a job on those tires."

"I can imagine."

Abby tightened her grip on Zeke and held her breath as two of the deputies charged forward as soon as the knife was safely tucked away and took Layla to the ground hard. She fought like a madwoman, but she was no match for her two captors. They had her subdued and handcuffed in record time. It was disturbing to watch, but also a huge relief.

"Abby! Answer me."

She realized the bellow was coming from her phone. How could she have forgotten about being on the phone with Tripp?

She hastened to reassure him. "Sorry, Tripp, the cavalry got here in record time. I'm fine. Really."

The yard was swarming with people in uniforms now. "The police have her in custody, and no one was hurt."

Scared spitless, maybe, but not hurt.

Tripp didn't sound convinced. "Are you sure?"

"Zeke sat right by my side the whole time, and she never got close to me."

His sigh of relief came across loud and clear. "You did a good job of keeping her engaged. But I've got to tell you, those were some of the longest minutes of my life."

"Mine, too."

Well, except for that time when she'd been alone in a deserted parking lot with a murderer and praying the cops would get there in time.

Evidently Tripp was flashing back to that same incident. "This isn't the first time I've been on the phone listening while you talk to someone out to do you harm."

His voice was a deep growl by that point. "I know, Tripp. I'm sorry."

Although it wasn't as if she'd invited Layla to come over. That had been totally out of her control.

"No more, okay?"

"Fine by me."

She'd been hugging Zeke hard while she talked to Tripp. It took her a few seconds to notice there were two grim-faced men standing at the front edge of her lawn. "Um, I've got to go now. Gage and Detective Earle just joined the party and will want to talk to me. I'll check in with you later."

"Glad to know they're with you. Personally, I'm going to go take a nap, because I'm pretty sure this little adventure took another five years off my life."

"Two, tops."

At least he was laughing as he hung up.

Chapter Twenty-Two

It took Abby two attempts to disconnect the call, but she finally succeeded. After sticking her phone back in her pocket, she stood up and waited for Ben and Gage to make their way across the yard to the porch. "Why don't you come in for coffee?"

They silently followed her inside and settled in at her kitchen table while she made coffee and filled a plate with slices of pumpkin bread. She appreciated them giving her a little time to calm down before they launched into their interrogation.

Ben took a bite of the bread. "We don't actually expect you to feed us every time we respond, but this is really good. Thanks."

She took a seat at the table. "Okay, I'm ready. Ask away."

Between consuming the refreshments and them making her repeat everything at least twice, it was almost an hour before they ran out of questions, or maybe the energy to ask any more. That was okay, but she had a few of her own.

"So, do you really think she wasn't the one who attacked my pumpkin?"

Although Gage looked doubtful, Ben nodded. "She admitted to everything else, so I'd be surprised if she picked that one thing to lie about."

"What about her finding the knife in her car?"

Ben shrugged and shook his head. "That seems weird, but there's not much about this case that's been normal. Someone could be setting her up to take the fall."

"Like they did Sergeant Montgomery?"

Ben looked less happy with that particular suggestion. "Could be. It would help if we could talk to him, but the man has a definite talent for hiding. We also don't have the available manpower to search the national forest and every other place where he could've gone to ground. If he stays on the move, that only makes it harder."

Surprised she'd gotten even that much of a concession from him, she didn't want to push him on the subject and so changed topics. "What will happen to Layla? She seemed a little out of it to me. You know, like she'd lost touch with reality or something."

Gage answered that one for her. "She'll likely be facing charges, but it will be up to the judge and the court what happens to her after that. All things considered, Jasper and his wife might prefer to handle their damages quietly if she's willing to make restitution. That might be the best-case scenario for everyone concerned if she also undergoes a court-ordered psych eval. I'll keep you posted."

She really hoped the woman got some kind of help. It was as if losing Jasper had broken Layla somehow. "I'd be glad to testify that she made no threatening moves toward me or Zeke. She said she'd thought about slashing my tires, too, but she didn't."

On second thought, that last part might not actually help Layla's case.

Ben carried his empty plate and cup over to the sink. "You've had quite the week, Abby. Are you going to be okay here by yourself?"

"Yeah, I'll be fine."

Even better once she popped the cork on the bottle of wine in the fridge, but she kept that part of the plan to herself.

"We'll be going. Don't hesitate to call if you need anything."

She dredged up another of her patented smiles she used to reassure lawmen and Tripp. "I will. Zeke and I have a quiet evening planned."

Of course, she'd also intended to spend a relaxing afternoon working in the yard, and just look how that had turned out.

As much as Abby liked and respected Gage Logan, and even Ben Earle, she would rather not find herself standing on the front porch and waving as a large part of the local police force drove away from her house again anytime soon. She suspected the neighbors felt the same way. This had always been a quiet street, but not so much since she'd moved in after her aunt's death.

Rather than return to her yard work, she called Zeke back inside. "Come on, boy. Let's pick out a movie and zone out in front of the television for the rest of the afternoon. Tomorrow is the last full day before the festival, sort of the calm before the storm."

Zeke woofed his agreement and headed straight for his favorite spot on the living room floor. No surprise there. He was always up for a good snooze. That thought had her genuinely smiling for the first time in what felt like hours. There were so many things she couldn't control in her life, it was nice to know some things never changed.

Abby jerked awake in the chair, not sure what had jarred her out of a sound sleep. She blinked several times and then squinted at the clock on the mantel to learn that it was after two in the morning. Wow, she'd been a bit drowsy when the second movie started, but she'd only meant to rest her eyes for a few minutes. She'd slept for nearly five hours.

All seemed quiet, so what had woken her up?

Zeke's usual spot on the floor was empty. Maybe he'd made a noise or something when he got up. Regardless, it was time to head upstairs to bed. She stood up and stretched before walking over to turn on the light over the staircase before turning off the lamps in the living room. Before she got that far, she noticed Zeke sitting in the entryway watching the front door with great interest. His tail was doing a slow sweep back and forth on the floor as he kept his attention riveted on something only he could hear.

Her pulse kicked it up a notch. Was there someone out on her porch? If so, Zeke clearly didn't view the person as any kind of threat. Maybe there was a cat or some other critter sneaking around out there. If so, Zeke's reaction would be a bit out of character for him, since he always took great offense whenever there was a feline incursion into his personal territory. It was a matter of personal honor to run off all cats while making dire threats at the top of his lungs.

She edged closer to the door to peer out the window. She'd left the front light on, so the porch

itself was well lit, but the glow from the single bulb by
the door didn't extend very far into the yard beyond.
It was a relief that she couldn't see any intruders,
whether two-legged or four. But then she glanced
down to the surface of the porch.

What was that?

Although she knew. There was a huge pumpkin sitting right where her previous one had been before it
was destroyed. With her heart in her throat, she unlocked the door and stepped outside. Zeke followed
right behind her, and his reaction was the same as it
had been the first time the mysterious artist had
gifted her with a portrait. He sniffed the pumpkin
and then the whole area around it, his tail a blur.
Clearly whoever had been there was someone Zeke
knew and liked.

She picked up the pumpkin and turned it toward
the light so she could see the face. It was almost
identical to the original, although maybe the smile
wasn't quite as happy-looking. Well, she'd been
through a lot lately, and maybe the artist had picked
up on that. When she went to set it back down, she
noticed something else sitting on the step below. It was
the same kind of container she used to store cookies
in her freezer. For some reason, her instincts were
telling her that she'd just discovered something important. But what?

Thanks to the late hour, it took her a few seconds
to put it all together. She kept a supply of those dis-
posable containers on hand all the time since she gave
away a large percentage of the cookies and other
things that she baked. However, this one was distinc-
tive because it was a new holiday pattern that had only
come on the market a couple of weeks ago. The only

two she'd given away were the couple she'd sent home with Tripp the day after she'd followed him out into the woods. He'd kept one, but he'd taken the other out to Sergeant Montgomery. With Tripp in jail, this couldn't have been his.

That left only one likely possibility. Kevin had brought his back. She held it out to Zeke to sniff. He barked softly and wagged his tail some more. With that, all the pieces came together, or at least she thought they had. If Sergeant Montgomery had returned her container, then he must have also carved her replacement portrait. Despite all of his problems, the vet had an amazing gift for creating real beauty and was secretly sharing it with the entire town.

Should she bring the pumpkin into the house, where it would be safe from harm, or leave it out where it could be admired? Her sleep-fogged brain kept going in circles—inside or outside? Finally, she set it back down on the porch, but where it couldn't be seen from the street. That should keep it safe enough for the rest of the night.

"Let's get to bed, Zeke. I have a busy day tomorrow."

He brushed past her and headed straight upstairs while she locked the door and turned off the lights on the first floor. As she made her way up the steps, it occurred to her to wonder how Sergeant Montgomery had found out about her original portrait being destroyed. Had he been the one to stab it to pieces? No, she rejected that idea out of hand. He might have some issues stemming from his time in combat, but she couldn't picture him slipping through town in the dark of night just to attack his own creation and scare her in the process.

But that didn't change the fact that he had been

around, or else he wouldn't have known she needed a replacement portrait. Well, she didn't actually *need* one, but it felt surprisingly good to have that new one sitting out there on the porch. Somehow its presence erased some of the ugliness from the vandalism and soothed her fear from seeing that combat knife shoved deep into the smiling face on the first one.

As she changed into her favorite pajamas, she kept thinking about the homeless vet. It made sense that he knew this was her house, since Tripp lived in the cottage on the back of her property. Clearly this wasn't the first time he'd been there at night, but how often had he come prowling around? Was he still out there somewhere?

She flipped off her bedroom light. Cloaked in darkness, she felt her way across the familiar territory of her bedroom to reach the window. The back of her property was surrounded on three sides by huge cedars and Douglas firs, which cast the entire yard in extra dark shadows. Anyone could be hiding out there. Oddly enough, she didn't feel threatened by that possibility. She lifted her hand and gave a quick wave, just like she did whenever she spotted Tripp out on the prowl.

Zeke joined her at the window and whined just a little, as if to ask what was going on. She patted his head and ruffled his fur. "It's okay, boy. I'm probably just being silly thinking the sergeant is out there watching over us."

After several more seconds passed without her spotting any sign of movement in either the yard or the surrounding trees, she crawled into bed and went to sleep.

* * *

It was a crisp fall morning with only a few wisps of clouds overhead in the bright blue sky. Rather than drive, Abby decided to walk the few blocks to her meeting at city hall. Sunny fall days could be a rarity in the Pacific Northwest, and she didn't want to miss out on a chance to enjoy one to the fullest. Any day now, clouds and rain would move in and stay for weeks at a time. With luck, the weather would hold for another few days. A little thing like rain wouldn't keep the trick-or-treaters from turning out in full force or interfere with the rest of the festival. Regardless, dry weather would make the events a lot more pleasant for everyone involved.

She set off at a brisk pace and didn't stop until she reached Main Street. There, she paused to catch her breath and to enjoy the view. Some of the houses she'd passed along the way had been decked out with all kinds of Halloween decorations, mostly jack-o'-lanterns, ghosts, and witches. The city itself had gone all-out in the business district. Every store and business on Main Street now sported seasonal finery. The decorations ran the gamut from planters full of brightly colored mums to strings of orange and black lights to carved pumpkins. There were even a few enormous inflatable black cats and ghosts.

She wasn't sure why, but her personal favorite was one of those tall inflatable dancing men waving its arms. He was ghostly white with black circles for eyes and a gaping mouth shaped to look as if he was booing. Cute.

It was time to get moving again. All of the various

committee heads were supposed to report to the
conference room at city hall for one last meeting to
make sure everything was in place for tomorrow's
events. She would be only too glad to report that her
groups had completed all their tasks on time.

If she hurried, she could pick up a latte on her way.
As she made her way down the block to Something's
Brewing, she spotted Dean and Kristy Hake walking
out of the bank a short distance ahead. She started to
wave but then dropped her hand back down to her
side. Every step Dean took reflected a lot of anger. His
hands were curled up in tight fists, and his face was
flushed bright red. Kristy tripped along behind him,
her expression worried when he kept ignoring everything she said to him.

Whatever business they'd had inside the bank
hadn't gone well. Had they tangled with Jasper Collins
over the Minter farm again?

She slowed down, not wanting to get any nearer
to where the pair had stopped beside their vehicle.
Dean was looking a little less agitated now, so maybe
whatever Kristy was saying was having a soothing
effect. She hoped so. Getting worked up like that
couldn't be good for him, especially considering he
had a heart condition.

Finally, they both got in their car and drove away,
headed in the opposite direction of city hall. Had
they forgotten about the meeting? Maybe they had
another stop to make before it started. She waved as
they passed by, but neither one acknowledged her
greeting. Writing it off to them having a bad day,
she hurried on down the street to Bridey's shop. After

the day she'd had yesterday, she was going to need a steady supply of caffeine to get through this one.

The meeting promised to be short and sweet. Once Connie had everyone's attention, she held up a list of things that still needed to get finished before the festival.

"So, as you can see, it's mostly small stuff, and I do want to thank everyone for all their hard work in getting us to this point."

Did everyone pick up on Connie's careful wording that made it clear that the items on the list were only *mostly* small, which meant some things weren't small at all? She braced herself for the other shoe to drop. It didn't take long.

"I'm sorry to say that Kristy and Dean Hake have been called out of town on personal business. From what I understand, they've already left, and there's no word on when we can expect them back. For sure, they're going to miss the festival this year."

One of the women shook her head. "I hope it's nothing too serious. I did hear rumors the bank foreclosed on Ronald Minter's place. If that's true, I guess that will leave Kristy and Dean out of luck. God knows Ronald probably didn't have much, but I think it's a shame his only family won't see a dime out of the estate."

That was really too bad if it was true. It would certainly account for why Dean had looked so upset when he had walked out of the bank. Connie ignored the comment, and instead she redirected the conversation back to the more pressing problem of finding someone to fill in for them at the festival.

In the meantime, Abby wasn't the only one who found something riveting to look at to avoid making eye contact with Connie. That didn't stop her from launching right into her recruitment efforts.

"Dean has already lined up volunteers to oversee the various activities at the high school, but he said someone else should be there to make sure everything goes smoothly. Knowing what a great job he's done in the past, this job should be a slam dunk for whoever volunteers to fill in for him."

One man at the far end of the table slowly raised his hand. "Fine, I'll do it. I've helped Dean in the past, so I'm familiar with how he does things."

It was too soon to breathe a sigh of relief. There was still Kristy's job to fill. Abby risked a quick glance in Connie's direction and instantly regretted it. The woman was staring straight at her, as if willing Abby to look up. Just that quickly, she was caught.

Connie's satisfied smile said she knew it, too. "Abby, I believe you said your two groups had all of their jobs done."

Clearly Connie was casting her line and hoping the compliment would encourage Abby to take the bait.

"Yes, that's right. Everyone pitched in and worked really hard." She didn't bother to mention all the nagging and prodding it had taken to make that happen.

"You obviously have a real talent for managing people."

Oh, yeah, the woman was working hard to set the hook.

Connie was still talking. "So, I really hate to ask this of you, but could you take over the pie-eating contest for Kristy? She's the one who suggested your name."

The crafty woman didn't pause long enough for Abby

to answer before launching into the full particulars of the contest as if it was already a done deal.

"The tables will already be set up, and the pies are scheduled to be delivered to the high school later this afternoon. They'll be stored in the walk-in refrigerator in the high school cafeteria. Kristy dropped off the sign-up sheets for the contestants and already has them organized by age group. The three divisions are juniors, adults, and seniors. Each contest takes about fifteen minutes to set up and five minutes to run. Add in another ten minutes to hand out the trophy after each level. Altogether, it shouldn't take more than two hours maximum, so easy-peasy. I have the trophies in my office and will bring them to the gym."

As she spoke, she slid several pieces of paper across the table. If Abby touched them, she was toast. Despite her recent resolution to avoid any new commitments, she found her hand reaching out to pick them up. Trying to rationalize her moment of weakness, she reminded herself that she'd be at the festival anyway. Might as well make herself useful while she was there.

She figured Connie was underestimating the amount of time the contest would involve, but there was no way to know for sure. "I'll do it."

Then she glanced at the people seated around the table, most of whom were doing their best to avoid looking at her now. "I would love to talk to anyone who has either helped with the contest or even participated in it. I've never even seen a pie-eating contest, so I'll take all the help I can get."

The same man who'd volunteered to fill in for Dean nodded. "I helped Kristy set up the first round last year and then watched the contest. I'll be glad to tell you what I remember about how it all played out."

Connie showed the good sense to call the meeting to a halt a few minutes later and then bolted out the door. There was no way she wanted to hang around and risk any of the people she'd just coerced into volunteering to fill in the last few gaps in her to-do list for the festival enough time to change their minds.

Abby wanted to be as crafty as Connie was when she grew up.

No one else seemed to be in much of a hurry to leave. As she gathered up her papers, including her new list of instructions regarding the pie competition, she caught snippets of the conversations going on around her. Most had something to do with the festival tomorrow, but one in particular caught her attention. The men involved were standing close enough that she could listen in without being obvious about it.

"Well, my wife asked me to stop over in the police department to see what the heck is going on with their investigation. I can't believe that between Gage's people and the county mounties they haven't managed to round up one homeless vet. God knows I feel bad for the guy, but we can't leave murderers running around loose in our town. Even if he did serve our country, that doesn't excuse what he did to Ronald Minter."

The other man looked uneasy with his companion's comments, but he didn't argue with him, either. "I'm sure they're doing their best, Barry. Besides, from what I've heard, he's just a person of interest. No one has said he's definitely the killer."

That was true, but Barry didn't seem to care about little things like facts.

"Regardless, I don't like the way he creeps around

town. One way or the other, I want him to move on down the road."

His companion had a different take on the situation. "I'd rather see him get some help. It can't be easy living out in the woods like he does, especially with winter coming on."

Barry didn't back down. "It doesn't help that the other idiot is sitting on his backside in jail at the tax-payers' expense just to protect his homeless buddy. If you ask me, they should both be run out of town."

Abby bit her lip to keep from responding. Nothing she said would change Barry's opinion on the subject, and she didn't need the added stress of getting into a very public argument defending Tripp and his friend. It would accomplish nothing except to tie her up in knots. Meanwhile, the two men drifted toward the exit.

The last thing she heard Barry say was, "I just keep thinking about all the kids who'll be out roaming the streets tomorrow night. I want them to be safe."

Abby did, too, but she really didn't think Kevin presented any danger to them. Like Barry, though, she would feel a lot better about things once they had the real culprit behind bars, especially if that meant Tripp could finally come home.

At least she was done for the day. After lunch, maybe she'd take Zeke out for a long walk. It would do them both good. They could do the trail through the national forest. It was more peaceful than the path that ran along the river in the city park. They should be safe enough, since more people were using the trail right now, thanks to the nice weather.

She'd heard rumors that some folks were reticent to go out at night since the police hadn't yet made an arrest in Ronald Minter's murder. Unlike Barry and

Dean, not everyone believed Sergeant Montgomery was behind the attack. However, Dean's comments about going around armed all the time was never far from her mind. She didn't want anyone to get hurt, especially Tripp's friend.

With that in mind, she'd refill Sergeant Montgomery's cookie container just in case their paths crossed again. If Tripp wouldn't ask his friend to talk to the police, maybe it was time she did.

Chapter Twenty-Three

The late-afternoon sun felt good on Abby's face. Zeke had been trotting along at a good clip, but then he suddenly insisted he needed to catch up on the latest doggy gossip and was busy sniffing a row of bushes that crowded close to the trail. That was all right with her. She was in no hurry to get anywhere, especially back home. She was normally quite content to putter around the house with only Zeke for company, but lately it felt as if she was rattling around in a huge cage.

It wasn't just because Tripp hadn't been around, although that was definitely part of the problem. Not knowing who'd destroyed her pumpkin also accounted for some of her restlessness, as did the fact that the murderer was still on the loose. But if she was being totally honest, she was having trouble filling her time. She'd spent years working with her husband to get their business up and running, and she missed the constant challenges that had presented. Eventually she was going to have to pick a goal and work toward it.

But not today.

Zeke tugged on his leash, finally ready to move on

down the trail. She let him set the pace as she gauged how far they'd come. It was probably another mile back to where she'd parked their car. From where they stood, the trail did a wide loop that skirted the back edges of several local farms.

Not wanting to linger in the area that stirred up bad memories, she kept walking. Every so often she stopped to study the surrounding woods. She'd seen a bunch of squirrels, two does with their fawns, and a bald eagle soaring out over the valley, but no sign of Sergeant Montgomery anywhere. On the off chance he was within listening range, she called his name several times, but there was no response.

Zeke was panting hard, so she called another brief halt so she could fill his water bowl. The trees had thinned out a bit, giving her a clear view of the closest farm. As soon as she spotted the pumpkins in the field, she realized she was standing directly behind Ronald Minter's place. It seemed a shame that all the hard work he had put into raising that crop was going to waste. It was too bad someone hadn't been able to harvest the field, but she suspected the bank had little interest in doing so.

As she waited for Zeke to finish up, she noticed someone moving around just inside the open door of the old barn down below, which seemed odd. It wasn't the one that Ronald Minter actually used, but an ancient structure located farther back on the property that looked as if a stiff wind would knock it over. The driveway that led up to the house was empty, making her wonder who would be hanging around the farm and how they'd gotten there in the first place. She shifted more to the left to get a better look at what was going on.

She could just make out the edge of a bumper. Moving another couple of steps, she leaned forward as if those additional few inches would make a huge difference in how well she could see. Surprisingly, it did help. There was a vehicle down there after all, which was parked alongside the ancient barn rather than in the driveway. It appeared to be a rental van with the side doors open. What's more, there were several more large boxes sitting on the ground still waiting to be loaded.

Should she give Gage a call and let him know someone was trespassing? Not yet; not until she was sure. For one thing, he might jump to the erroneous conclusion that she was out snooping around when all she was doing was taking her dog for a walk. Before she could decide the best course of action, a familiar figure walked out of the barn carrying two bags. Judging from the effort it took her to lift them into the back of the van, the bags appeared to be quite heavy.

What on earth was Kristy doing down there anyway? Adding what she'd heard at the meeting about the foreclosure on the farm to how upset Dean had been when he'd walked out of the bank, she had to wonder if Kristy had any right to be there at all, much less loading up that van.

Abby stayed right where she was until the woman finished shoving the boxes into the vehicle and then drove away. When she pulled out onto the road, she headed away from Snowberry Creek. Interesting. If she and Dean were in such a hurry to respond to a family emergency out of town, why were they still hanging around?

Abby was halfway down the slope toward the old barn before she even realized she had decided to investigate. If she saw anything suspicious, anything at all, she'd be on the phone to Gage or Ben Earle in a heartbeat. Zeke took lead, his nose to the ground as they made their way to the open barn door. It took several seconds for Abby's eyes to adjust to the dim light inside. Unlike the more modern barn where Mr. Minter stored his tractor and other equipment, this one had a dirt floor. There was some old furniture piled in the corner, a bunch of rusty tools hanging on the wall, and clear evidence that some kind of varmints had taken up residency in the barn over the years.

Toward the back, several inches of the dirt floor had been scraped away to uncover what appeared to be a heavy metal trapdoor. It was rectangular and hinged along one side. The underside had a handle in the shape of a steering wheel that would allow someone to secure it from below. That was odd. Who would need to lock themselves underground? Well, maybe it would make sense if it was a storm cellar, the kind people who lived in tornado alley had. That didn't make sense, though. This area sometimes got high winds, but it wasn't prone to having twisters go roaring through.

She peeked down the opening, using her cell phone's flashlight app to illuminate the area below. It only got more intriguing. There was a steel staircase that led down to another door.

Retreating to the entrance to the barn, she took one more quick look around outside before returning to the steps.

"Zeke, you stay up here. I'll be back in a second."

He obligingly flopped down in the dirt and rested his head on his paws to watch as she descended into the shadowy depths below. At the bottom of the steps, she hesitated before turning the handle on the door. Should she knock? Instead, she rested her ear against the metal to listen for any sign that someone was moving around on the other side.

Nothing.

She turned the handle and pushed the door open, cringing at the loud creak from the rusty hinges. Stepping over the raised sill, she spotted a light switch and flipped it on. The overhead lights illuminated a short . . . "tunnel" was the best word she could come up with to describe it. She left the door open to ensure she could make a quick exit if necessary. Once again, she had to wonder why anyone would feel compelled to have a door like that on a cellar. It looked like what she imagined a door would look like on a military ship, or maybe even a submarine.

At the other end of the passageway, she opened the next door and reached through to the wall inside to find another light switch. As soon as the lights came on, she stood and stared as she finally made sense of what she was seeing. Then she stepped across the threshold right into a life-sized time capsule.

Chapter Twenty-Four

For the longest time, all Abby could do was stand and stare. Those heavy doors had been designed to seal airtight, which meant this was no cellar meant to keep someone safe from the odd tornado or two. No, this was a genuine, certified fallout shelter. Other than the air smelling a bit musty, it was totally intact, right down to all the furnishings that would have looked right at home in one of the old black-and-white sitcoms that her aunt used to watch. If Abby was right, this place had to have been built sometime in the early 1960s.

There were shelves of food off to the right—mostly cold cereals, fruit punch, canned meat, and soup. Not exactly the healthiest diet for a long-term stay underground. The next bank of shelves held a variety of board games and a stack of magazines. It was nice that someone had thought to provide some form of entertainment, but how many rounds of bingo and solitaire could one person play without going crazy?

How long would the person who built this place have expected to live down here? And what kind of world would've been waiting for them when they finally crawled back up into the sunlight?

She ventured farther into the room. The bright red bedspreads on the two sets of bunk beds were a nice touch, but they did little to relieve the gloomy atmosphere. She doubted there was much anyone could do to make concrete walls and steel floors look warm and cozy. Even though the ceiling was about seven feet high, she found herself hunching as she walked the length of the room. There was a bathroom of sorts, a kitchen with a camp stove, a small sink, and a set of aluminum pots and pans hanging from hooks overhead.

Several of the shelves were empty. There were dust-free spots where things had been sitting, but it was impossible to tell what was missing. No doubt the items were now in Kristy's van.

She checked out a couple of the drawers. One held flatware and cooking utensils. The other was filled with various medications. She picked up a couple at random to read the labels. Aspirin and antacids had been good, practical choices, as had the large first aid kit hanging on the wall. There had to be some historians or even archeologists who would give anything to study this place. In its own way, it was a microcosm of the world as it existed six decades ago.

There were several bins shoved under the bunk beds, while two others had padded tops, probably pulling double duty as seats. The one she pulled out from under the bed was filled with men's clothing—everything from socks to shirts and pants. Nothing fancy; just practical. The next bin held women's clothing, and the last one must have been intended for a couple of boys, since there were different sizes. On the other hand, maybe they thought they'd be down there long enough for their son to grow several inches.

That was a scary thought.

After shoving the container back to where it belonged, she lifted the lid on one of the other bins. Of all her amazing discoveries, this one topped them all. She picked up a small bar of gold, one of at least a dozen stacked in a neat pile. There was space around it that might have held another stack or two. No wonder those bags Kristy had been carrying had looked so heavy.

In addition to the gold, there were a bunch of jewelry boxes. She flipped open the top couple. One held a gold chain and pendant much like the one she'd noticed Kristy wearing that last time they crossed paths at the park. The other one contained another set of flowered earrings and matching necklace, this time in bright yellow and orange rather than the black-and-white set Kristy had worn the day they worked on scrubbing the tables.

The costume jewelry might not be worth a lot of money, but the gold bars and gold jewelry were a different matter. She was willing to bet Mr. Minter hadn't known about the fallout shelter. If he had, he could have easily sold off enough stuff to fix his money problems. So how had Kristy and Dean found out about it?

The image of them with their metal detectors flashed through her mind. Had they been snooping around in the barn above and run across the recessed trapdoor? If Ronald Minter and Dean weren't close and had little contact, what had the Hakes been doing in the barn in the first place? And having seen Mr. Minter go ballistic over the theft of a few pumpkins, she could only imagine what he would've done if he'd learned his cousin was stealing real treasure right out from under his nose.

She rubbed her arms to ward off both the chill of the dank shelter and the realization that she might have stumbled into something far more dangerous than simple theft. If the couple had been slipping into the barn after dark to steal valuables from down below, they might be the reason behind Sergeant Montgomery's belief that enemy troops had been moving through the area at night.

To cover her tracks, Abby hurried to put everything back where she'd found it. It was time to contact Gage and Ben Earle. When she tried Gage's number, the call wouldn't go through. She was about to try again but realized she wasn't getting any reception. When was the last time that had happened? Maybe it was because she was underground and surrounded by concrete and thick metal. Whatever the problem was, she really needed to get out of there, and pronto. Once she was back outside on the trail, she'd try again.

She turned off the lights and shut the door. Picking up speed, she hustled to the other door and stepped through, stopping only long enough to pull the second door closed. The squeaky hinges sounded even louder, but that was probably her imagination at work now that she might have discovered the real motive behind the pumpkin farmer's death.

Zeke was watching her from the top of the steps. Unfortunately, he wasn't alone.

She dusted her hands off on her jeans and smiled. "Dean, so nice to see you again."

Of course, that was a lie, but what was she supposed to say? *Dean, you sure don't look like a murderer?* Or maybe,

Did you find that big, ugly pistol in the fallout shelter? If so, whoever stocked the place sure thought of everything.

She was equally unhappy to notice he was also wearing one of those combat knives that kept popping up everywhere lately. Meanwhile, he wiggled the fingers on his free hand, motioning her to keep moving. "Come on the rest of the way out of there, Abby."

She had no choice but to do as he asked. The only alternative would be to charge back down the steps and hope that she could get back inside the shelter and slam the door closed before Dean caught up with her. Even if she succeeded, he'd simply wait her out. She could only live on stale cornflakes and outdated fruit punch for so long.

"It's really unfortunate that you had to go poking your nose where it doesn't belong. Kristy really likes you, and I don't relish telling her that there's been another unfortunate death." He paused, perhaps pondering how best to break that tragic news to his wife. Then he shrugged and added, "Still, we plan to enjoy our retirement now that we can afford to do everything we've always wanted to do."

She'd reached the top step, and she waited for Dean to move out of her way so she could leave the staircase behind. Zeke licked her hand to show at least he was glad to see her. She considered trying to sic him on Dean but immediately rejected the idea. If Dean felt no compunction about the idea of killing her, there was every chance he would shoot her dog as well. Nothing about this situation was Zeke's fault, and she didn't want him to die for her mistakes.

Maybe she could keep Dean talking long enough to figure out some way to escape. It was worth a try.

"I assume you discovered the fallout shelter using

your metal detectors. How did you even know to look for it?"

"Ronnie's grandfather was my great-uncle, Vincent. There were always rumors in the family that he had some serious money squirreled away, but no one ever knew what he'd done with it. He and his wife died in a car accident while Ronnie's dad was in the army and the family was living out of state. All we can figure is that the old man had built the fallout shelter while they were overseas and never had a chance to tell them about it. This farm sat vacant for years until Ronnie's dad retired from the military. Ronnie inherited it when his father died a few years back."

"So they never knew about the missing money."

Dean gave their surroundings a pointed look. "You've seen the house and the farm. Does it look like the kind of place a rich man would live? I don't know about cousin Ronnie, but his dad just thought it was all crazy talk."

Then Dean laughed.

"Looks like we proved him wrong. Kristy and I started slipping in after dark and carrying out a load at a time on foot to keep Ronnie from figuring out what we were up to. Everything was going according to plan until that crazy veteran started sneaking out of the woods to pick pumpkins and carry them off. Poor Ronnie must have been going nuts trying to figure out who was stealing his precious crop. One night, he finally decided to stake out the place." Dean shrugged. "Instead of the soldier, he caught us."

Maybe it would help if she sympathized with their plight. "I'm guessing he wasn't at all reasonable about the situation."

Dean's laugh was ugly. "That's putting it mildly.

We offered to split the loot with him, even promised to give him a higher percentage of the take, but Ronnie wouldn't hear of it. He had the guts to actually demand we return everything we'd taken. Even then he planned to turn us in to the authorities as if we were common criminals instead of family. Well, that wasn't going to happen, not when we'd done all the work to find the stuff in the first place. Besides, we'd already spent most of the money we'd gotten from selling off the stuff we'd taken. We also spent a lot of time and energy driving to different parts of the region so we didn't unload too much in any one place. We wanted to be careful not to draw too much attention to ourselves, you know."

She could easily imagine the hissy fit Mr. Minter would've had over finding out that he'd been sitting on a fortune all this time only to have it stolen. The unfortunate man had signed his own death warrant the second he'd threatened to call the police, and poor Sergeant Montgomery had made for an easy scapegoat.

There were a few more details she'd like to have explained. "So I'm guessing you're the one who trashed the pumpkin on my front porch and left a combat knife in Layla's car."

"Yeah, we thought all of that would keep the cops spinning in circles while we finished up our business here at the farm."

He took another step toward her. "Come on, Abby, let's get this over with. Thanks to you poking your nose where it doesn't belong, we're going to have to hurry to get everything worth taking out of the shelter before your body is discovered."

Did he expect her to apologize for rushing their

getaway? So not happening. At least he wasn't going to kill her right there and leave her body in the fallout shelter where it would never be found.

When he made a grab for her arm, Zeke surprised them both and went on the attack. It seemed as if he'd only been biding his time to make his move at the right moment. He lunged at Dean, clamping his teeth on his arm. From the way the man screamed, Zeke's powerful jaws had bitten right through his jacket and deep into the muscle in his forearm.

When Dean dropped the gun, it clattered down the steps to the shelter entrance below. There was no time to go after it, so Abby yanked on Zeke's leash. "Let go, boy. We've got to run."

The two of them bolted out the door and headed for the trail in the forest. Even if they didn't run into someone who could help, she stood a better chance of finding a place to hide in the national forest. Regretfully, the damage to Dean's arm didn't slow him down all that much. He was already out of the barn and pounding up the hillside right behind her. From what she could tell, it didn't appear that he'd gone after the gun, but he still had that knife.

She and Zeke were making good time, but so was he. Surprisingly so, for a man who allegedly had a heart condition. When they reached the tree line, she turned in the direction that led back toward her car. There wasn't much chance of them making it that far, but a woman could always hope.

They'd gone a short distance when someone lurched out into the trail from behind a cluster of bushes and saplings. She barely recognized an enraged Sergeant Montgomery as he charged past her to take Dean down to the ground hard. The other man put up a fight, but he was no match for the determined veteran. When he drew his knife, the sergeant flipped Dean over facedown in the dirt and then twisted his arm up behind him with a powerful jerk. Dean bellowed as he struggled without success to throw him off. Kevin yanked his arm up higher and forced Dean to release his hold on the knife, sending it flying a short distance away.

"Keep it up, mister, and I'll dislocate your shoulder for you."

Kevin issued the threat with a surprising amount of calm. Dean quit fighting but didn't shut up. "Get off me! I'll sue you for damages. You'll both rot in jail."

Abby picked up the knife and then waited just long enough to make sure Sergeant Montgomery had Dean under control before calling for help. "Detective Earle, this is Abby. I'm on the trail on the hillside directly behind the Minter farm. Sergeant Montgomery and I have the murderer in custody."

He started to rattle off a bunch of questions, but she cut him off. "I'll give you the short version. Dean and Kristy Hake killed Mr. Minter over treasure they found on his property. Right now Kristy's driving westbound toward the interstate in a rented van that's loaded down with more of the loot they've stolen. I'll answer everything else when you get here."

After she disconnected the call, she went over to stand next to both of her intrepid saviors. Zeke lay sprawled in the dirt next to Sergeant Montgomery and growled in Dean's face every time the man tried to move or even opened his mouth. She ignored their prisoner while she studied the veteran.

"Sergeant, thank you for coming to my rescue. I don't know how Zeke and I will repay you."

Once again, he seemed uncomfortable with looking straight at her, but finally his gaze connected briefly with hers. "Tripp would have my hide if I let something happen to you."

The faint sound of sirens in the distance caught his attention. She suspected that he was considering bolting back to the safety of the trees, but then he gave a quick nod. "Don't worry, Ms. Abby. I won't desert you. I know my duty and will see it done."

When the first police officer came charging down the trail toward them, she reached down and took his rough hand in hers. "We'll get through this together, Sergeant."

He stared at their joined hands for a few seconds and then looked up at her again. "Yeah, we will."

Chapter Twenty-Five

By the time Abby finally got home, she was running on fumes. By now, she shouldn't have been surprised by the amount of time it took to make her statement to the police. They had plenty of questions for both her and Sergeant Montgomery. Gage had shown up a bit late to the party, so she'd ended up repeating a lot of what she'd already told Detective Earle and his people. She did her best to cooperate but didn't much appreciate it that Ben was pretty evasive when she asked if this meant he'd drop the charges against Tripp. He'd mumbled something about talking to the judge.

It was no surprise that both men had been as fascinated by the fallout shelter as she had been. In fact, she suspected everyone who could find a legitimate excuse had made a trip down the steps to look around.

The EMTs had been called in to treat Dean's dog bite. When he kept muttering threats under his breath about suing Abby over Zeke attacking him, Ben redeemed himself by getting right up in the man's face and telling him to shut up. He also suggested the money it would cost to hire a personal injury attorney would be better spent on one who was well-versed in defending him and Kristy against first-degree murder and armed robbery charges. Dean got real quiet after that.

She worried more about Sergeant Montgomery than herself, but he handled everything pretty well. Zeke remained right at his side through the entire ordeal, which seemed to keep him anchored in the moment. The former soldier answered all of their questions as if reporting back to a superior officer on the outcome of a combat mission.

Gage volunteered to take Abby home, but he first called Jack Haliday to come to the scene to be with Sergeant Montgomery. The pastor's congregation had recently converted a small outbuilding on the church property into a temporary shelter for when people like Kevin needed a place to stay. Abby made a point of telling him that she'd sleep better knowing he wasn't alone out in the woods at least for a night or two.

When she offered to let Zeke come with him, he gave both her and the dog a quick hug and assured her he'd be all right on his own.

Gage insisted on walking her inside the house to make sure everything was safe and sound, even though Dean was already behind bars. Ben had also called to let them know that they'd just caught up with Kristy. Not only had they recovered the items she still had in the van, but a search of their house had netted even more items that they'd taken from the shelter. She was now in custody and on her way to jail.

Abby took her usual spot at the kitchen table while Gage made himself at home in the kitchen. After feeding Zeke, he poured two glasses of iced tea and made each of them a sandwich.

As she waited for him to finish, she said, "That's a real shame about the Hakes. I can hardly get my head around the idea of them being thieves, much less killers. They seemed like such nice people who did a lot for the community."

Gage set her plate down in front of her. "No one has ever said that criminals have to be unlikable."

The tea felt good going down her throat. "I guess that's true. Still, to kill his own cousin and leave him lying in a corn maze like that was pretty darn cold-hearted. I just don't get it."

"That's because you're not wired up to ever do something like that, Abby." He pointed toward her plate. "Now, eat that. You'll feel better."

As it turned out, he was right about that. "Thanks, Gage. That hit the spot."

He pushed his own empty plate out of the way. Just that quickly the concerned friend disappeared and the hard-nosed cop took his place. "So, are you ready for your 'what on earth were you thinking' lecture now, or do you want me to come back later?"

Why wait until tomorrow when she could get yelled at today? Besides, she'd already been threatened with a gun and chased by a killer who'd stabbed his own flesh and blood. By those standards, having an angry cop ranting in her kitchen would be a piece of cake.

"Go ahead, Chief Logan. I'm listening."

And with that, Gage launched right in.

It was no surprise that the news of the arrests spread through Snowberry Creek like wildfire. Her phone had started ringing before the sun came up and still hadn't stopped by the time she left for the festival. While the whole town had been shocked to learn the Hakes were guilty of murder and theft, it was quickly decided that the Halloween Festival should go on as planned. There was no reason to disappoint the kids, and everyone was ready to take a big step back toward normal.

The only thing that still worried her was there was no sign of Tripp. She didn't know what to make of that fact, but she'd have to take action of some kind if he didn't show up soon. She knew Ben was probably busy, but the least he could do was let an innocent man out of jail. Since staging a jailbreak would only land her in the cell next to Tripp's, she'd have to settle for hiring an attorney to spring him. That would have to wait until tomorrow. She had commitments, promises to keep, miles to go, and all of that stuff.

She managed to find a spot in the already crowded parking lot at the high school. Before getting out of the car, she checked her image in the rearview mirror. Two days ago, desperation had driven her into the depths of the attic, where Aunt Sybil had kept steamer trunks full of old clothes. Inspiration had hit when she'd uncovered a wool greatcoat. It sported more than a few moth holes, but beggars couldn't be choosers. Coupled with a magnifying glass and the deerstalker hat she'd paid big bucks to have overnighted to the house, she was the spitting image of Sherlock Holmes.

Well, not really, but it was the best she could do. From the looks they gave her from across the gym, neither Ben nor Gage found the thought of Detective Abby McCree amusing, but too bad. When she did a quick pirouette to give them the full effect, they shook their heads and immediately turned away. She suspected they were hiding the fact that they were both laughing.

It was time to get set up for her first round of pie-eating contestants. She'd watched videos of a few online and learned a lot—hopefully enough to get her through the next two hours without a disaster happening.

With everything that had happened, she should've known that other people would pitch in to help. That's the kind of town Snowberry Creek was. The tables were already set up and waiting, just as Connie had promised. Two members of the Committee on Senior Affairs volunteered to fetch the pumpkin pies from the cooler, while three others helped cover the tables with butcher paper to make cleanup easier.

Everything was in place when her first group was checked in and ready to go. In one of the videos, the twenty young contestants wore large trash bags with a hole cut through the bottom for their heads. The bags served the dual purposes of protecting the wearers' clothing and preventing them from using their hands.

The junior competitors had a great time, even if more of their pies ended up on their faces and the floor than in their stomachs. The mayor stopped by to award the trophy to the ten-year-old who won. There was a lot of laughter and applause involved, which seemed to lift everyone's spirits.

The people signed up for the second round had already started lining up. When Abby glanced around to see who was participating, she almost dropped the pie she'd just picked up off the cart. She closed her eyes and then opened them again to make sure she wasn't seeing things. No, that really was Tripp standing at the back of the line dressed in his camos. He grinned and waved, as did the other man in uniform standing right next to him.

It took her a little longer to realize that she actually knew the second guy, too. It was Sergeant Montgomery, but he looked radically different. Sometime between last night and right then, he'd showered, shaved, and gotten a haircut. His uniform looked new, too. She wanted to do more than just wave back at both of them, but she had this silly contest to run.

Soon, though.

Tripp took a spot at the table, while Sergeant Montgomery stepped back out of range of the mess that was sure to ensue.

"Everyone to your places and put on your fine dining attire. When you're ready, I'll count down from five. At one, dig in and enjoy your pie!"

A few seconds later, she started the countdown. "On your mark: Five, four, three, two, one, go!"

This group was far more focused or maybe had more practice at eating a pie without their hands. The preferred method seemed to be to grab the pie plate with their teeth and flip it over to dump the pie out onto the table. Although it was a close call, Tripp took first place, beating out Zoe's husband and his two friends by half a pie.

Once again the mayor was on hand to award the prize. Tripp immediately held the trophy up over his head as Sergeant Montgomery and several other men in uniform applauded and hooted up a storm. As the person in charge, Abby was probably supposed to be neutral, but she joined right in the celebration.

Tripp made his way over to her. "I'm out."

"I see that. It's about time. That uniform looks better on you than jailhouse orange."

He looked down at his camos. "Yeah, I guess it does. Just so you know, Kevin has been giving me heck for pulling what he described as a stupid stunt that worried my nice landlady."

"Good for him."

He studied her outfit but made no comment about it. "Are you doing okay after last night?"

She didn't even have to think about it. "I am now."

Tripp still looked a little rough around the edges, as if he hadn't slept well in a long time. She'd planned to hang around the festival for a while after she finished up her pie-eating contest duties, but maybe that wasn't a good idea.

"I'm pretty tired, though. I have one more round in the contest to finish up. After that, I'd like to go home. Does that sound good?"

His relief was obvious. "Yeah, it does. Kevin also wants to talk to you, so we'll meet you outside. Being around this many people is making him a bit twitchy." Then he grinned. "Me, too, for that matter. All that time in solitary has an effect on a man."

So not funny. She punched his arm hard. "I'll meet you by the sign out in the front of the parking lot as soon as I get done here."

"Sounds good."

To her surprise, Kevin rode back to the house with them. He had a heavy-looking bag with him. When they got out of the car, he carried it over to the front porch and then took out another large jack-o'-lantern

that looked just like Tripp. He set it beside hers and
stood back to let her and Tripp admire his work.

She gave him her honest appraisal. "Sergeant,
you're an amazingly talented man."

He shuffled his feet a little, clearly uneasy with
her praise. "Look, I have to be somewhere in a little
while, but I wanted to say goodbye to you both before
I leave."

She hoped he wasn't heading back out into the
forest or, worse yet, moving on down the highway.
"Where are you going?"

Kevin's gaze slid past hers to lock onto Tripp's.
"The sergeant here has been trying to get me to come
back in, and I think maybe he's right. Pastor Jack
found me a spot at a group home up near Tacoma,
so not all that far away. He said it's a good place.
Guess I'll find out."

Clearly his decision was news to Tripp, who looked
both relieved and a little bit sad. "I'll be pulling for
you, Sergeant. You have my number. Call and I'll
come running."

The older vet gave Tripp a rough hug. "I know
you've got my back, Master Sergeant, but don't worry
about me. You've got enough on your plate just keeping this lady out of trouble."

The two men stood shoulder to shoulder and
glared down at her. Before she could respond, Tripp
launched right in. "Huff and puff all you want, Abby
McCree, but he's right. How many times do you think
you can brush up against a murderer and walk away
unscathed? I swear, keeping you in line is a full-time
job, which means you need a full-time keeper."

As she sputtered in outrage, Kevin laughed and

clapped his friend on the shoulder. "I'll leave you two to iron this out."

He walked away, leaving them both staring after him as he disappeared into the darkness.

She knew Tripp would miss his friend, but there wasn't much she could do about it. Maybe a hug would help.

When she slipped her arms around him, Tripp pulled her in close and surprised her with another one of his rare hit-and-run kisses, the kind that fried her brain and curled her toes in the process. When he broke off the embrace, he picked her up and set her back down at arm's length.

"He's right, you know. You're trouble with a capital T."

Then he stalked off. "Go inside, lock the door, and stay there. I'll need a few hours of sleep before I have enough energy to keep an eye on you."

It was tempting to laugh, but she suspected he wasn't kidding. Rather than argue, she went into the house and shared the good news with Zeke that his buddy was finally back home. When she let him out the back door, the dog charged across the yard to greet Tripp, who must have been watching for him. They both disappeared into the cottage. She suspected it would be morning before she saw either of them again.

For now, she was too restless to go to bed. Maybe she'd bake some brownies, the extra fudgy ones Tripp liked so much. In fact, a double batch might be a real good idea.

After all, she hadn't yet told Tripp about his starring role in the bachelor auction.

Connect with Us

Visit us online at
KensingtonBooks.com
to read more from your favorite authors, see books
by series, view reading group guides, and more.

for sneak peeks, chances to win books and prize packs,
and to share your thoughts with other readers.

facebook.com/kensingtonpublishing
twitter.com/kensingtonbooks

Tell us what you think!

To share your thoughts, submit a review,
or sign up for our eNewsletters, please visit:
KensingtonBooks.com/TellUs.